THE SIGN of the BLACK ROCK

THREE THIEVES · BOOK TWO

Kids Can Press acknowledges the financial support of the Government of Ontario, through the Ontario Media Development Corporation's Ontario Book Initiative; the Ontario Arts Council; the Canada Council for the Arts; and the Government of Canada, through the BPIDP, for our publishing activity.

Published in Canada by
Kids Can Press Ltd.
25 Dockside Drive
Toronto, ON M5A 0B5

Published in the U.S. by
Kids Can Press Ltd.
2250 Military Road
Tonawanda, NY 14150

www.kidscanpress.com

Edited by Karen Li
Designed by Rachel Di Salle and Scott Chantler
Pages lettered with Blambot comic fonts

The hardcover edition of this book is smyth sewn casebound.
The paperback edition of this book is limp sewn with a drawn-on cover.
Manufactured in Buji, Shenzhen, China, in 4/2011 by WKT Company

CM 11 0 9 8 7 6 5 4 3 2 1
CM PA 11 0 9 8 7 6 5 4 3 2 1

Library and Archives Canada Cataloguing in Publication

Chantler, Scott
     The sign of the black rock / Scott Chantler.

(Three thieves ; bk. 2)
ISBN 978-1-55453-416-6 (bound). —ISBN 978-1-55453-417-3 (pbk.)

I. Title. II. Series: Chantler, Scott. Three thieves ; bk. 2.

PN6733.C53S54 2011   j741.5   C2011 900091-1

Kids Can Press is a *l'©r\Js*™ Entertainment company

THE SIGN of the BLACK ROCK

THREE THIEVES · BOOK TWO

Scott Chantler

Kids Can Press

ACT ONE
STORM

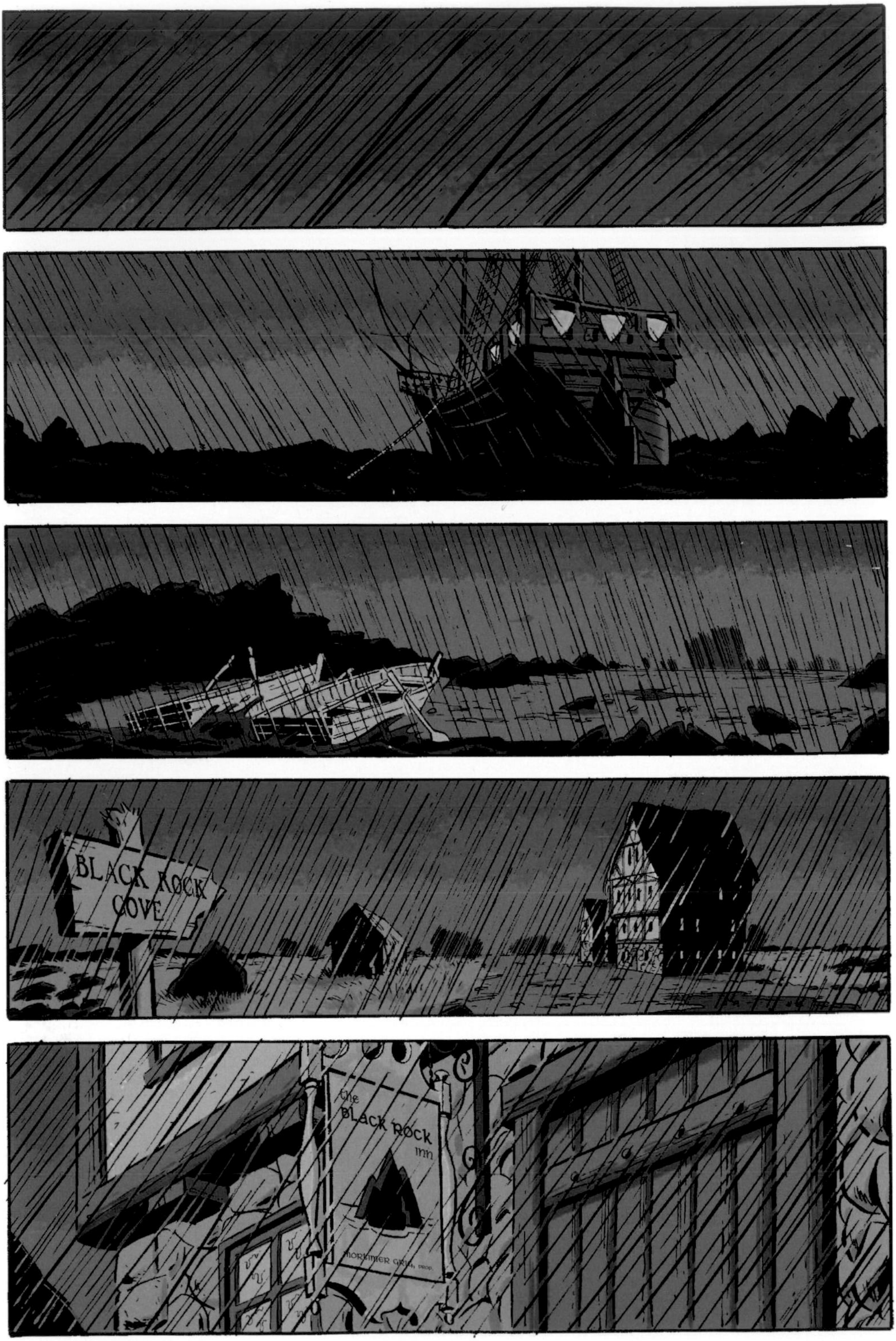
BLACK ROCK
COVE
the
BLACK ROCK
inn
MORTIMER GRIM, PROP.

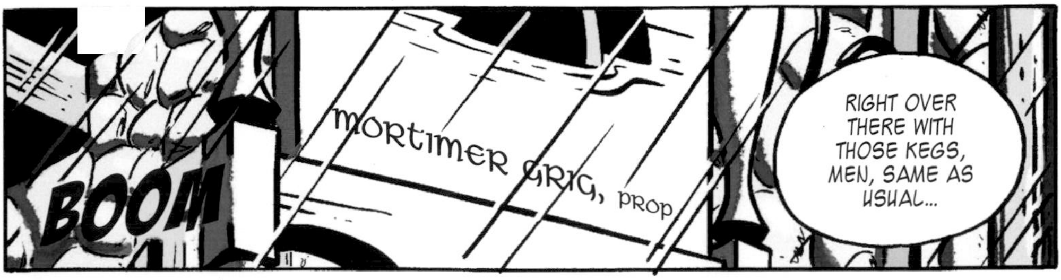
BOOM
MORTIMER GRIG, prop
RIGHT OVER THERE WITH THOSE KEGS, MEN, SAME AS USUAL...

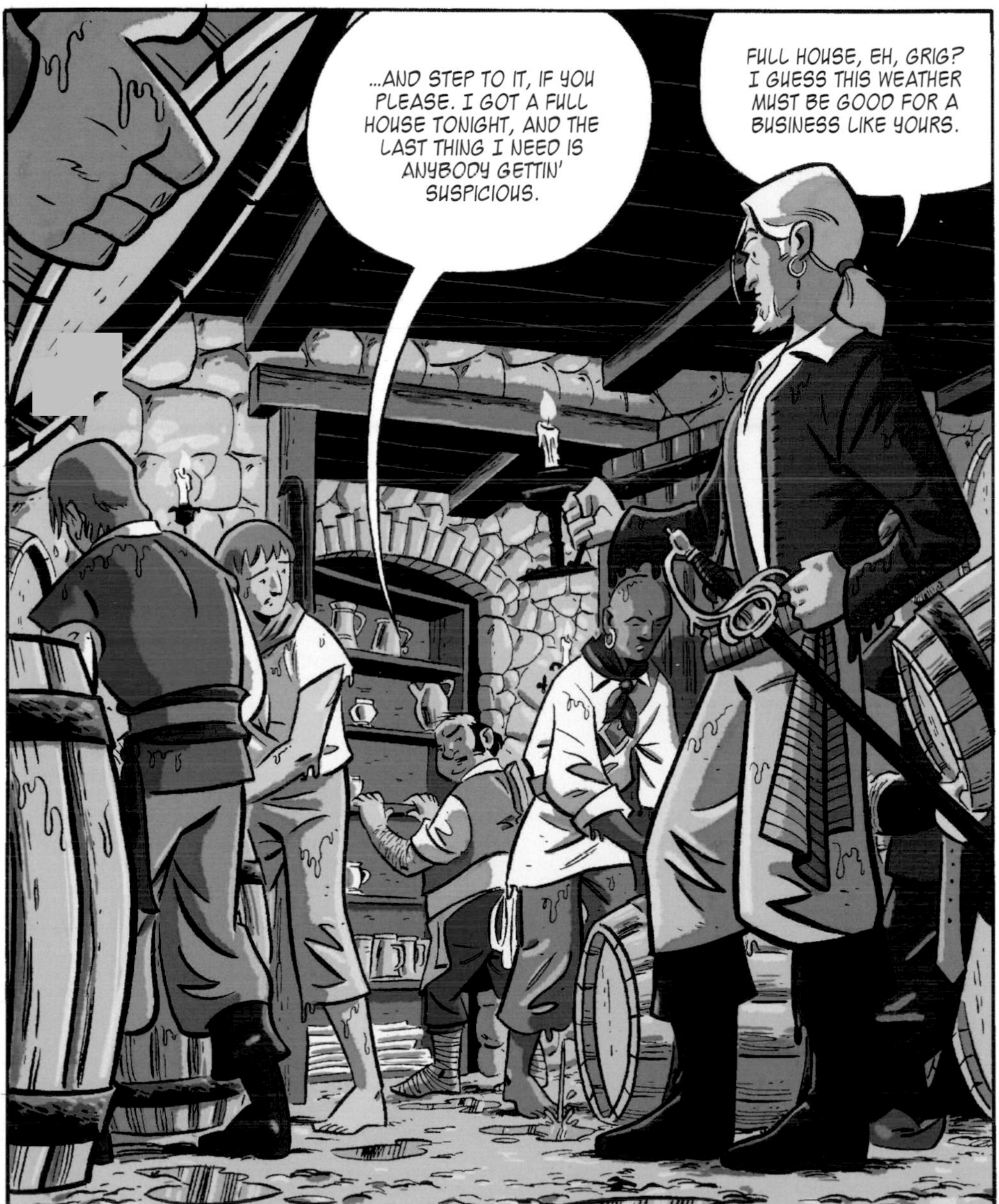
...AND STEP TO IT, IF YOU PLEASE. I GOT A FULL HOUSE TONIGHT, AND THE LAST THING I NEED IS ANYBODY GETTIN' SUSPICIOUS.
FULL HOUSE, EH, GRIG? I GUESS THIS WEATHER MUST BE GOOD FOR A BUSINESS LIKE YOURS.

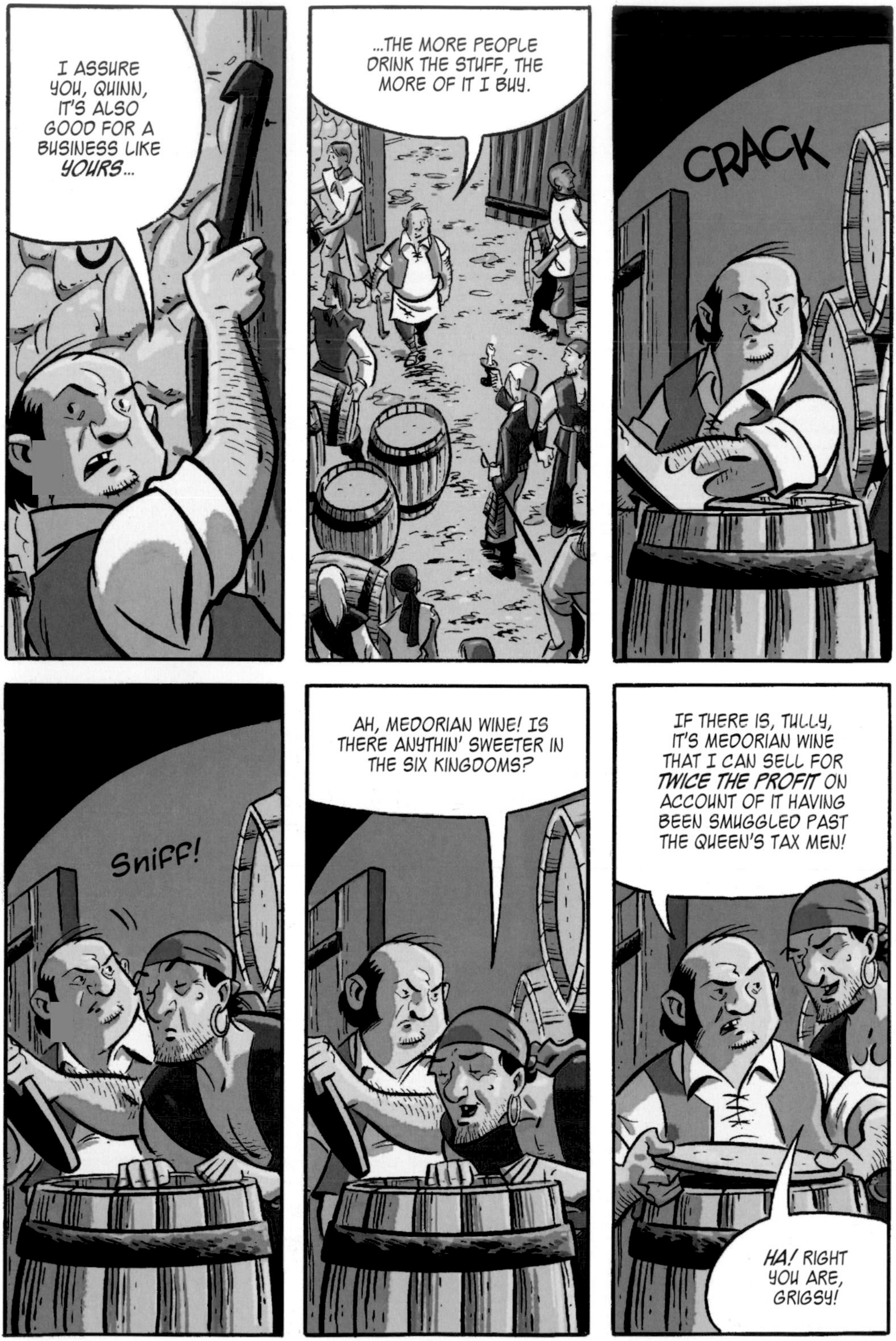
I ASSURE YOU, QUINN, IT'S ALSO GOOD FOR A BUSINESS LIKE *YOURS*...
...THE MORE PEOPLE DRINK THE STUFF, THE MORE OF IT I BUY.
CRACK
Sniff!
AH, MEDORIAN WINE! IS THERE ANYTHIN' SWEETER IN THE SIX KINGDOMS?
IF THERE IS, TULLY, IT'S MEDORIAN WINE THAT I CAN SELL FOR *TWICE THE PROFIT* ON ACCOUNT OF IT HAVING BEEN SMUGGLED PAST THE QUEEN'S TAX MEN!
HA! RIGHT YOU ARE, GRIGSY!

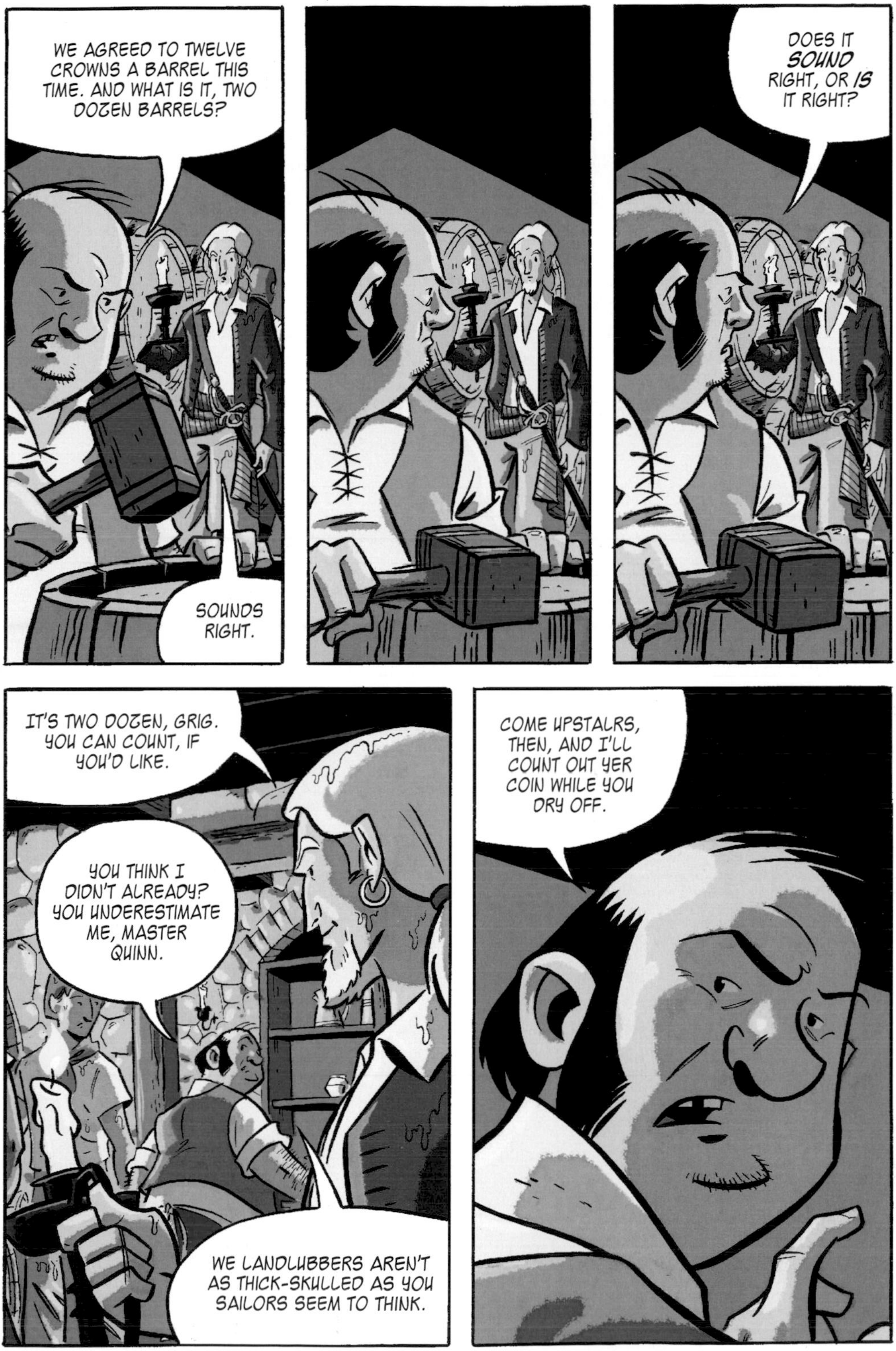
WE AGREED TO TWELVE CROWNS A BARREL THIS TIME. AND WHAT IS IT, TWO DOZEN BARRELS?
SOUNDS RIGHT.
DOES IT *SOUND* RIGHT, OR *IS* IT RIGHT?
IT'S TWO DOZEN, GRIG. YOU CAN COUNT, IF YOU'D LIKE.
YOU THINK I DIDN'T ALREADY? YOU UNDERESTIMATE ME, MASTER QUINN.
WE LANDLUBBERS AREN'T AS THICK-SKULLED AS YOU SAILORS SEEM TO THINK.
COME UPSTAIRS, THEN, AND I'LL COUNT OUT YER COIN WHILE YOU DRY OFF.

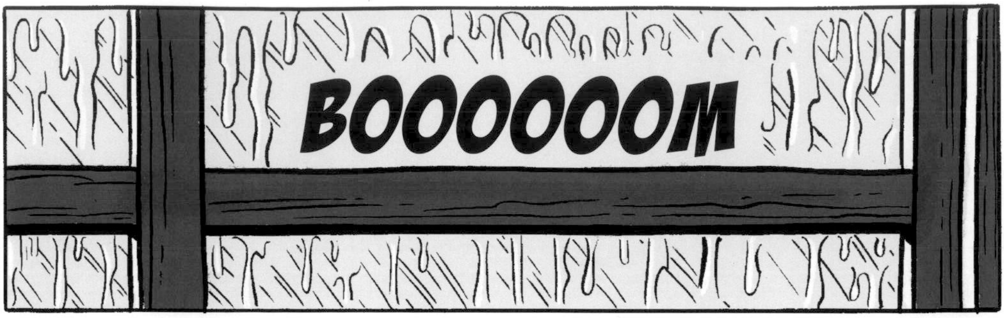
BOOOOOOM

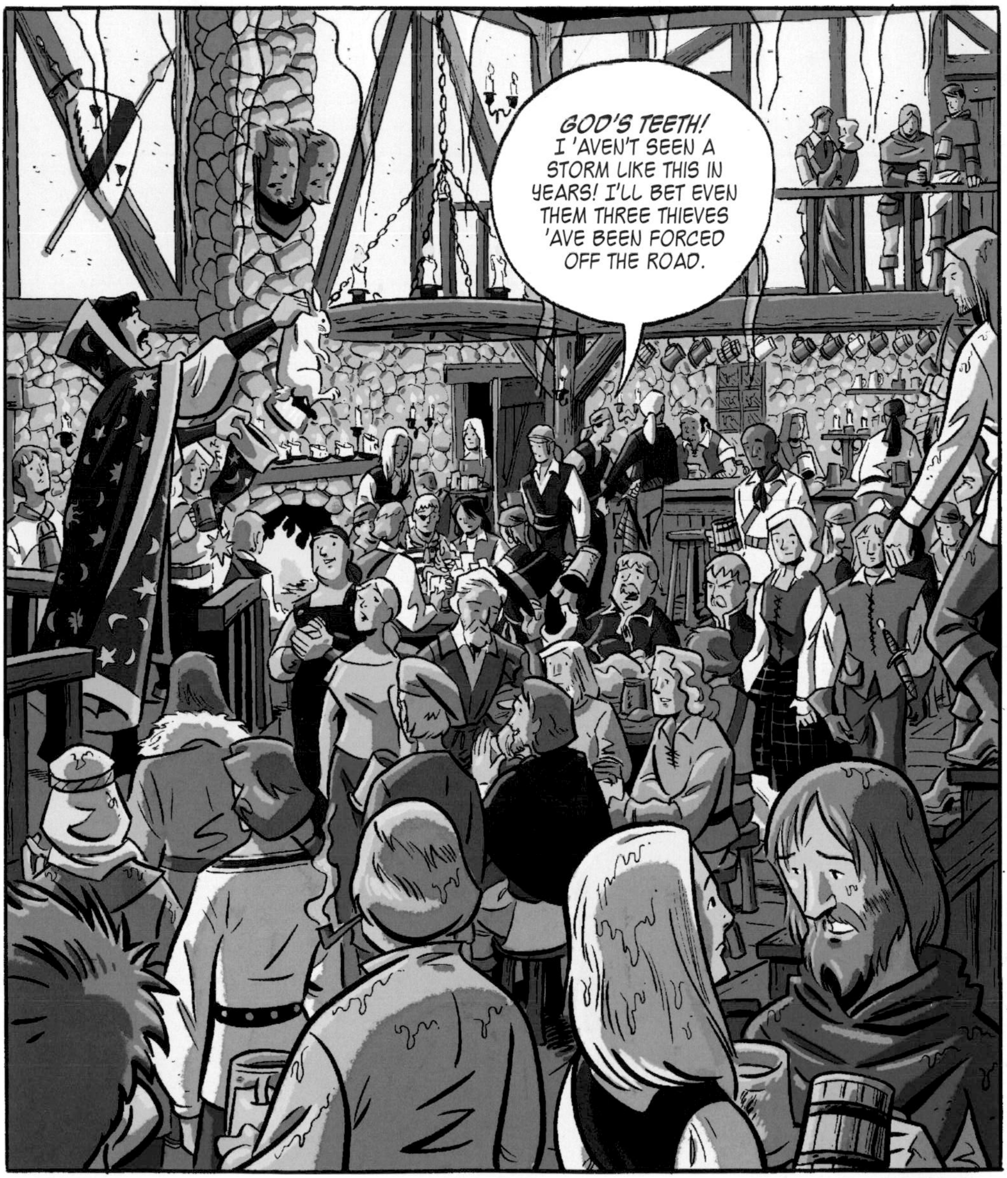
GOD'S TEETH! I 'AVEN'T SEEN A STORM LIKE THIS IN YEARS! I'LL BET EVEN THEM THREE THIEVES 'AVE BEEN FORCED OFF THE ROAD.

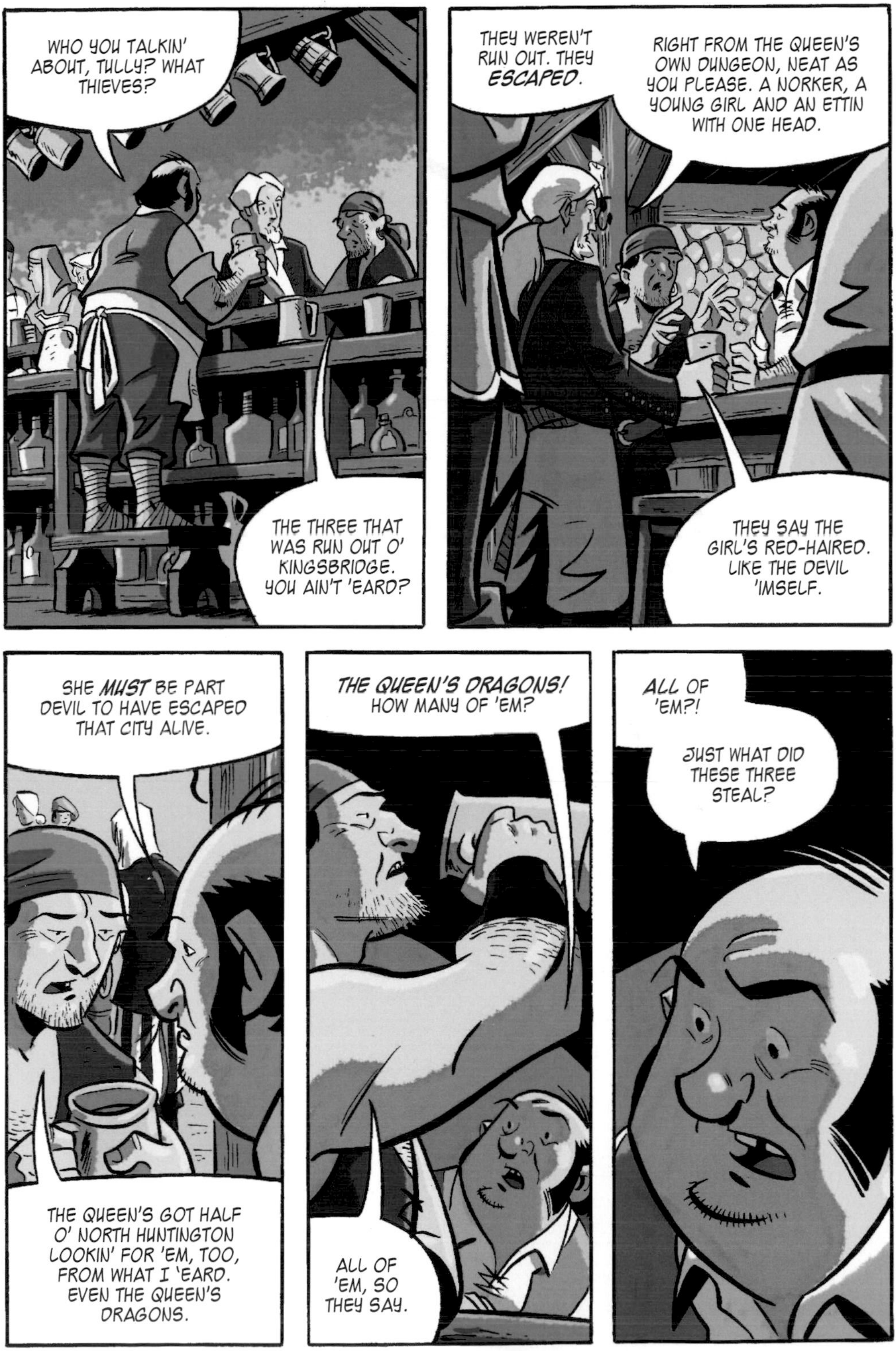
WHO YOU TALKIN' ABOUT, TULLY? WHAT THIEVES?
THE THREE THAT WAS RUN OUT O' KINGSBRIDGE. YOU AIN'T 'EARD?
THEY WEREN'T RUN OUT. THEY *ESCAPED*.
RIGHT FROM THE QUEEN'S OWN DUNGEON, NEAT AS YOU PLEASE. A NORKER, A YOUNG GIRL AND AN ETTIN WITH ONE HEAD.
THEY SAY THE GIRL'S RED-HAIRED. LIKE THE DEVIL 'IMSELF.
SHE *MUST* BE PART DEVIL TO HAVE ESCAPED THAT CITY ALIVE.
THE QUEEN'S GOT HALF O' NORTH HUNTINGTON LOOKIN' FOR 'EM, TOO, FROM WHAT I 'EARD. EVEN THE QUEEN'S DRAGONS.
THE QUEEN'S DRAGONS! HOW MANY OF 'EM?
ALL OF 'EM, SO THEY SAY.
ALL OF 'EM?!
JUST WHAT DID THESE THREE STEAL?

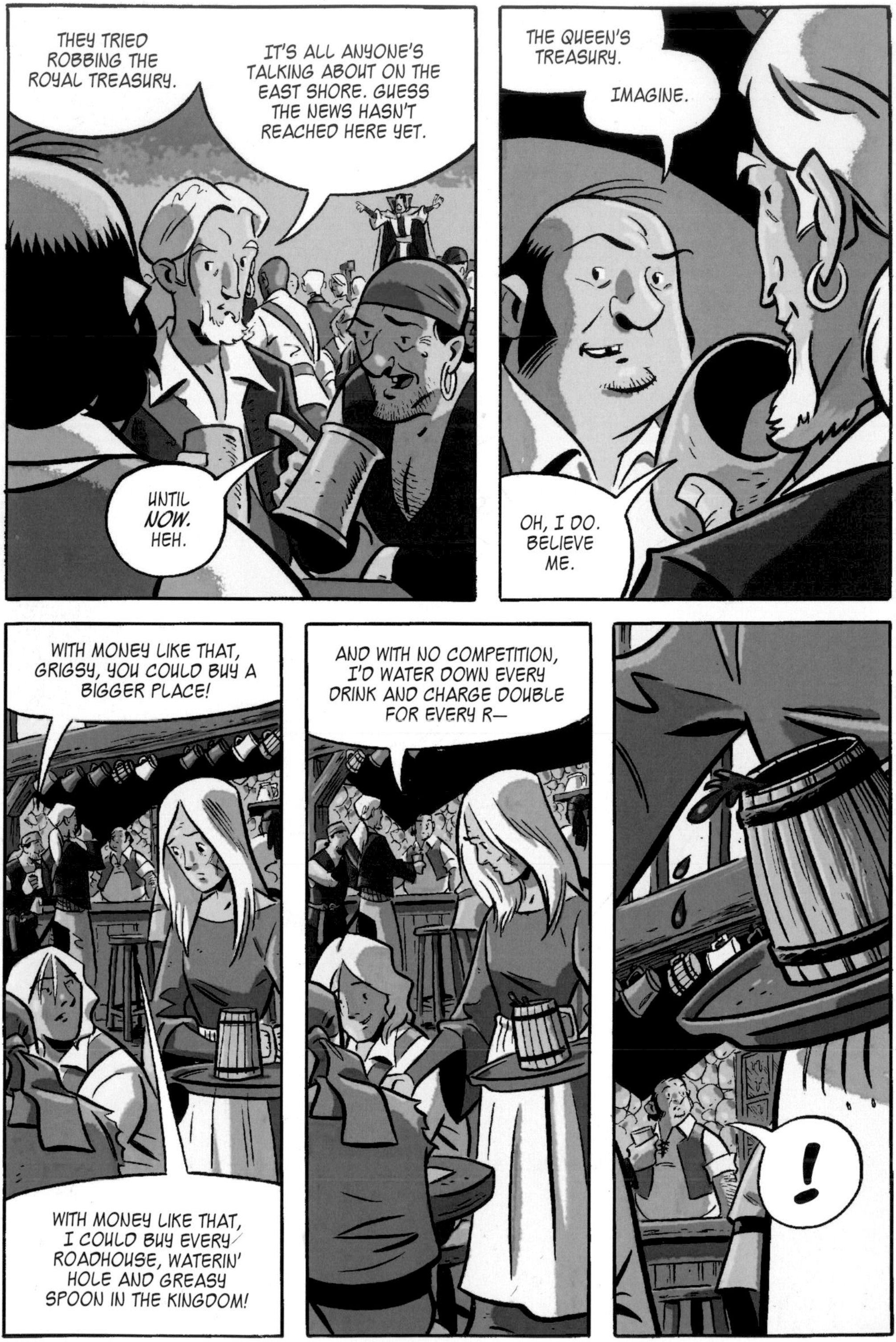
THEY TRIED ROBBING THE ROYAL TREASURY.
IT'S ALL ANYONE'S TALKING ABOUT ON THE EAST SHORE. GUESS THE NEWS HASN'T REACHED HERE YET.
UNTIL *NOW.* HEH.
THE QUEEN'S TREASURY.
IMAGINE.
OH, I DO. BELIEVE ME.
WITH MONEY LIKE THAT, GRIGSY, YOU COULD BUY A BIGGER PLACE!
WITH MONEY LIKE THAT, I COULD BUY EVERY ROADHOUSE, WATERIN' HOLE AND GREASY SPOON IN THE KINGDOM!
AND WITH NO COMPETITION, I'D WATER DOWN EVERY DRINK AND CHARGE DOUBLE FOR EVERY R—
!

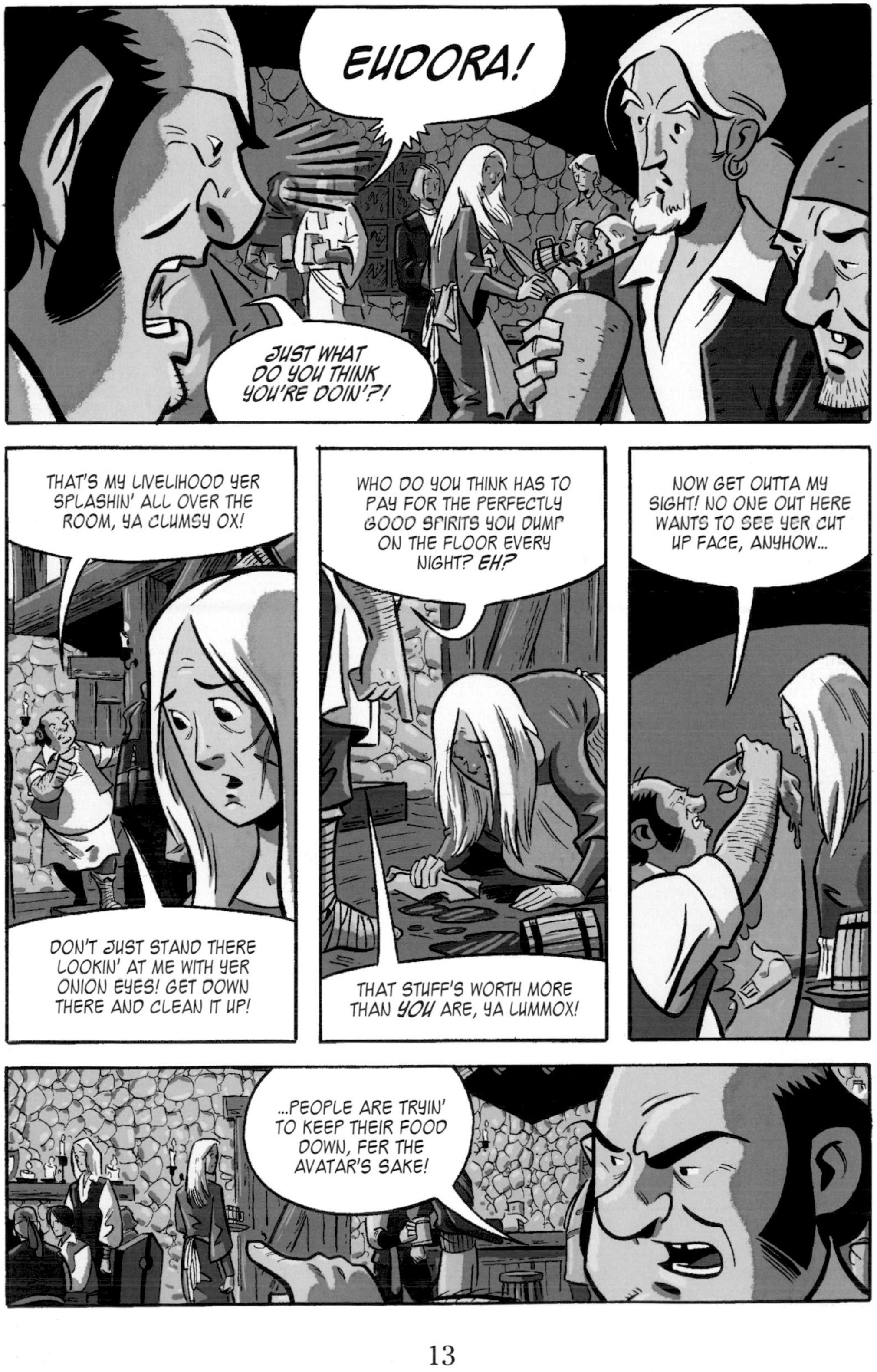
EUDORA!
JUST WHAT DO YOU THINK YOU'RE DOIN'?!
THAT'S MY LIVELIHOOD YER SPLASHIN' ALL OVER THE ROOM, YA CLUMSY OX!
DON'T JUST STAND THERE LOOKIN' AT ME WITH YER ONION EYES! GET DOWN THERE AND CLEAN IT UP!
WHO DO YOU THINK HAS TO PAY FOR THE PERFECTLY GOOD SPIRITS YOU DUMP ON THE FLOOR EVERY NIGHT? EH?
THAT STUFF'S WORTH MORE THAN YOU ARE, YA LUMMOX!
NOW GET OUTTA MY SIGHT! NO ONE OUT HERE WANTS TO SEE YER CUT UP FACE, ANYHOW...
...PEOPLE ARE TRYIN' TO KEEP THEIR FOOD DOWN, FER THE AVATAR'S SAKE!

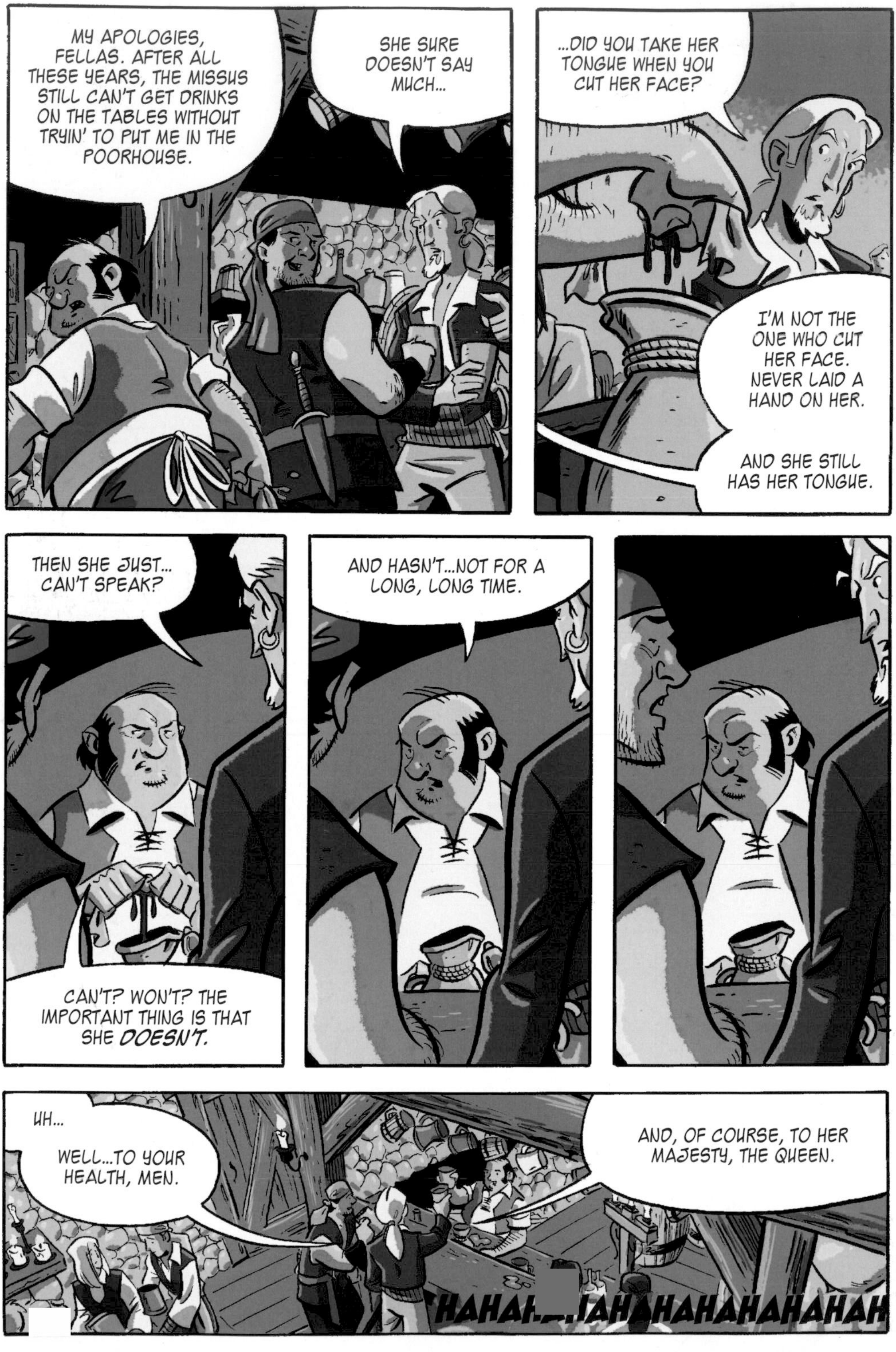
MY APOLOGIES, FELLAS. AFTER ALL THESE YEARS, THE MISSUS STILL CAN'T GET DRINKS ON THE TABLES WITHOUT TRYIN' TO PUT ME IN THE POORHOUSE.
SHE SURE DOESN'T SAY MUCH...
...DID YOU TAKE HER TONGUE WHEN YOU CUT HER FACE?
I'M NOT THE ONE WHO CUT HER FACE. NEVER LAID A HAND ON HER.
AND SHE STILL HAS HER TONGUE.
THEN SHE JUST... CAN'T SPEAK?
CAN'T? WON'T? THE IMPORTANT THING IS THAT SHE *DOESN'T.*
AND HASN'T...NOT FOR A LONG, LONG TIME.
UH...
WELL...TO YOUR HEALTH, MEN.
AND, OF COURSE, TO HER MAJESTY, THE QUEEN.
HAHAH
AHAHAHAHAHAHAH

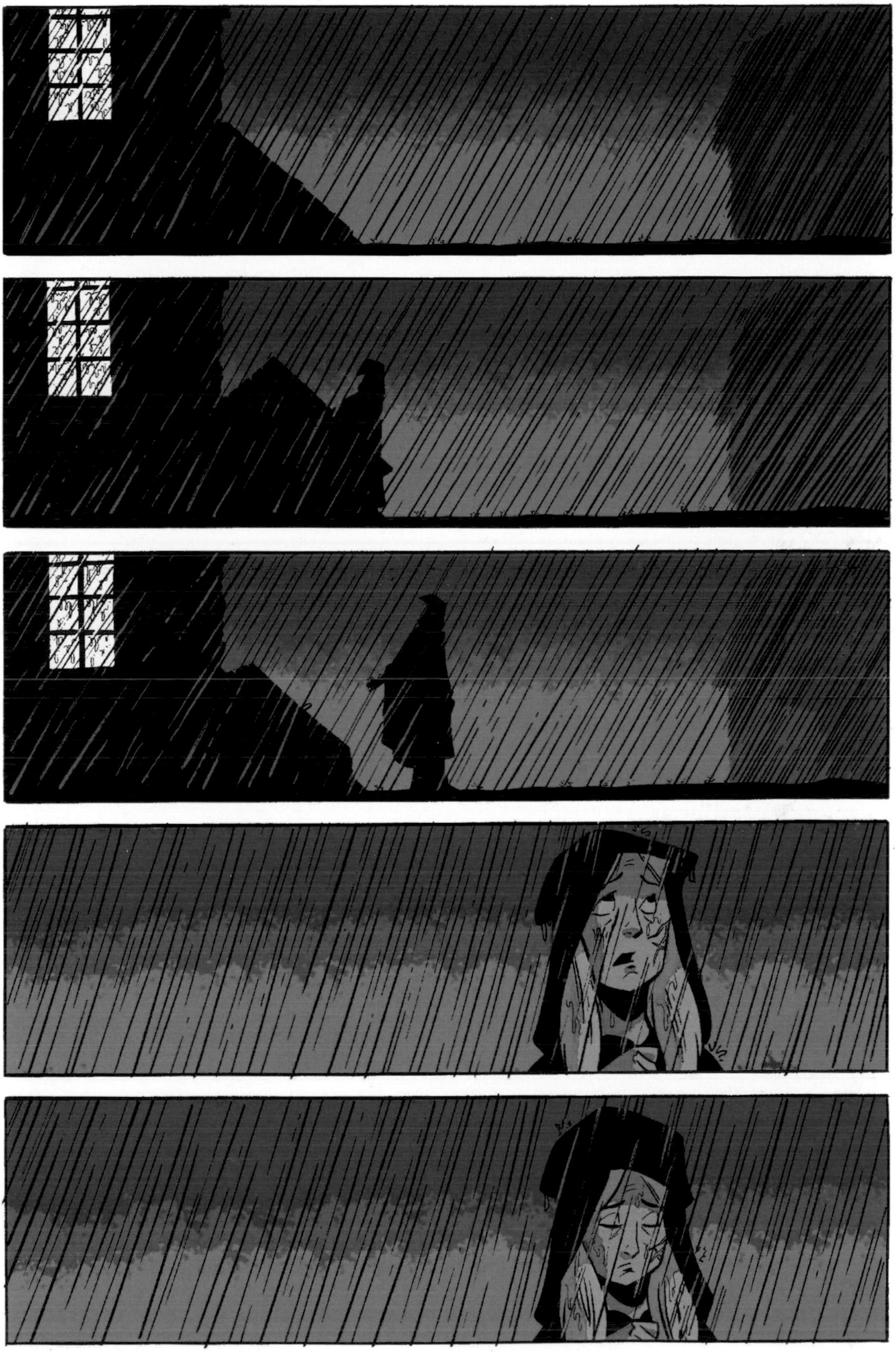

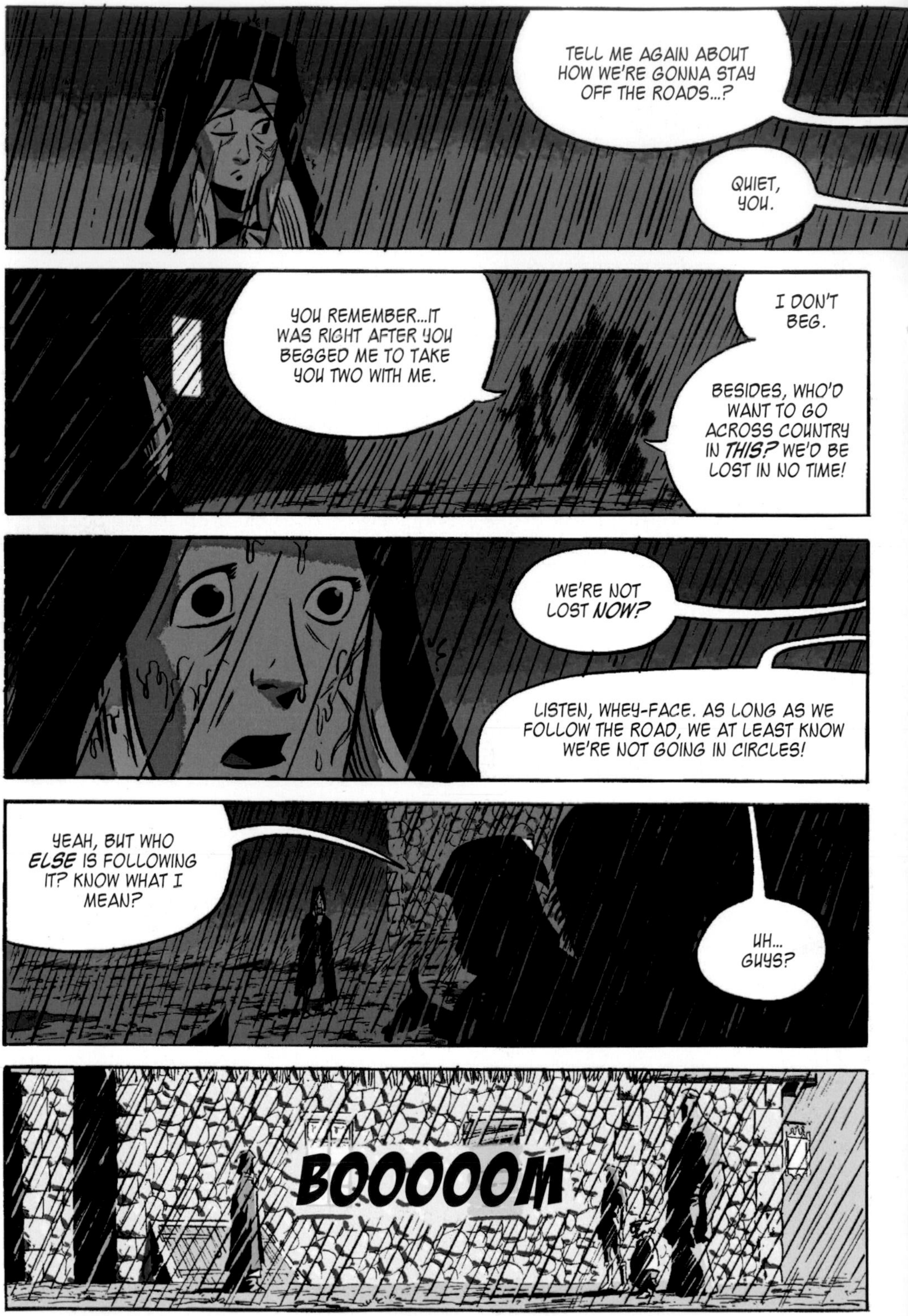
TELL ME AGAIN ABOUT HOW WE'RE GONNA STAY OFF THE ROADS...?
QUIET, YOU.
YOU REMEMBER...IT WAS RIGHT AFTER YOU BEGGED ME TO TAKE YOU TWO WITH ME.
I DON'T BEG.
BESIDES, WHO'D WANT TO GO ACROSS COUNTRY IN THIS? WE'D BE LOST IN NO TIME!
WE'RE NOT LOST NOW?
LISTEN, WHEY-FACE. AS LONG AS WE FOLLOW THE ROAD, WE AT LEAST KNOW WE'RE NOT GOING IN CIRCLES!
YEAH, BUT WHO ELSE IS FOLLOWING IT? KNOW WHAT I MEAN?
UH... GUYS?
BOOOOOM

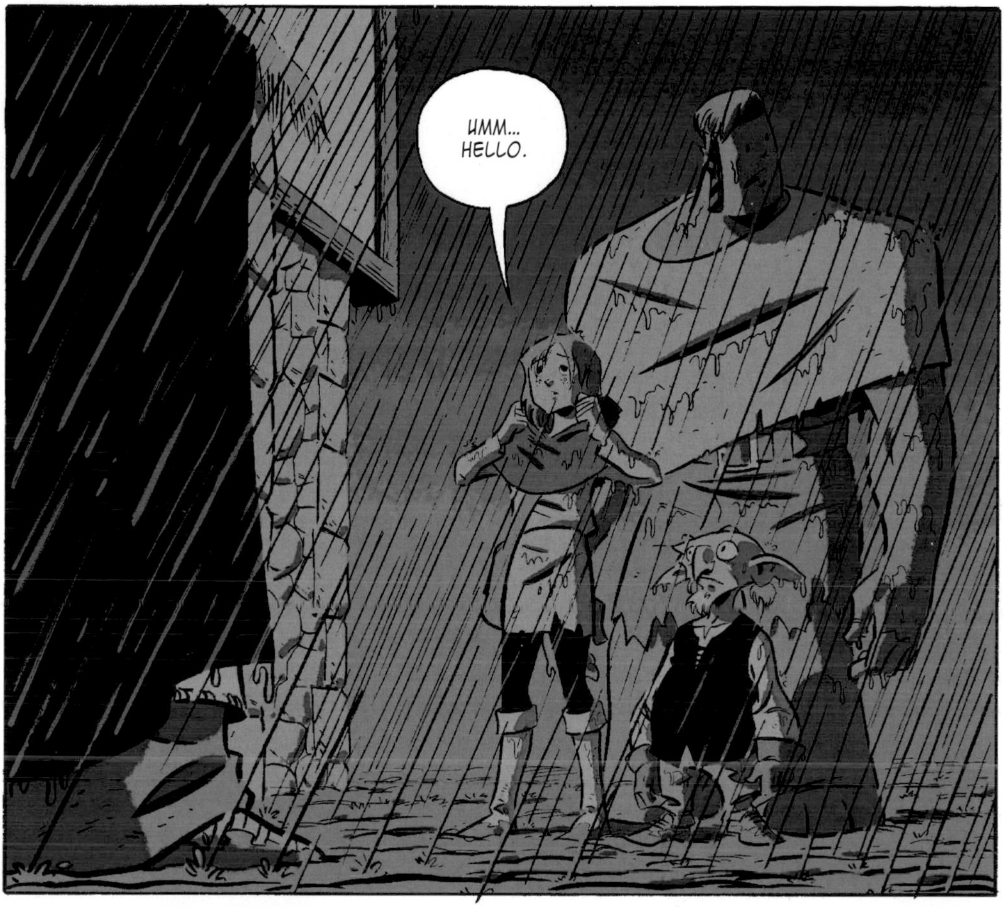
UMM... HELLO.
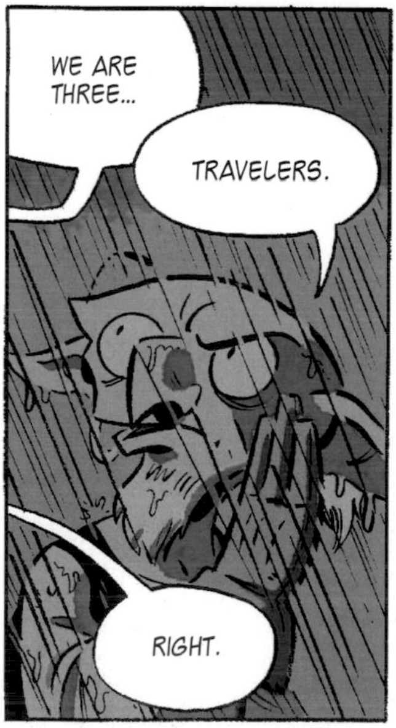
WE ARE THREE...
TRAVELERS.
RIGHT.
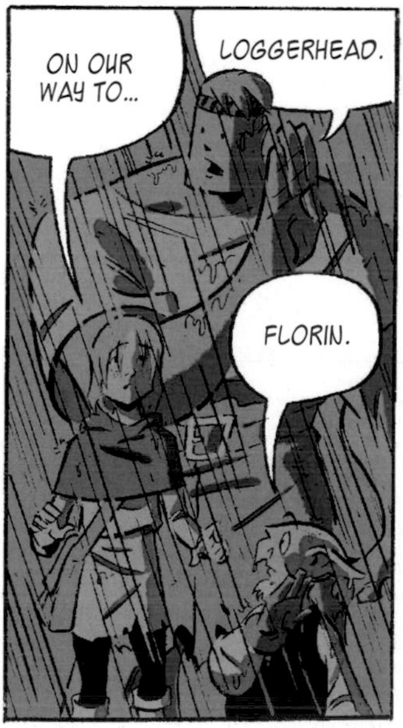
ON OUR WAY TO...
LOGGERHEAD.
FLORIN.
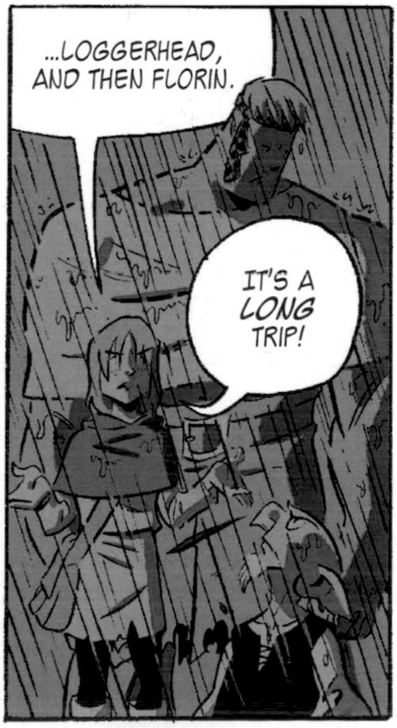
...LOGGERHEAD, AND THEN FLORIN.
IT'S A *LONG* TRIP!

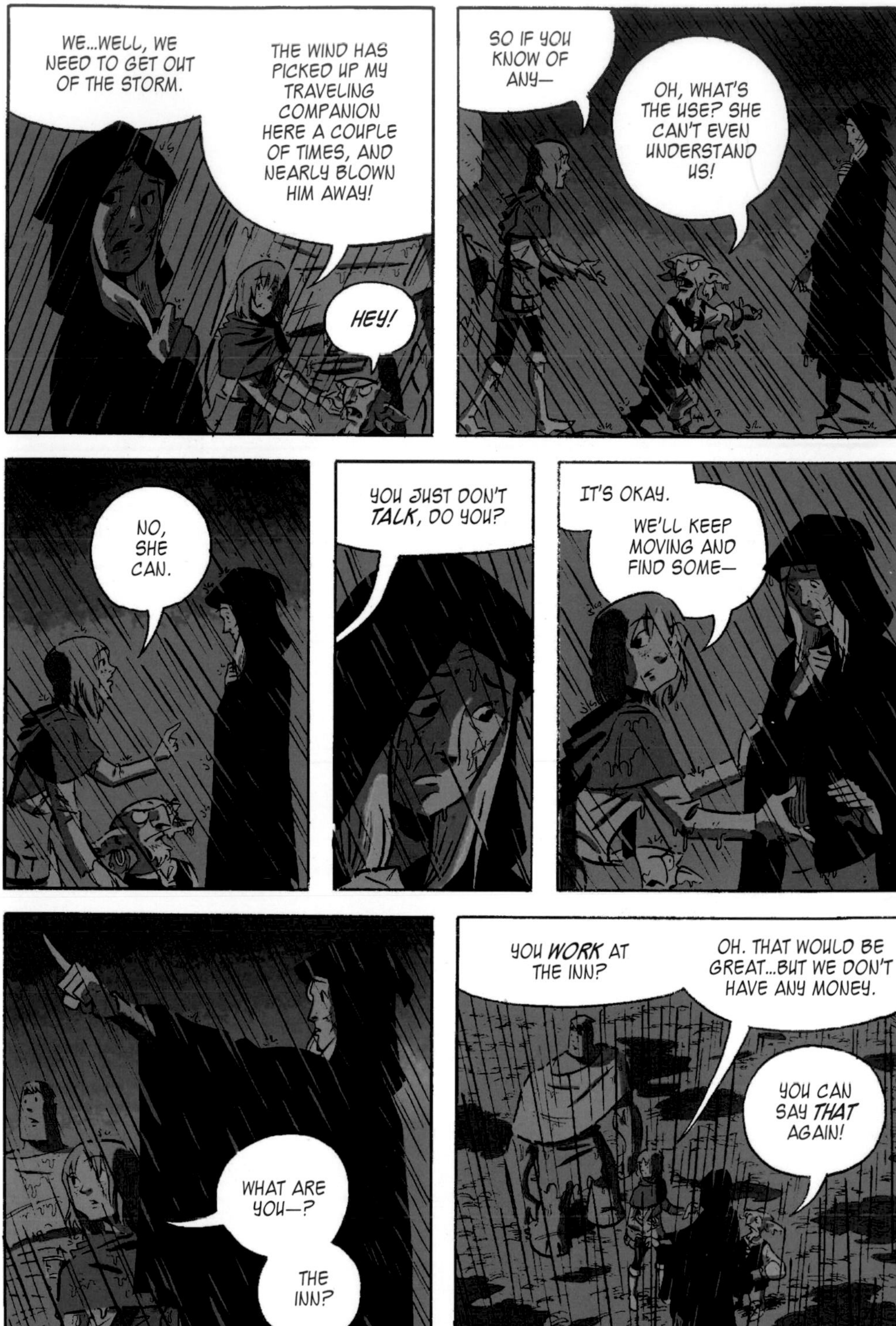
WE...WELL, WE NEED TO GET OUT OF THE STORM.
THE WIND HAS PICKED UP MY TRAVELING COMPANION HERE A COUPLE OF TIMES, AND NEARLY BLOWN HIM AWAY!
HEY!
SO IF YOU KNOW OF ANY—
OH, WHAT'S THE USE? SHE CAN'T EVEN UNDERSTAND US!
NO, SHE CAN.
YOU JUST DON'T TALK, DO YOU?
IT'S OKAY.
WE'LL KEEP MOVING AND FIND SOME—
WHAT ARE YOU—?
THE INN?
YOU WORK AT THE INN?
OH. THAT WOULD BE GREAT...BUT WE DON'T HAVE ANY MONEY.
YOU CAN SAY THAT AGAIN!

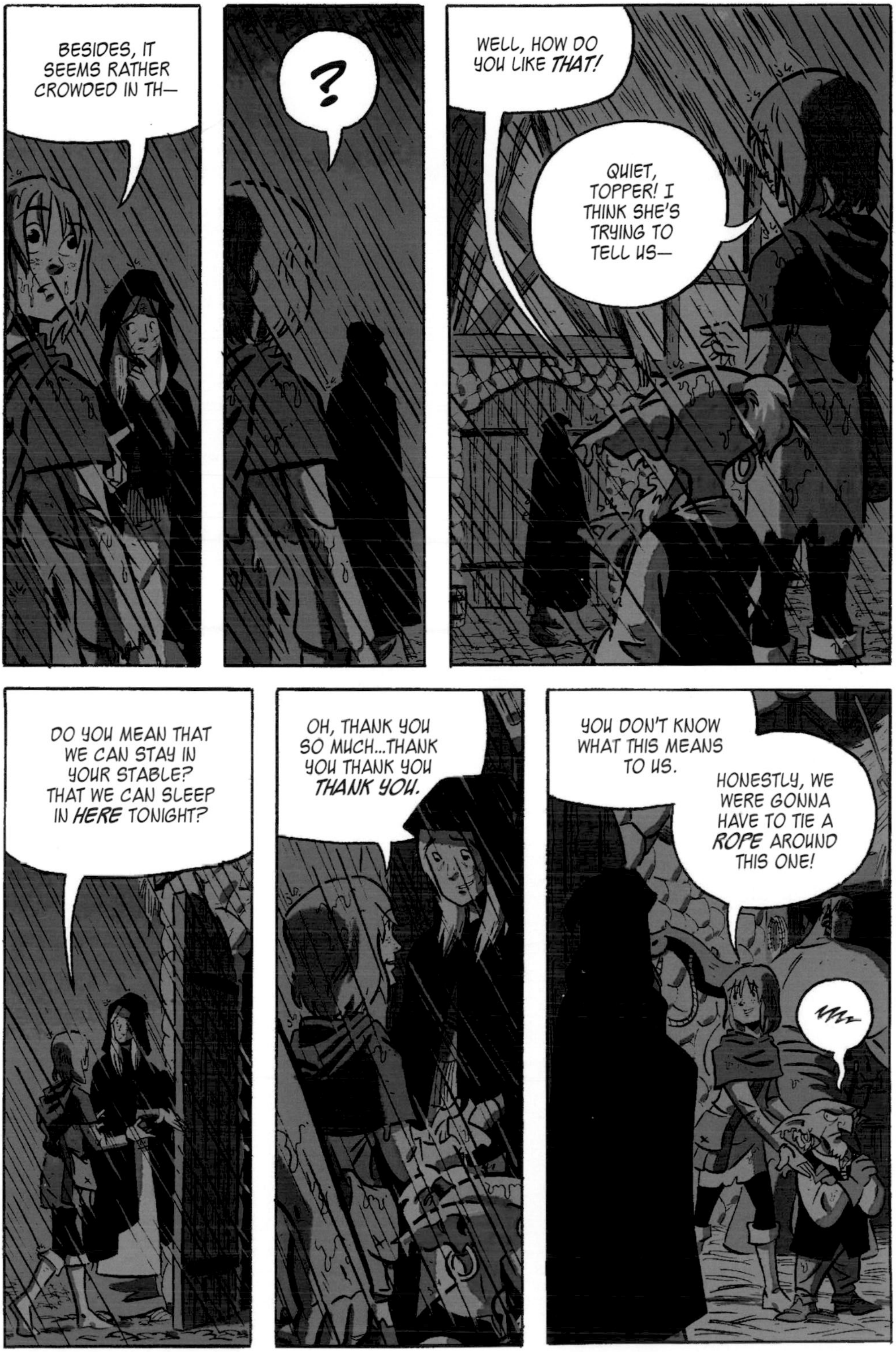
BESIDES, IT SEEMS RATHER CROWDED IN TH—
?
WELL, HOW DO YOU LIKE THAT!
QUIET, TOPPER! I THINK SHE'S TRYING TO TELL US—
DO YOU MEAN THAT WE CAN STAY IN YOUR STABLE? THAT WE CAN SLEEP IN HERE TONIGHT?
OH, THANK YOU SO MUCH...THANK YOU THANK YOU THANK YOU.
YOU DON'T KNOW WHAT THIS MEANS TO US.
HONESTLY, WE WERE GONNA HAVE TO TIE A ROPE AROUND THIS ONE!

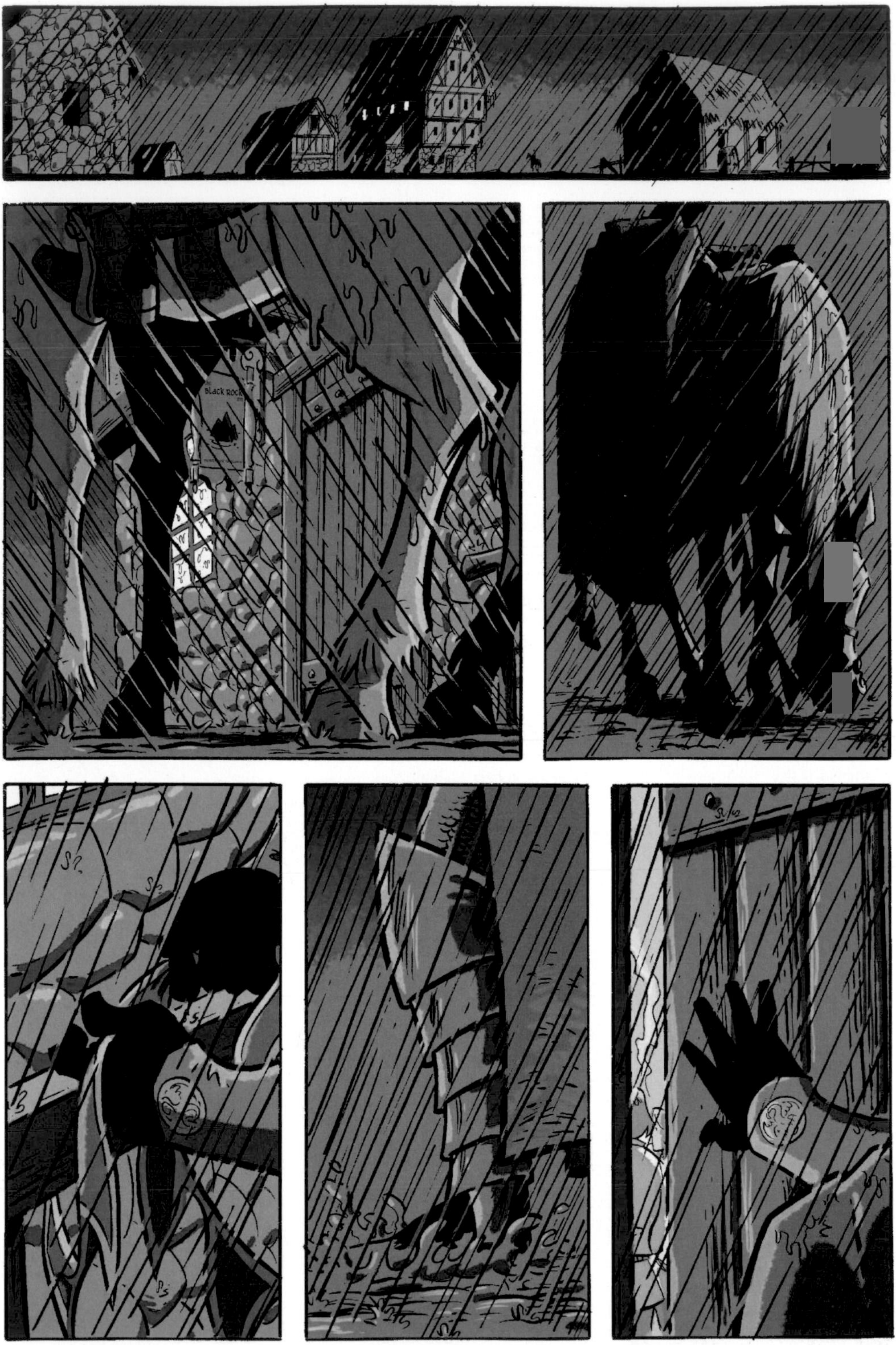
BLACK ROCK

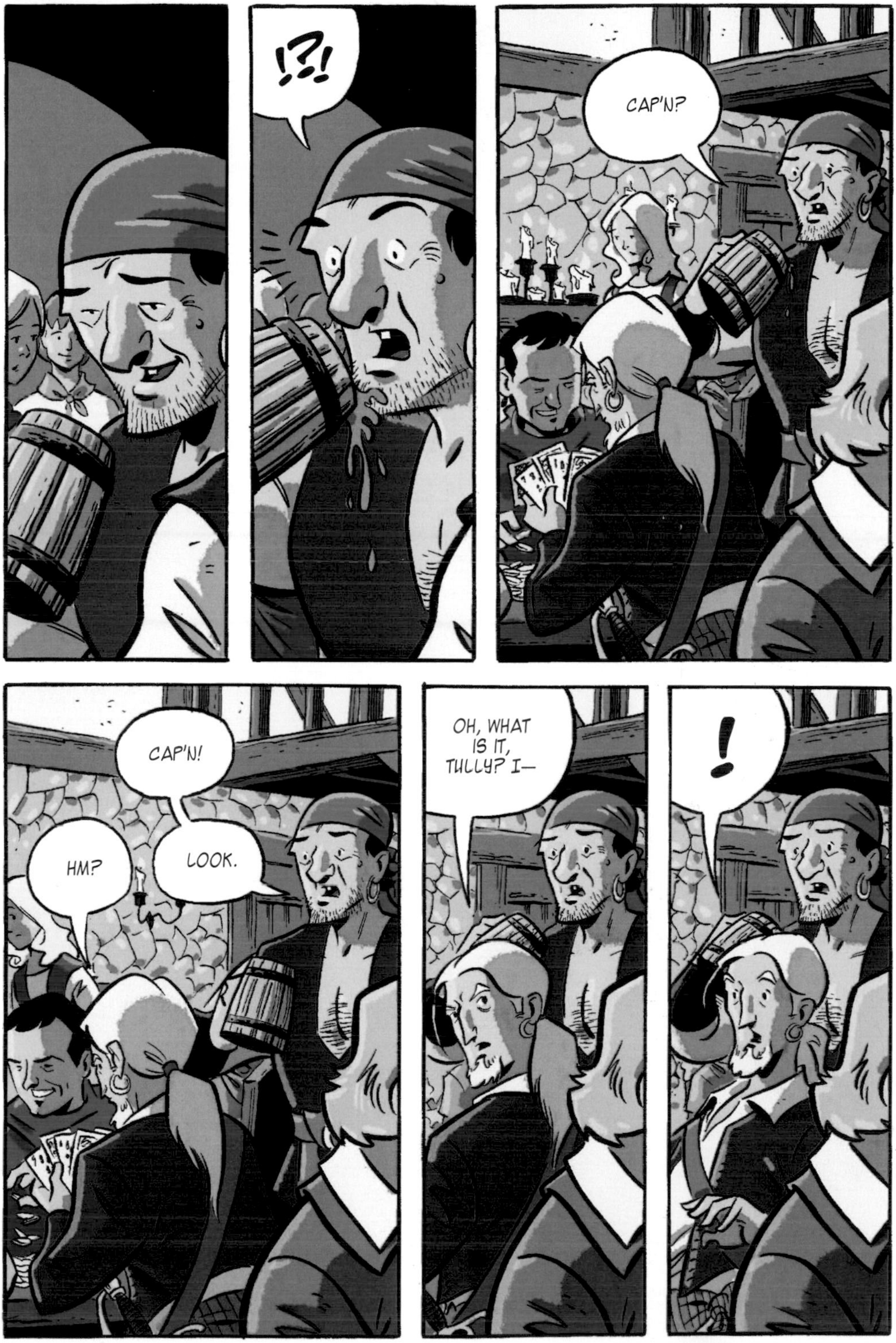
!?!
CAP'N?
CAP'N!
HM?
LOOK.
OH, WHAT IS IT, TULLY? I—
!

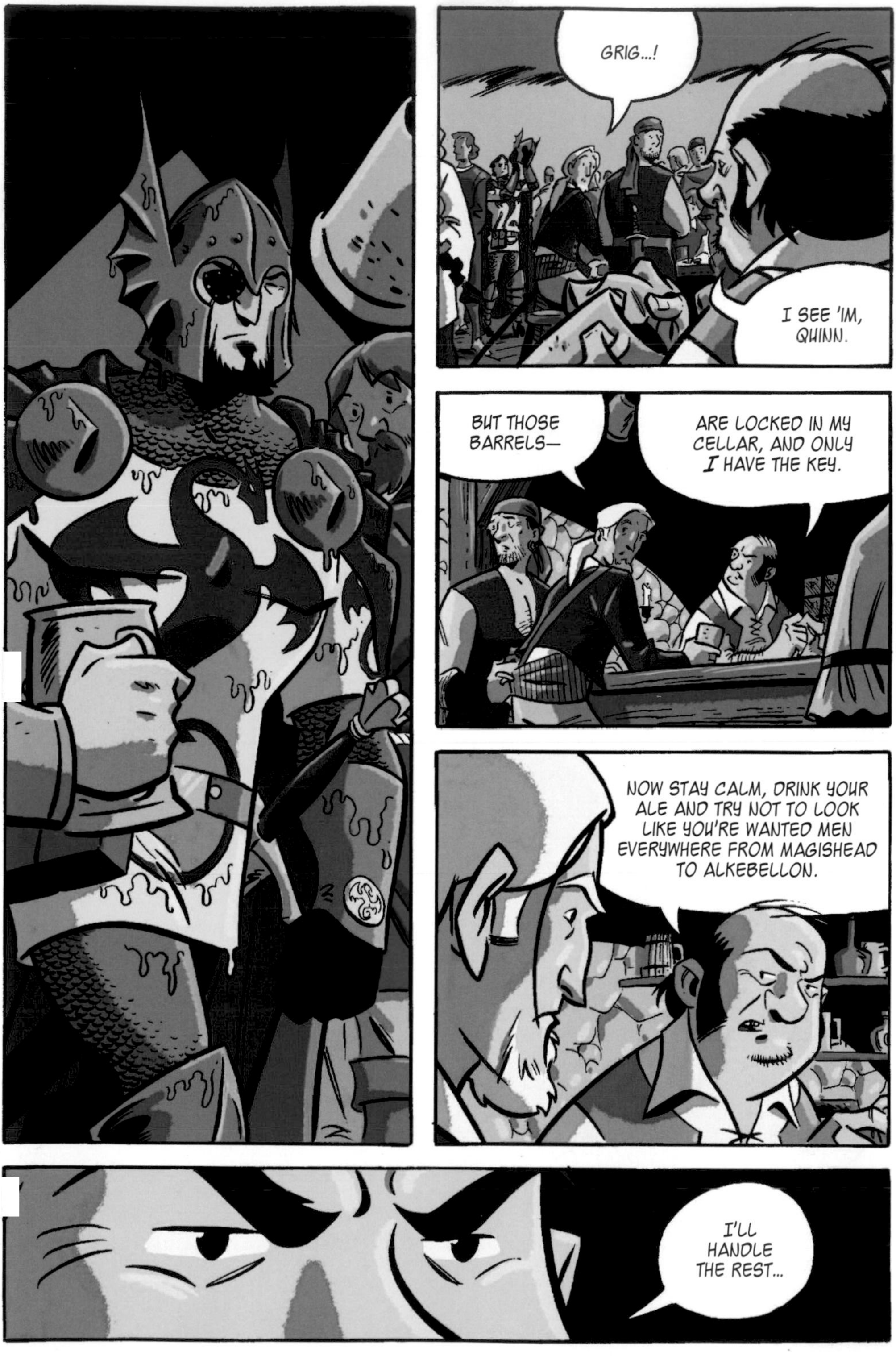
GRIG...!
I SEE 'IM, QUINN.
BUT THOSE BARRELS—
ARE LOCKED IN MY CELLAR, AND ONLY I HAVE THE KEY.
NOW STAY CALM, DRINK YOUR ALE AND TRY NOT TO LOOK LIKE YOU'RE WANTED MEN EVERYWHERE FROM MAGISHEAD TO ALKEBELLON.
I'LL HANDLE THE REST...

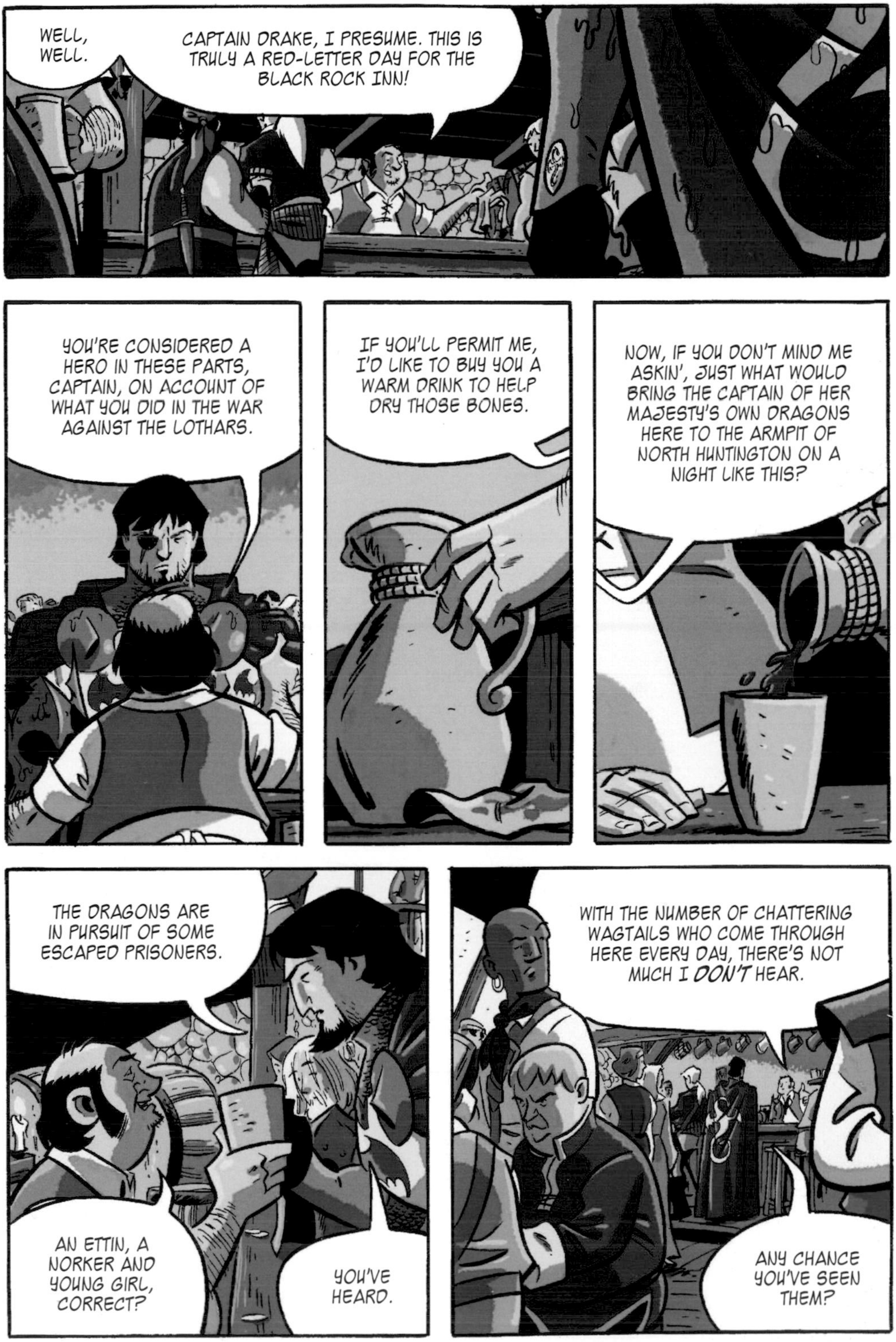
WELL, WELL.
CAPTAIN DRAKE, I PRESUME. THIS IS TRULY A RED-LETTER DAY FOR THE BLACK ROCK INN!
YOU'RE CONSIDERED A HERO IN THESE PARTS, CAPTAIN, ON ACCOUNT OF WHAT YOU DID IN THE WAR AGAINST THE LOTHARS.
IF YOU'LL PERMIT ME, I'D LIKE TO BUY YOU A WARM DRINK TO HELP DRY THOSE BONES.
NOW, IF YOU DON'T MIND ME ASKIN', JUST WHAT WOULD BRING THE CAPTAIN OF HER MAJESTY'S OWN DRAGONS HERE TO THE ARMPIT OF NORTH HUNTINGTON ON A NIGHT LIKE THIS?
THE DRAGONS ARE IN PURSUIT OF SOME ESCAPED PRISONERS.
AN ETTIN, A NORKER AND YOUNG GIRL, CORRECT?
YOU'VE HEARD.
WITH THE NUMBER OF CHATTERING WAGTAILS WHO COME THROUGH HERE EVERY DAY, THERE'S NOT MUCH I *DON'T* HEAR.
ANY CHANCE YOU'VE SEEN THEM?

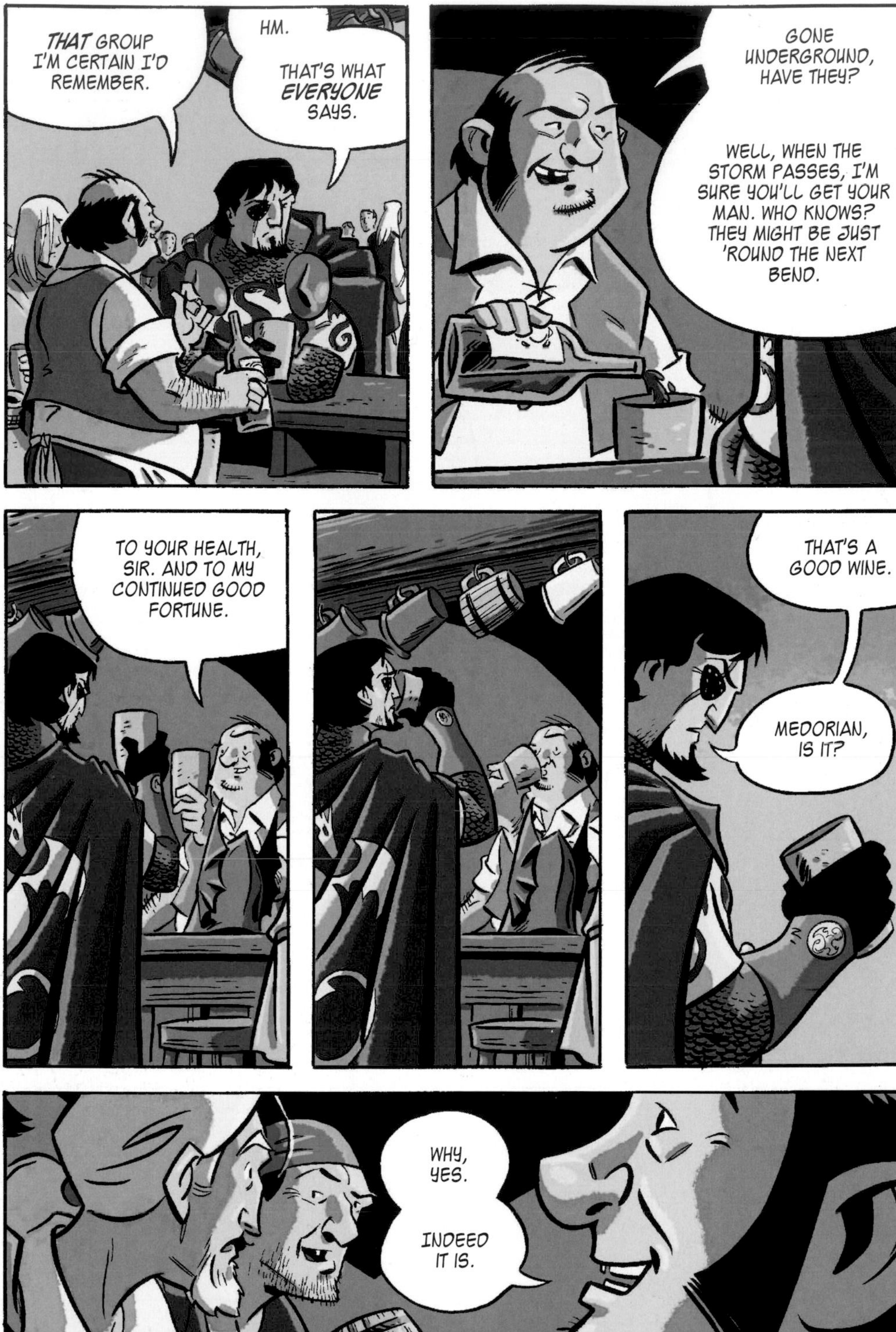
THAT GROUP I'M CERTAIN I'D REMEMBER.
HM.
THAT'S WHAT EVERYONE SAYS.
GONE UNDERGROUND, HAVE THEY?
WELL, WHEN THE STORM PASSES, I'M SURE YOU'LL GET YOUR MAN. WHO KNOWS? THEY MIGHT BE JUST 'ROUND THE NEXT BEND.
TO YOUR HEALTH, SIR. AND TO MY CONTINUED GOOD FORTUNE.
THAT'S A GOOD WINE.
MEDORIAN, IS IT?
WHY, YES.
INDEED IT IS.

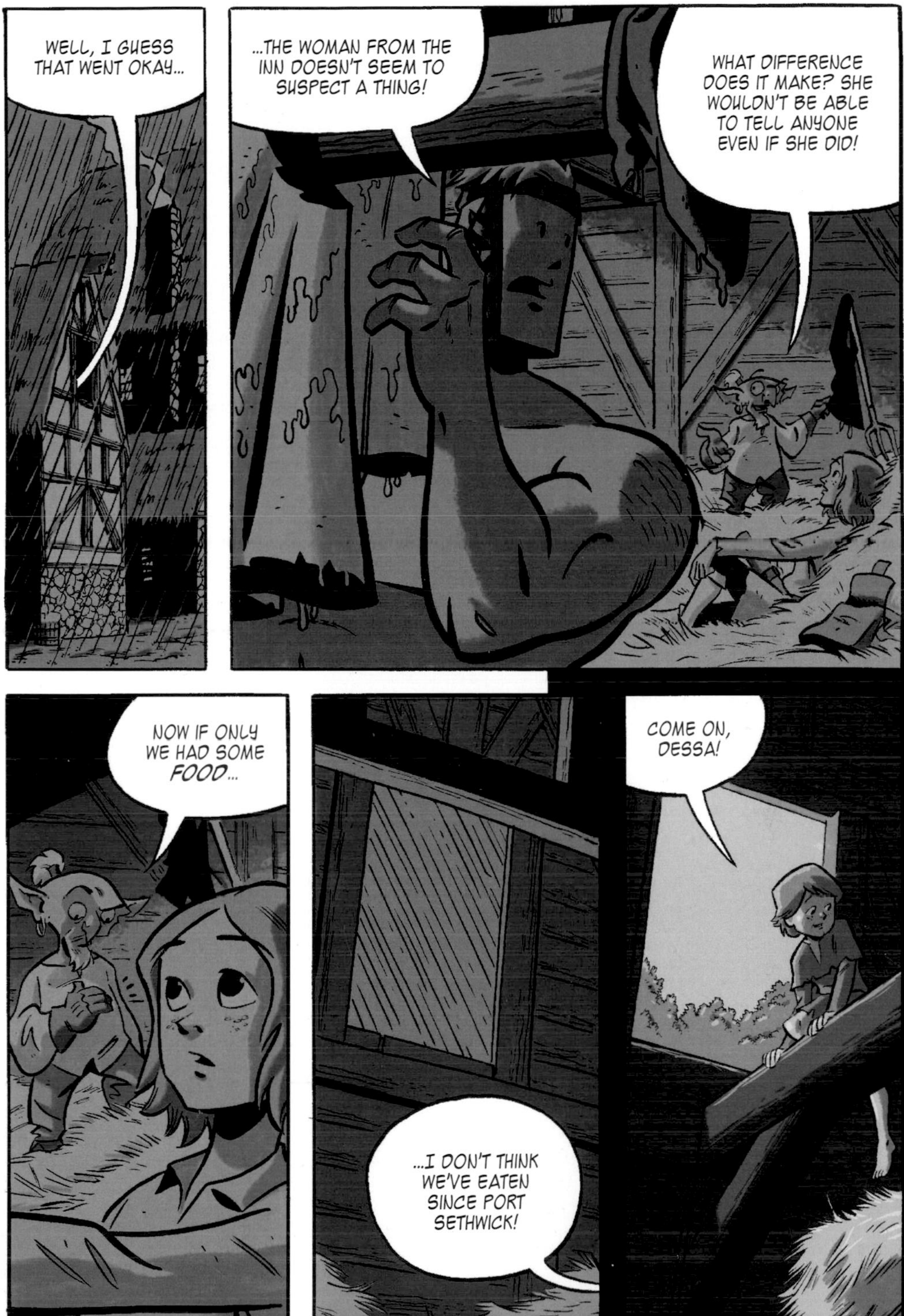
WELL, I GUESS THAT WENT OKAY...
...THE WOMAN FROM THE INN DOESN'T SEEM TO SUSPECT A THING!
WHAT DIFFERENCE DOES IT MAKE? SHE WOULDN'T BE ABLE TO TELL ANYONE EVEN IF SHE DID!
NOW IF ONLY WE HAD SOME *FOOD*...
...I DON'T THINK WE'VE EATEN SINCE PORT SETHWICK!
COME ON, DESSA!

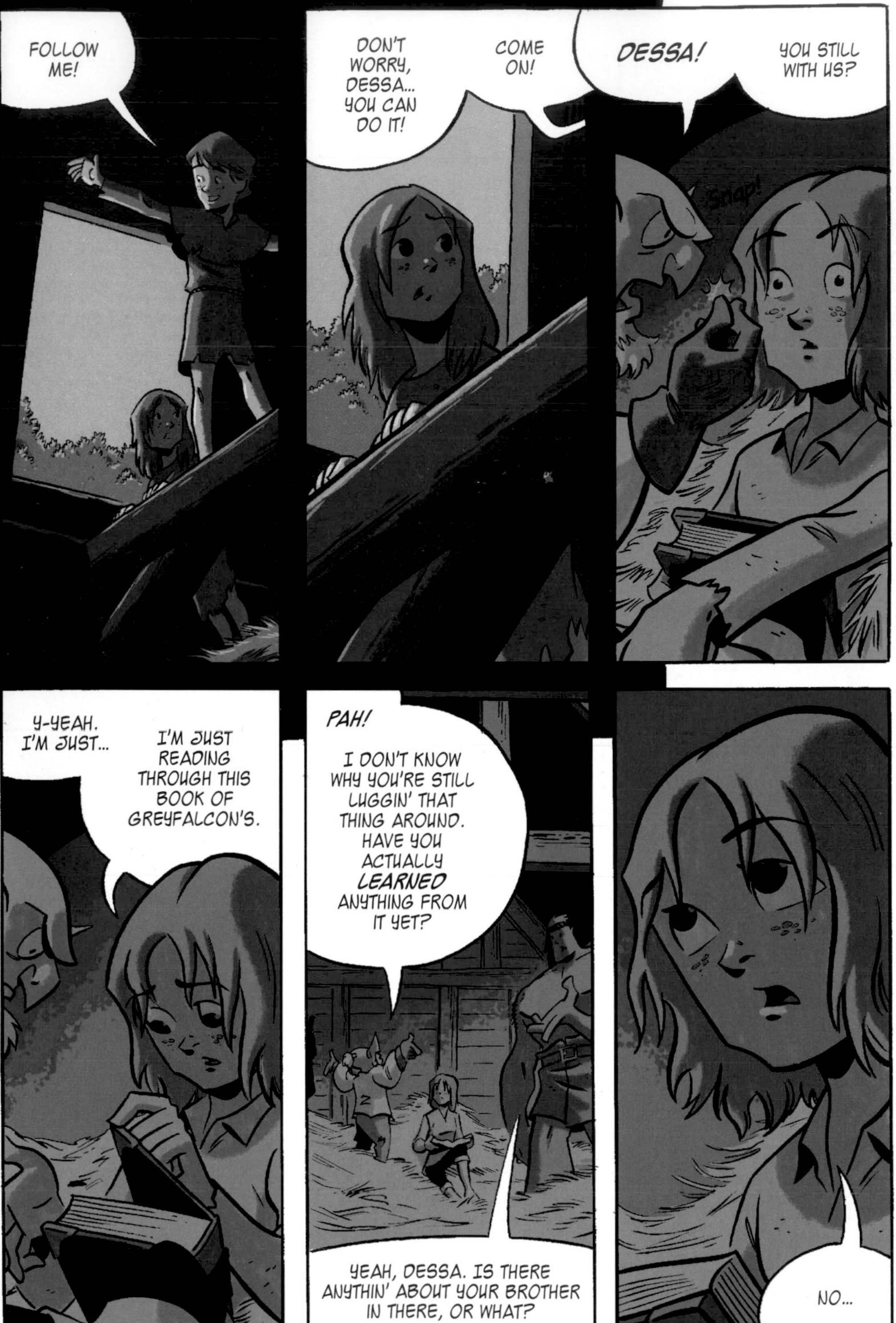
FOLLOW ME!
DON'T WORRY, DESSA... YOU CAN DO IT!
COME ON!
DESSA!
YOU STILL WITH US?
Snap!
Y-YEAH. I'M JUST...
I'M JUST READING THROUGH THIS BOOK OF GREYFALCON'S.
PAH!
I DON'T KNOW WHY YOU'RE STILL LUGGIN' THAT THING AROUND. HAVE YOU ACTUALLY LEARNED ANYTHING FROM IT YET?
YEAH, DESSA. IS THERE ANYTHIN' ABOUT YOUR BROTHER IN THERE, OR WHAT?
NO...

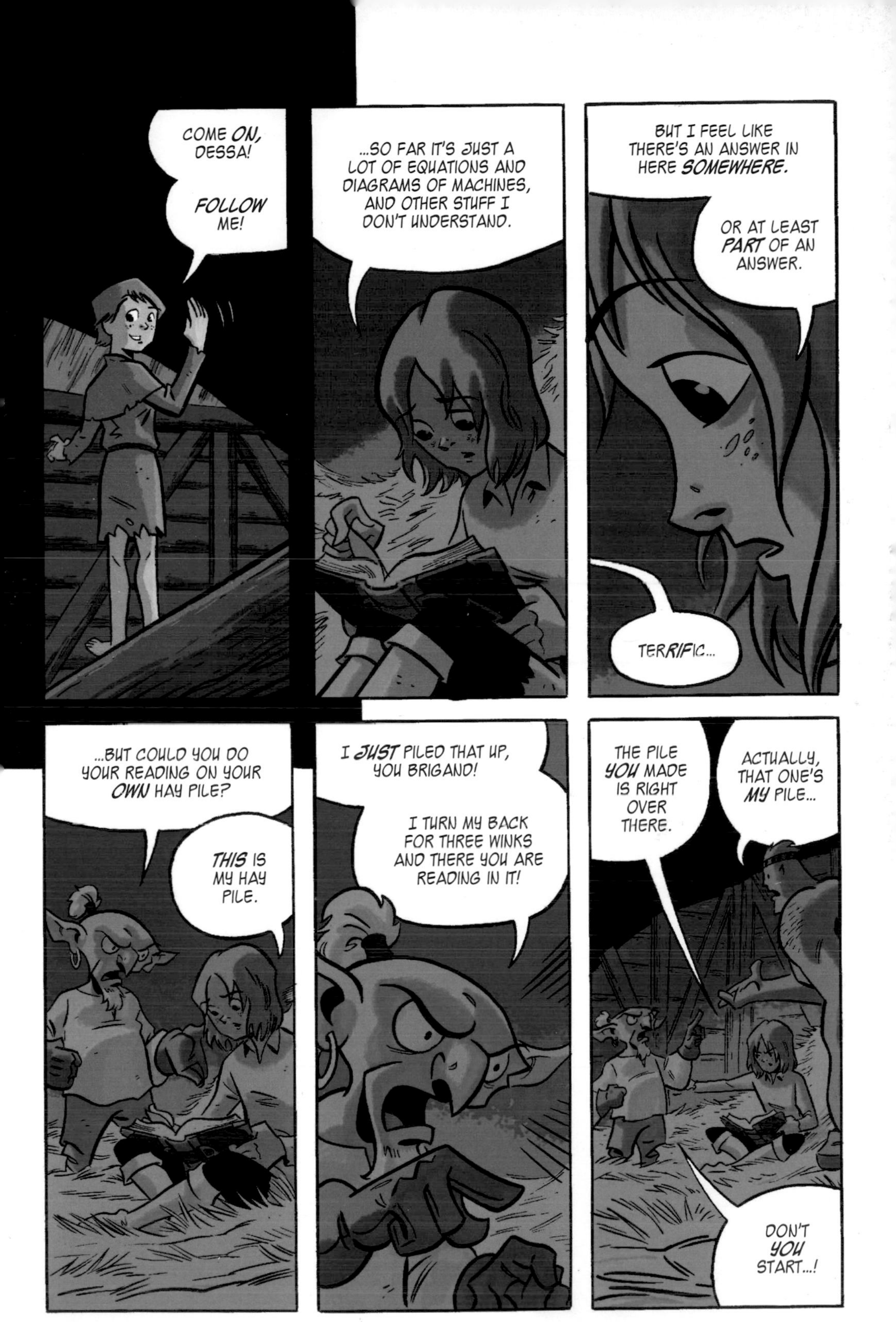
COME *ON,* DESSA!
FOLLOW ME!
...SO FAR IT'S JUST A LOT OF EQUATIONS AND DIAGRAMS OF MACHINES, AND OTHER STUFF I DON'T UNDERSTAND.
BUT I FEEL LIKE THERE'S AN ANSWER IN HERE *SOMEWHERE.*
OR AT LEAST *PART* OF AN ANSWER.
TER*RIF*IC...
...BUT COULD YOU DO YOUR READING ON YOUR *OWN* HAY PILE?
THIS IS MY HAY PILE.
I *JUST* PILED THAT UP, YOU BRIGAND!
I TURN MY BACK FOR THREE WINKS AND THERE YOU ARE READING IN IT!
THE PILE *YOU* MADE IS RIGHT OVER THERE.
ACTUALLY, THAT ONE'S *MY* PILE...
DON'T *YOU* START...!

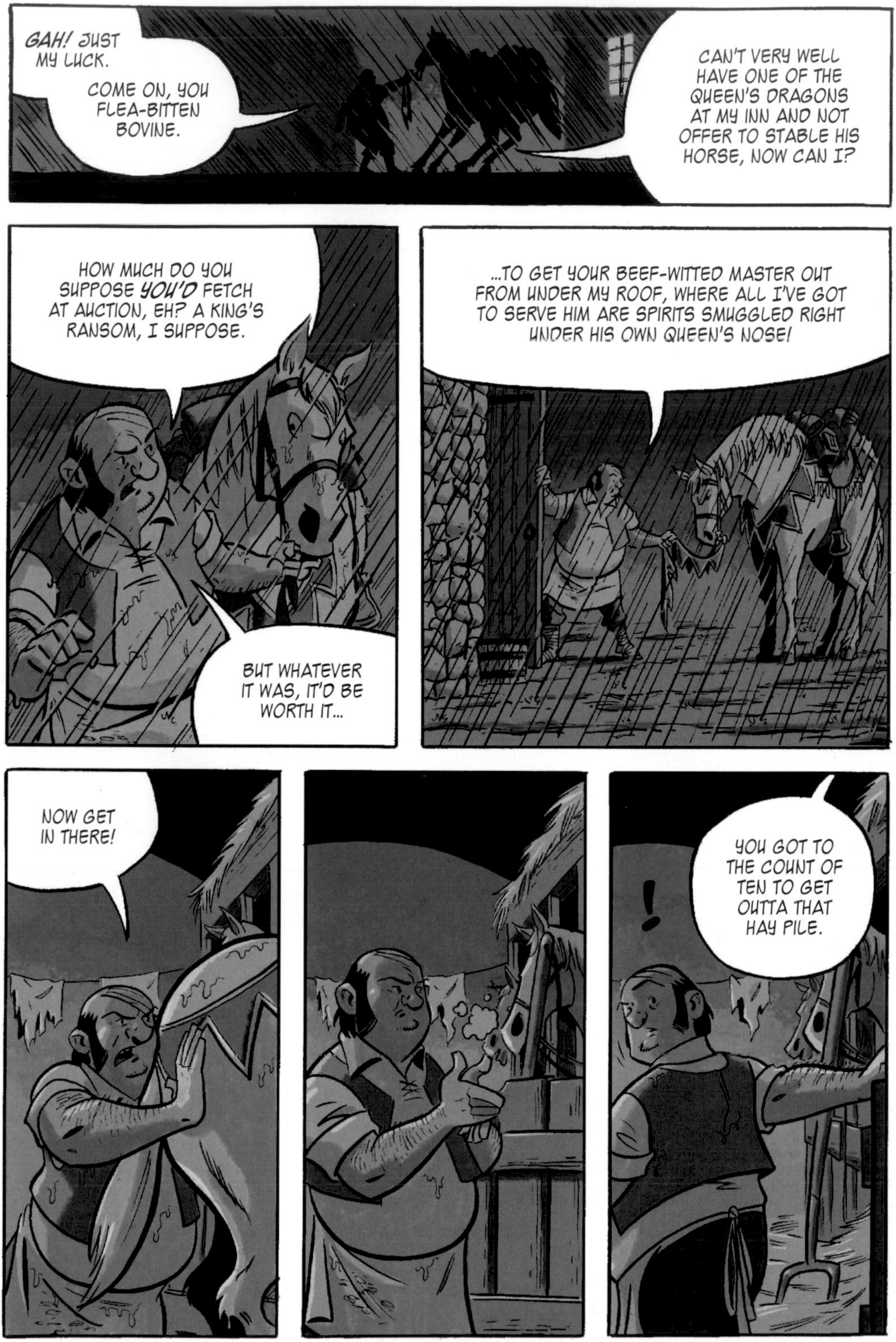
GAH! JUST MY LUCK.
COME ON, YOU FLEA-BITTEN BOVINE.
CAN'T VERY WELL HAVE ONE OF THE QUEEN'S DRAGONS AT MY INN AND NOT OFFER TO STABLE HIS HORSE, NOW CAN I?
HOW MUCH DO YOU SUPPOSE YOU'D FETCH AT AUCTION, EH? A KING'S RANSOM, I SUPPOSE.
BUT WHATEVER IT WAS, IT'D BE WORTH IT...
...TO GET YOUR BEEF-WITTED MASTER OUT FROM UNDER MY ROOF, WHERE ALL I'VE GOT TO SERVE HIM ARE SPIRITS SMUGGLED RIGHT UNDER HIS OWN QUEEN'S NOSE!
NOW GET IN THERE!
!
YOU GOT TO THE COUNT OF TEN TO GET OUTTA THAT HAY PILE.

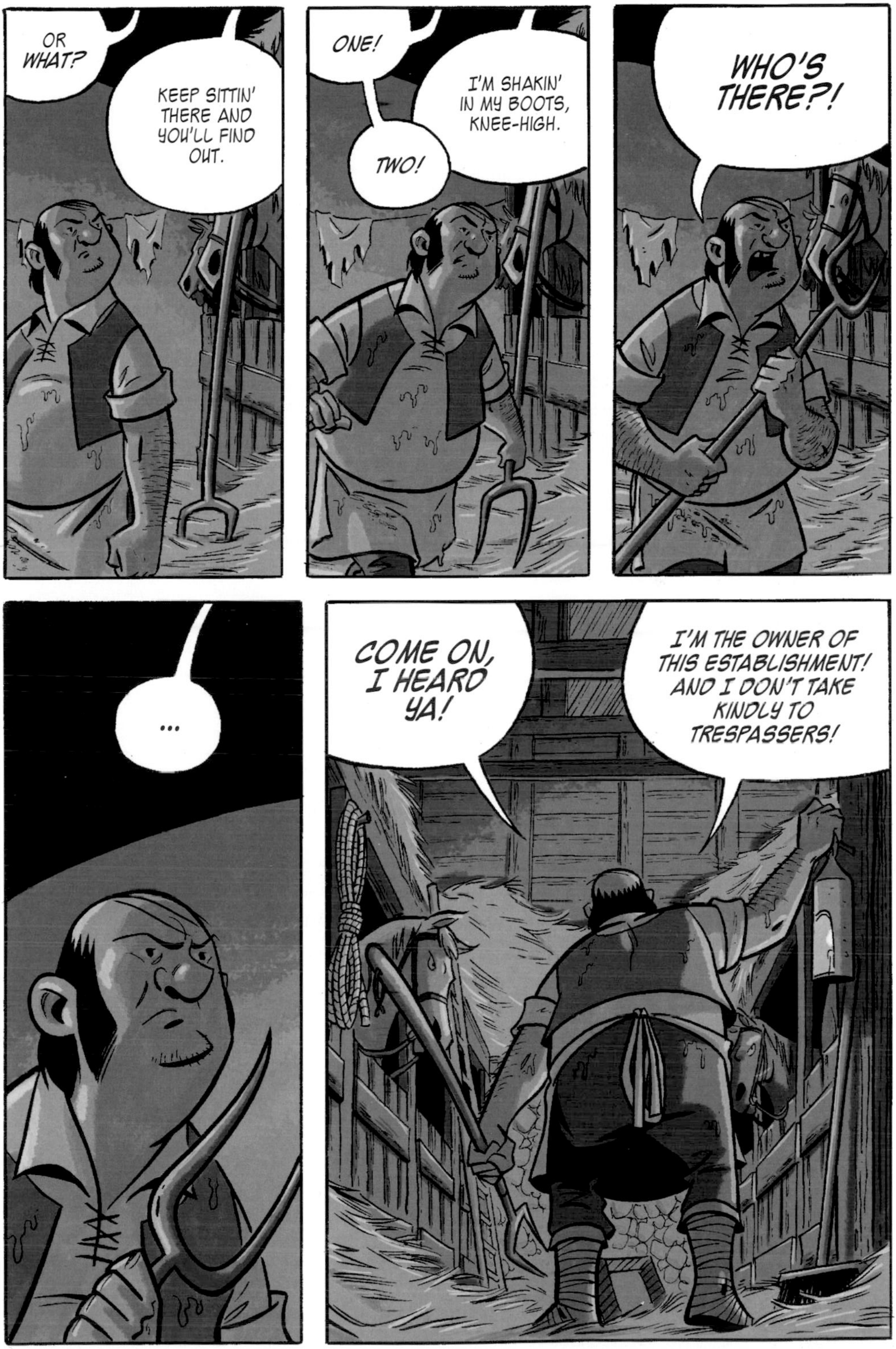
OR WHAT?
KEEP SITTIN' THERE AND YOU'LL FIND OUT.
ONE!
I'M SHAKIN' IN MY BOOTS, KNEE-HIGH.
TWO!
WHO'S THERE?!
...
COME ON, I HEARD YA!
I'M THE OWNER OF THIS ESTABLISHMENT! AND I DON'T TAKE KINDLY TO TRESPASSERS!

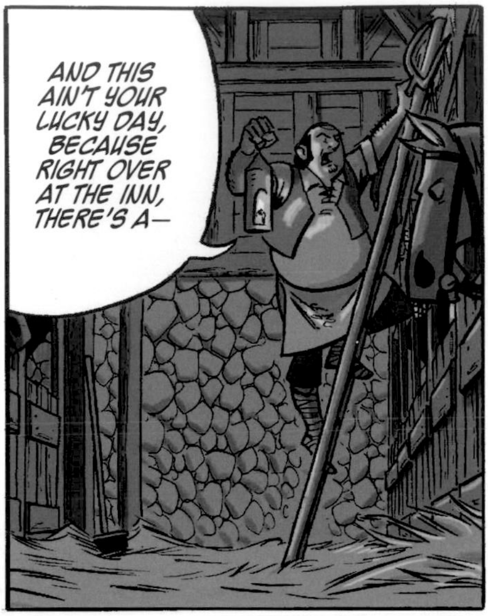
AND THIS AIN'T YOUR LUCKY DAY, BECAUSE RIGHT OVER AT THE INN, THERE'S A—

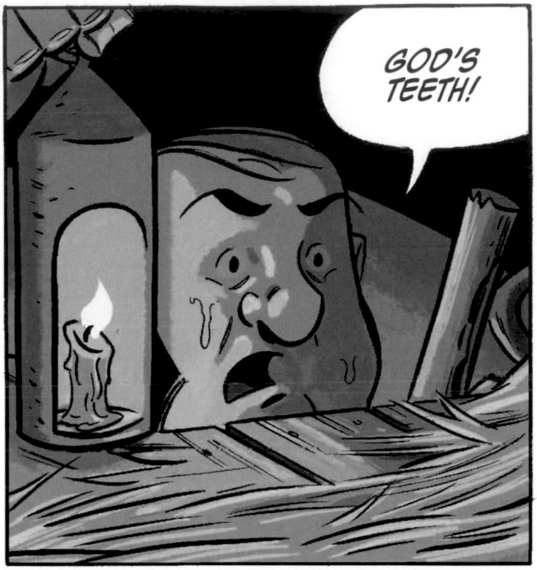
GOD'S TEETH!

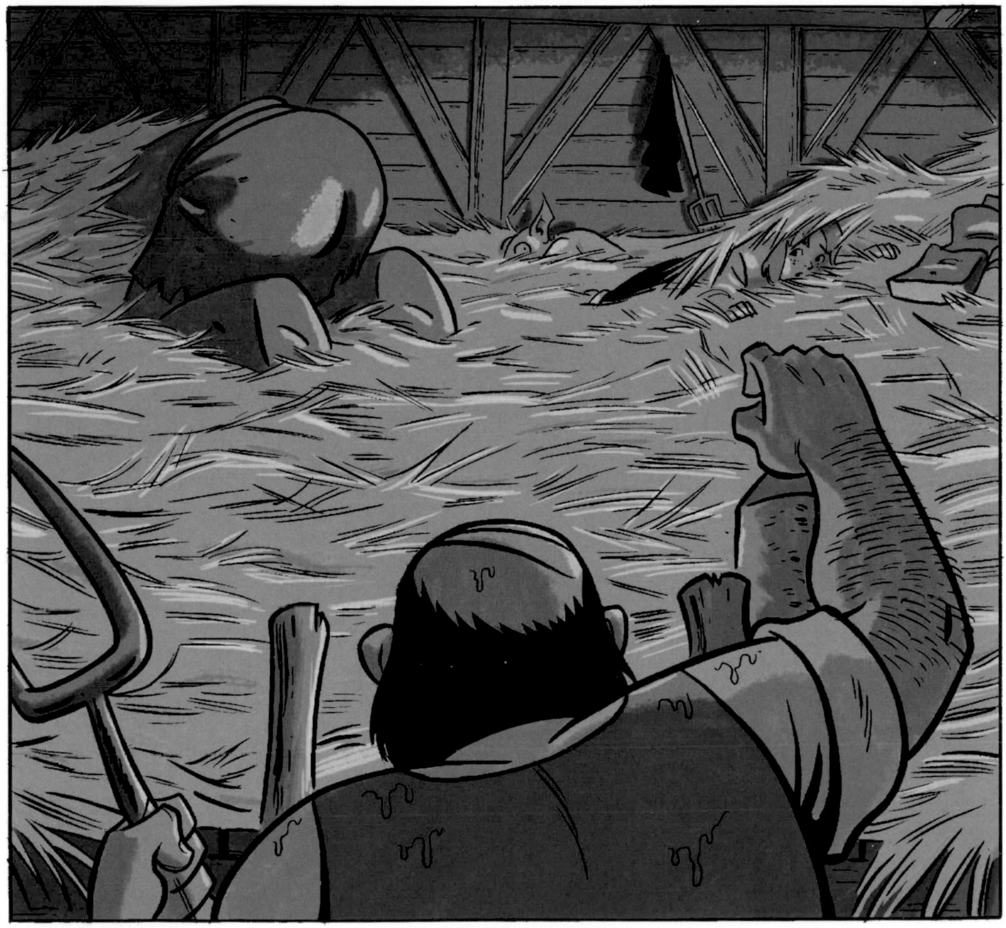

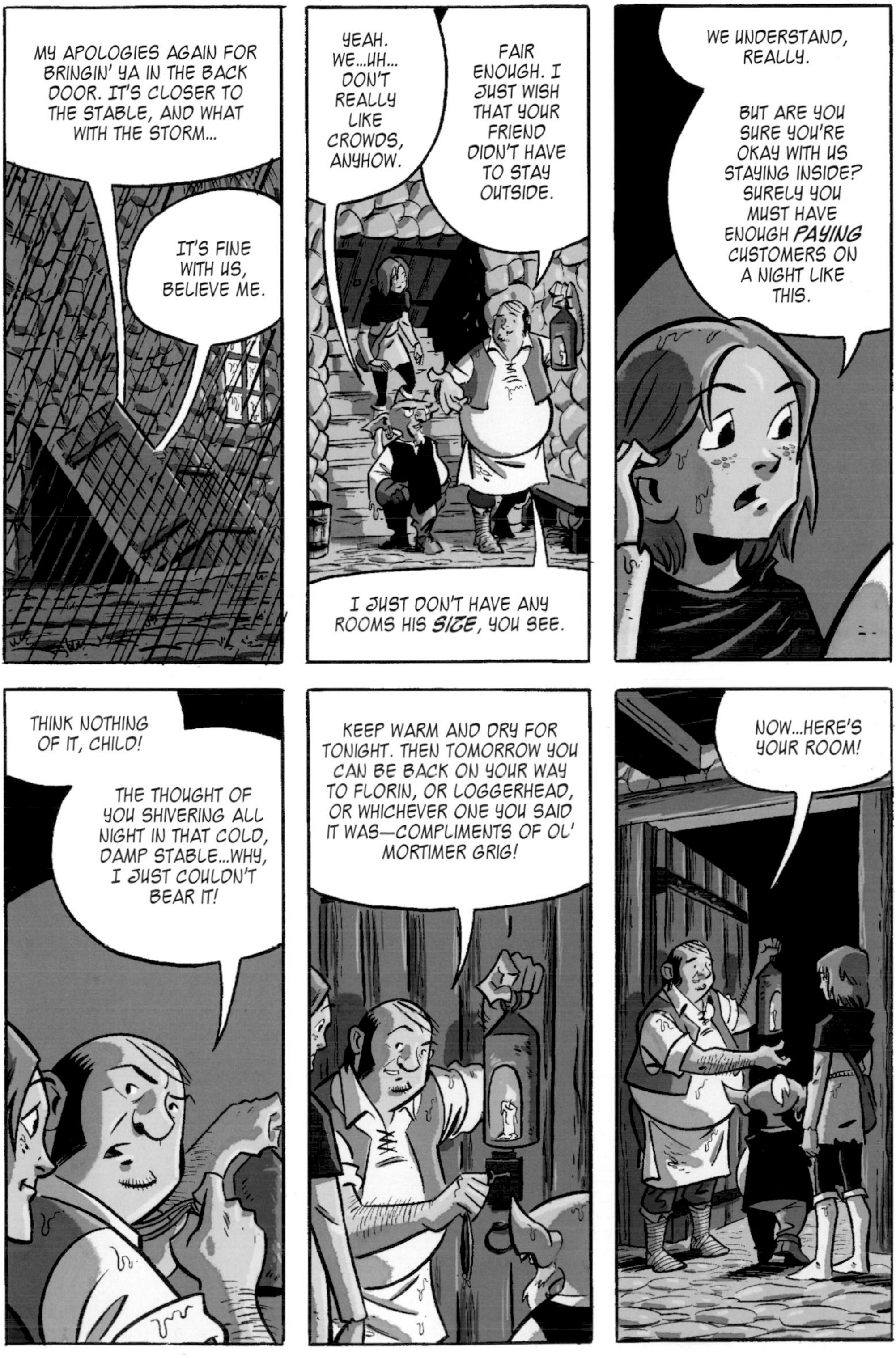
MY APOLOGIES AGAIN FOR BRINGIN' YA IN THE BACK DOOR. IT'S CLOSER TO THE STABLE, AND WHAT WITH THE STORM...
IT'S FINE WITH US, BELIEVE ME.
YEAH. WE...UH... DON'T REALLY LIKE CROWDS, ANYHOW.
FAIR ENOUGH. I JUST WISH THAT YOUR FRIEND DIDN'T HAVE TO STAY OUTSIDE.
I JUST DON'T HAVE ANY ROOMS HIS SIZE, YOU SEE.
WE UNDERSTAND, REALLY.
BUT ARE YOU SURE YOU'RE OKAY WITH US STAYING INSIDE? SURELY YOU MUST HAVE ENOUGH PAYING CUSTOMERS ON A NIGHT LIKE THIS.
THINK NOTHING OF IT, CHILD!
THE THOUGHT OF YOU SHIVERING ALL NIGHT IN THAT COLD, DAMP STABLE...WHY, I JUST COULDN'T BEAR IT!
KEEP WARM AND DRY FOR TONIGHT. THEN TOMORROW YOU CAN BE BACK ON YOUR WAY TO FLORIN, OR LOGGERHEAD, OR WHICHEVER ONE YOU SAID IT WAS—COMPLIMENTS OF OL' MORTIMER GRIG!
NOW...HERE'S YOUR ROOM!

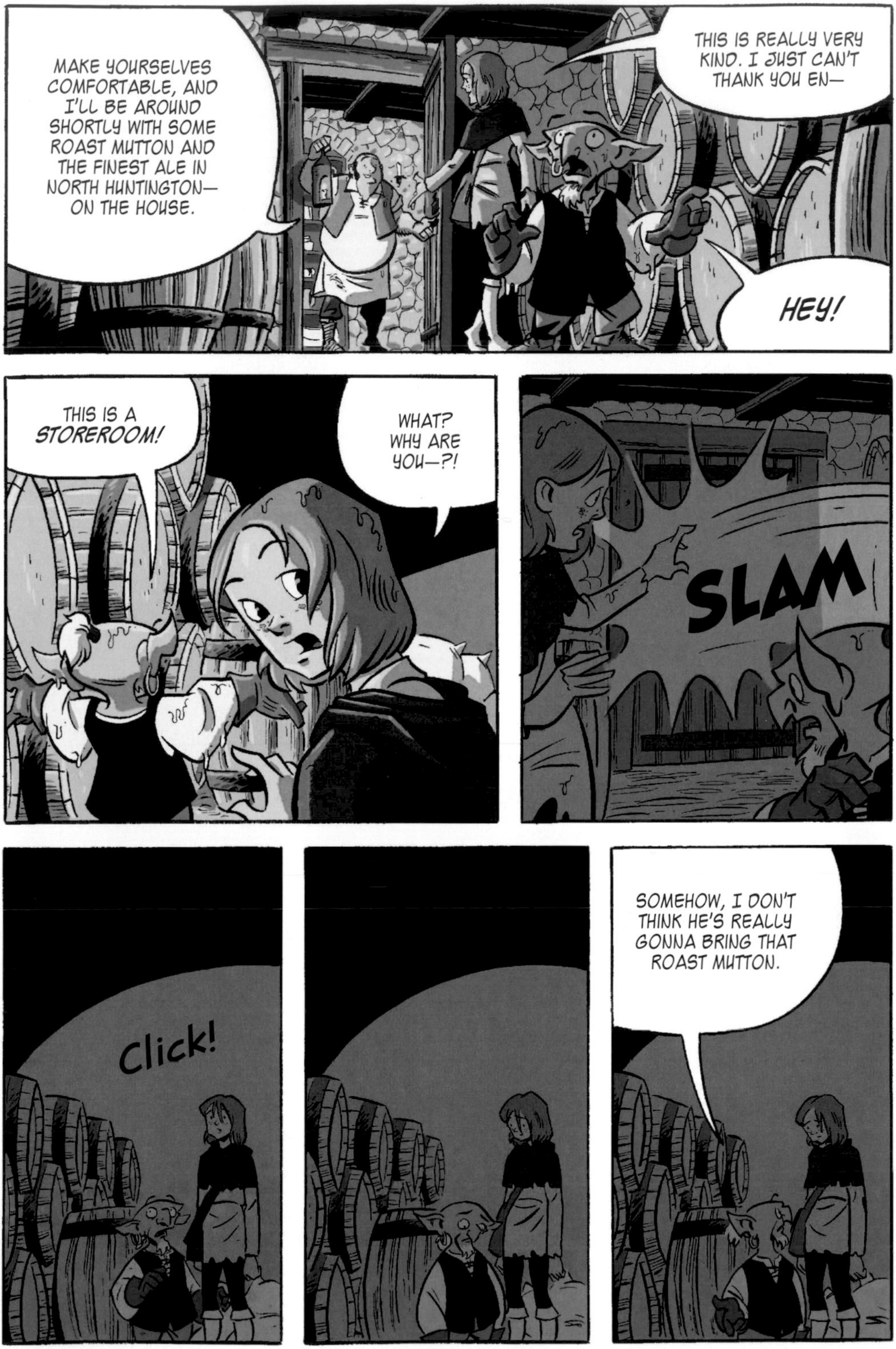
MAKE YOURSELVES COMFORTABLE, AND I'LL BE AROUND SHORTLY WITH SOME ROAST MUTTON AND THE FINEST ALE IN NORTH HUNTINGTON— ON THE HOUSE.
THIS IS REALLY VERY KIND. I JUST CAN'T THANK YOU EN—
HEY!
THIS IS A STOREROOM!
WHAT? WHY ARE YOU—?!
SLAM
Click!
SOMEHOW, I DON'T THINK HE'S REALLY GONNA BRING THAT ROAST MUTTON.

ACT TWO
DISAPPEARING ACT

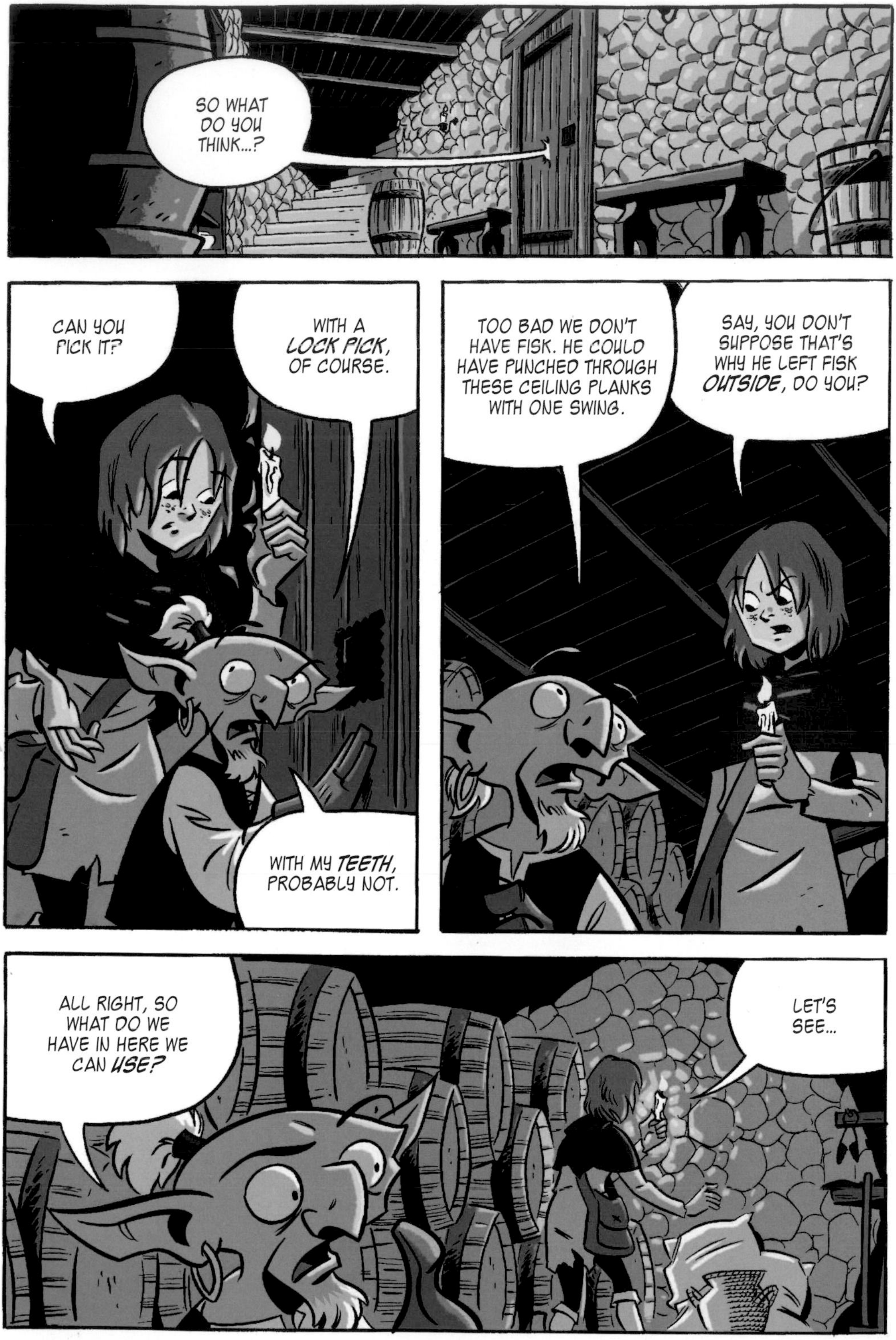
SO WHAT DO YOU THINK...?
CAN YOU PICK IT?
WITH A LOCK PICK, OF COURSE.
WITH MY TEETH, PROBABLY NOT.
TOO BAD WE DON'T HAVE FISK. HE COULD HAVE PUNCHED THROUGH THESE CEILING PLANKS WITH ONE SWING.
SAY, YOU DON'T SUPPOSE THAT'S WHY HE LEFT FISK OUTSIDE, DO YOU?
ALL RIGHT, SO WHAT DO WE HAVE IN HERE WE CAN USE?
LET'S SEE...

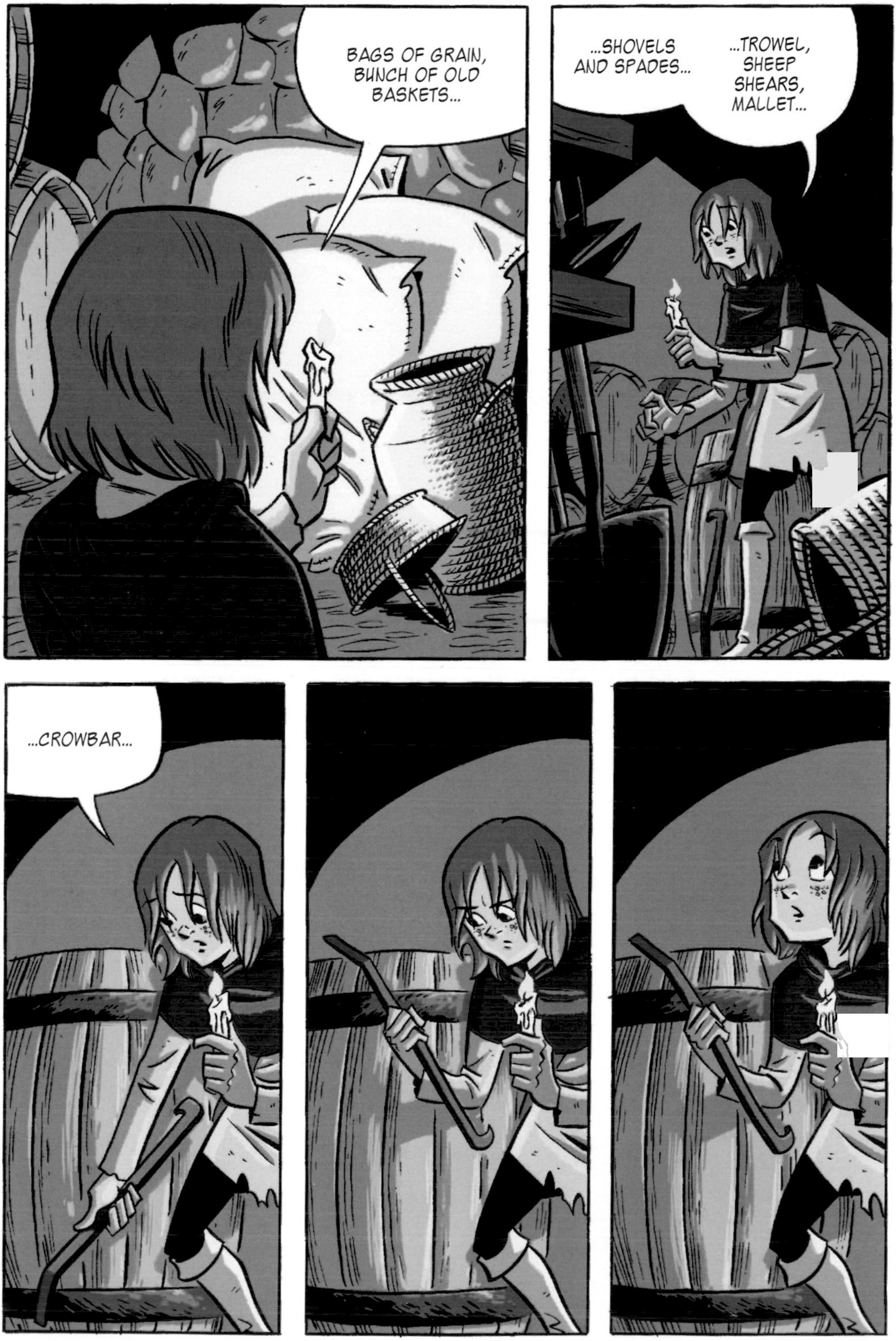
BAGS OF GRAIN, BUNCH OF OLD BASKETS...
...SHOVELS AND SPADES...
...TROWEL, SHEEP SHEARS, MALLET...
...CROWBAR...

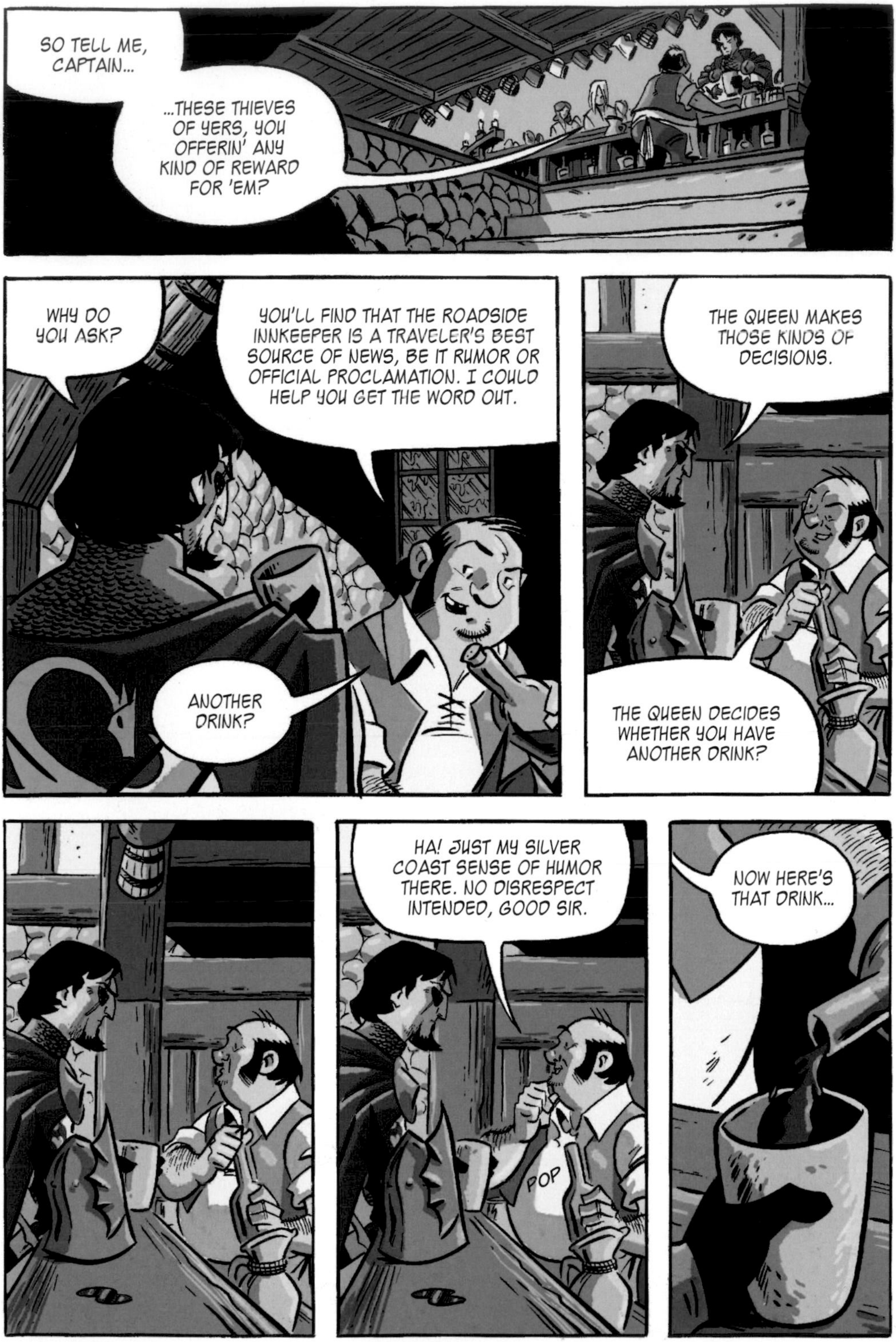
SO TELL ME, CAPTAIN...
...THESE THIEVES OF YERS, YOU OFFERIN' ANY KIND OF REWARD FOR 'EM?
WHY DO YOU ASK?
YOU'LL FIND THAT THE ROADSIDE INNKEEPER IS A TRAVELER'S BEST SOURCE OF NEWS, BE IT RUMOR OR OFFICIAL PROCLAMATION. I COULD HELP YOU GET THE WORD OUT.
ANOTHER DRINK?
THE QUEEN MAKES THOSE KINDS OF DECISIONS.
THE QUEEN DECIDES WHETHER YOU HAVE ANOTHER DRINK?
HA! JUST MY SILVER COAST SENSE OF HUMOR THERE. NO DISRESPECT INTENDED, GOOD SIR.
POP
NOW HERE'S THAT DRINK...

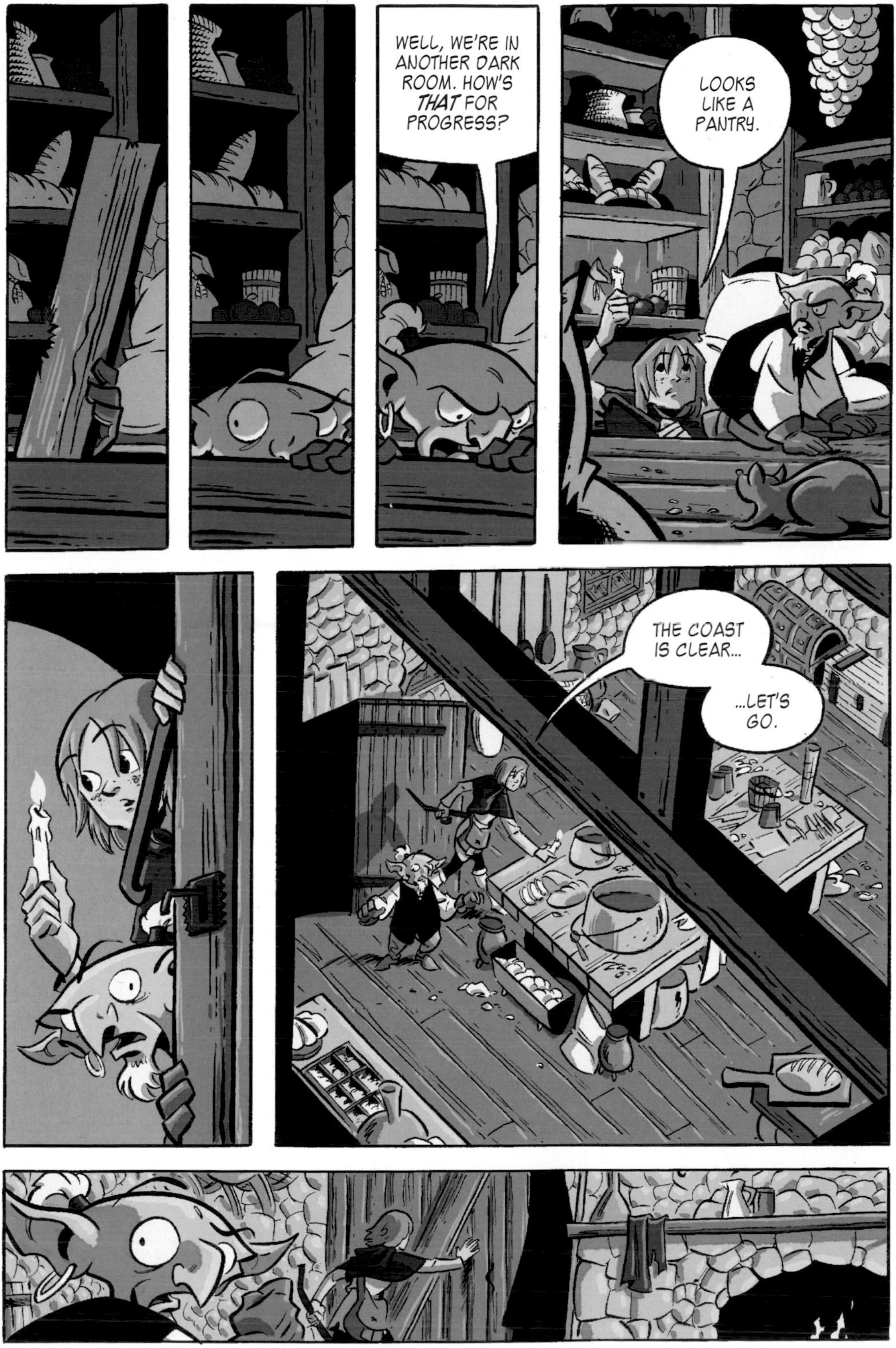
WELL, WE'RE IN ANOTHER DARK ROOM. HOW'S *THAT* FOR PROGRESS?
LOOKS LIKE A PANTRY.
THE COAST IS CLEAR...
...LET'S GO.

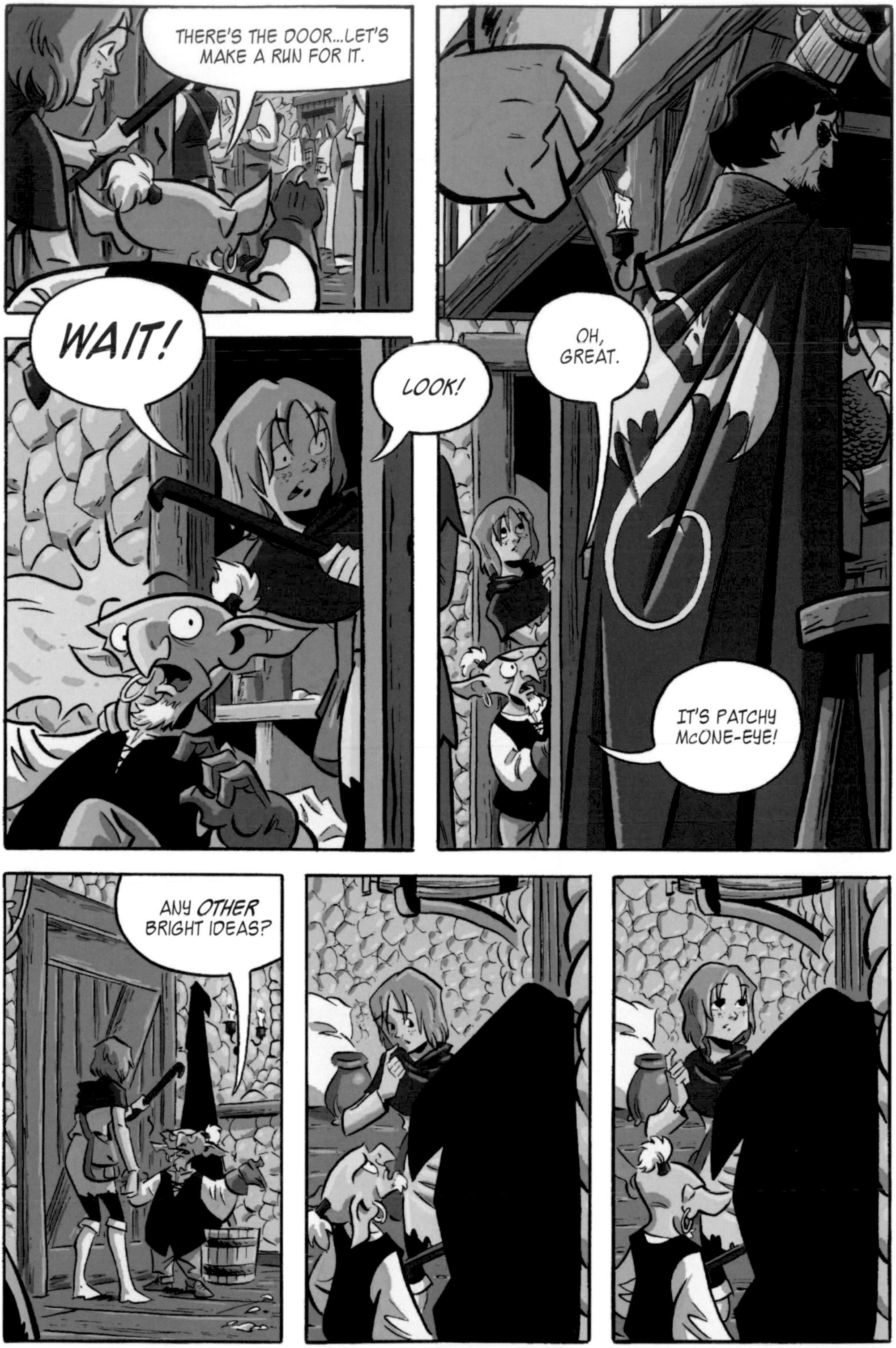
THERE'S THE DOOR...LET'S MAKE A RUN FOR IT.
WAIT!
LOOK!
OH, GREAT.
IT'S PATCHY McONE-EYE!
ANY *OTHER* BRIGHT IDEAS?

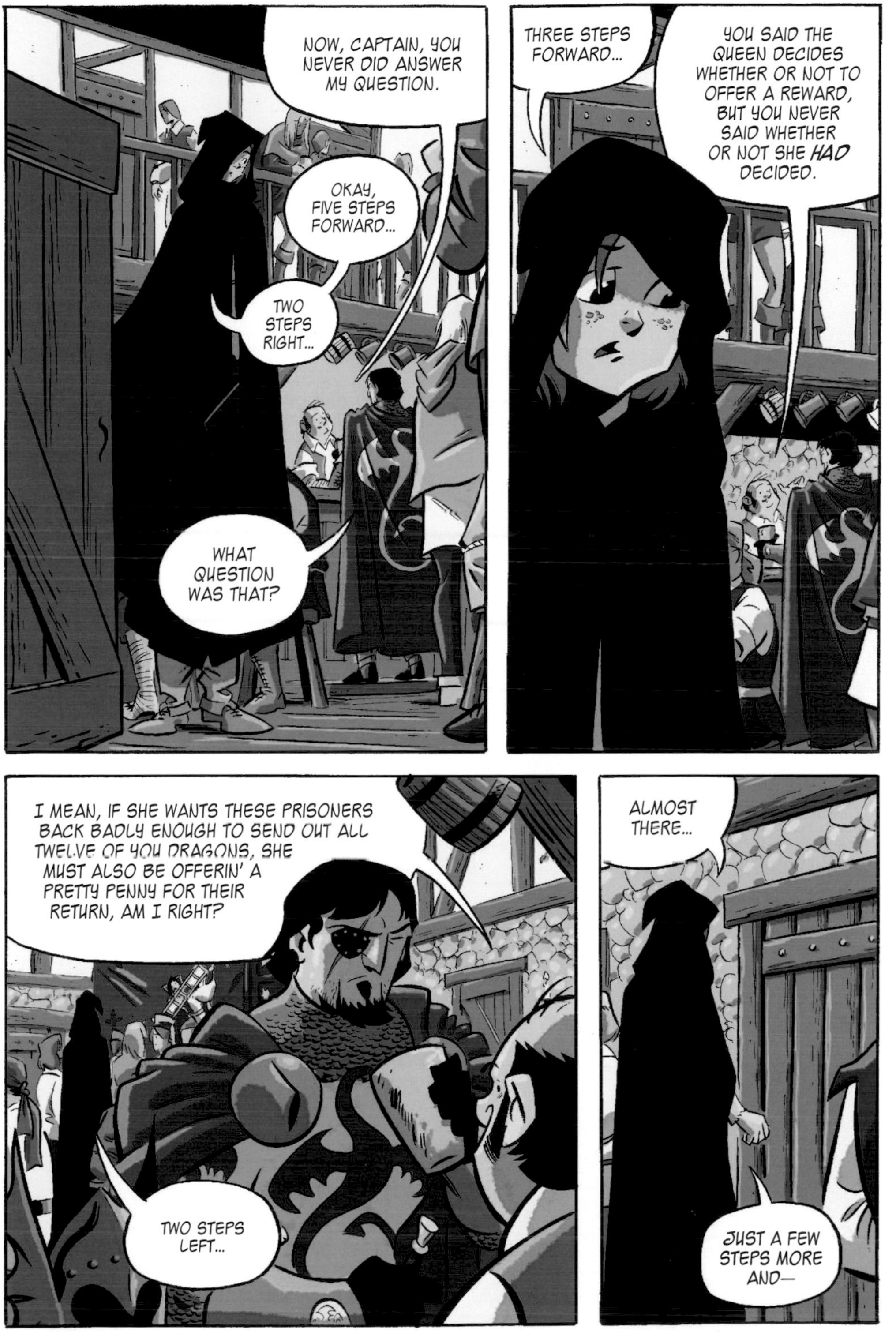

NOW, CAPTAIN, YOU NEVER DID ANSWER MY QUESTION.
OKAY, FIVE STEPS FORWARD...
TWO STEPS RIGHT...
WHAT QUESTION WAS THAT?
THREE STEPS FORWARD...
YOU SAID THE QUEEN DECIDES WHETHER OR NOT TO OFFER A REWARD, BUT YOU NEVER SAID WHETHER OR NOT SHE HAD DECIDED.
I MEAN, IF SHE WANTS THESE PRISONERS BACK BADLY ENOUGH TO SEND OUT ALL TWELVE OF YOU DRAGONS, SHE MUST ALSO BE OFFERIN' A PRETTY PENNY FOR THEIR RETURN, AM I RIGHT?
TWO STEPS LEFT...
ALMOST THERE...
JUST A FEW STEPS MORE AND—

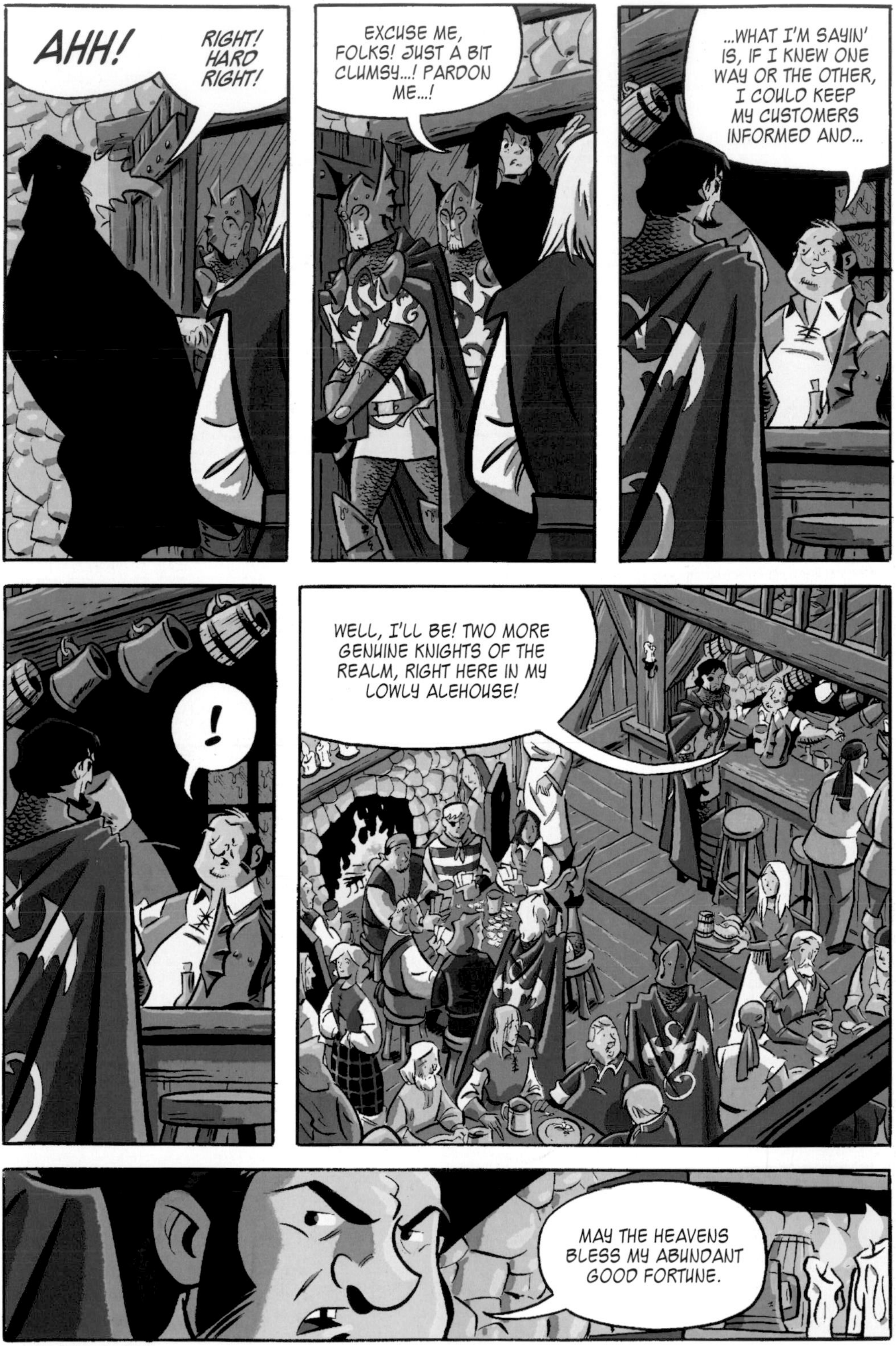
AHH!
RIGHT! HARD RIGHT!
EXCUSE ME, FOLKS! JUST A BIT CLUMSY...! PARDON ME...!
...WHAT I'M SAYIN' IS, IF I KNEW ONE WAY OR THE OTHER, I COULD KEEP MY CUSTOMERS INFORMED AND...
!
WELL, I'LL BE! TWO MORE GENUINE KNIGHTS OF THE REALM, RIGHT HERE IN MY LOWLY ALEHOUSE!
MAY THE HEAVENS BLESS MY ABUNDANT GOOD FORTUNE.

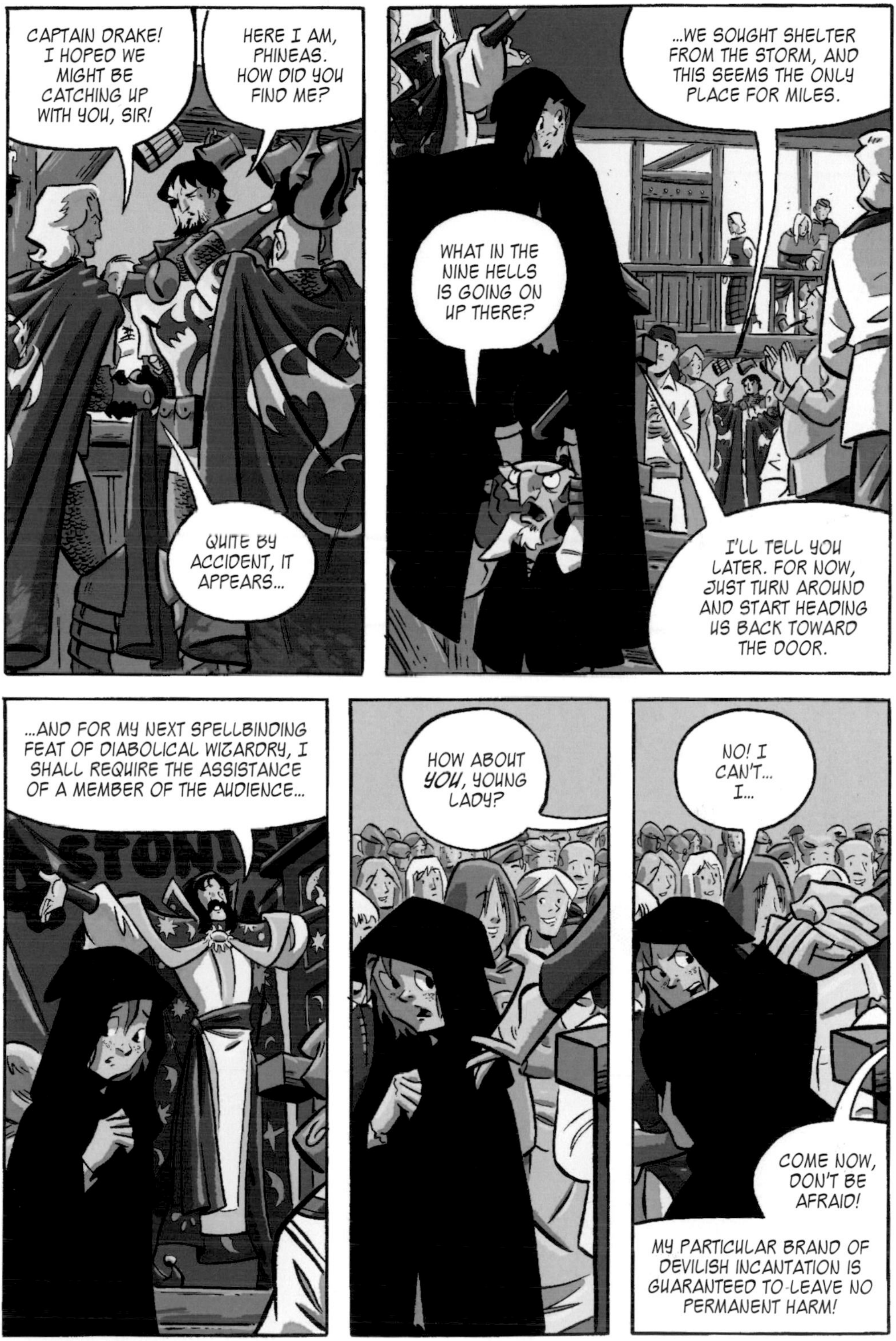
CAPTAIN DRAKE! I HOPED WE MIGHT BE CATCHING UP WITH YOU, SIR!
HERE I AM, PHINEAS. HOW DID YOU FIND ME?
QUITE BY ACCIDENT, IT APPEARS...
...WE SOUGHT SHELTER FROM THE STORM, AND THIS SEEMS THE ONLY PLACE FOR MILES.
WHAT IN THE NINE HELLS IS GOING ON UP THERE?
I'LL TELL YOU LATER. FOR NOW, JUST TURN AROUND AND START HEADING US BACK TOWARD THE DOOR.
...AND FOR MY NEXT SPELLBINDING FEAT OF DIABOLICAL WIZARDRY, I SHALL REQUIRE THE ASSISTANCE OF A MEMBER OF THE AUDIENCE...
HOW ABOUT *YOU*, YOUNG LADY?
NO! I CAN'T... I...
COME NOW, DON'T BE AFRAID!
MY PARTICULAR BRAND OF DEVILISH INCANTATION IS GUARANTEED TO LEAVE NO PERMANENT HARM!

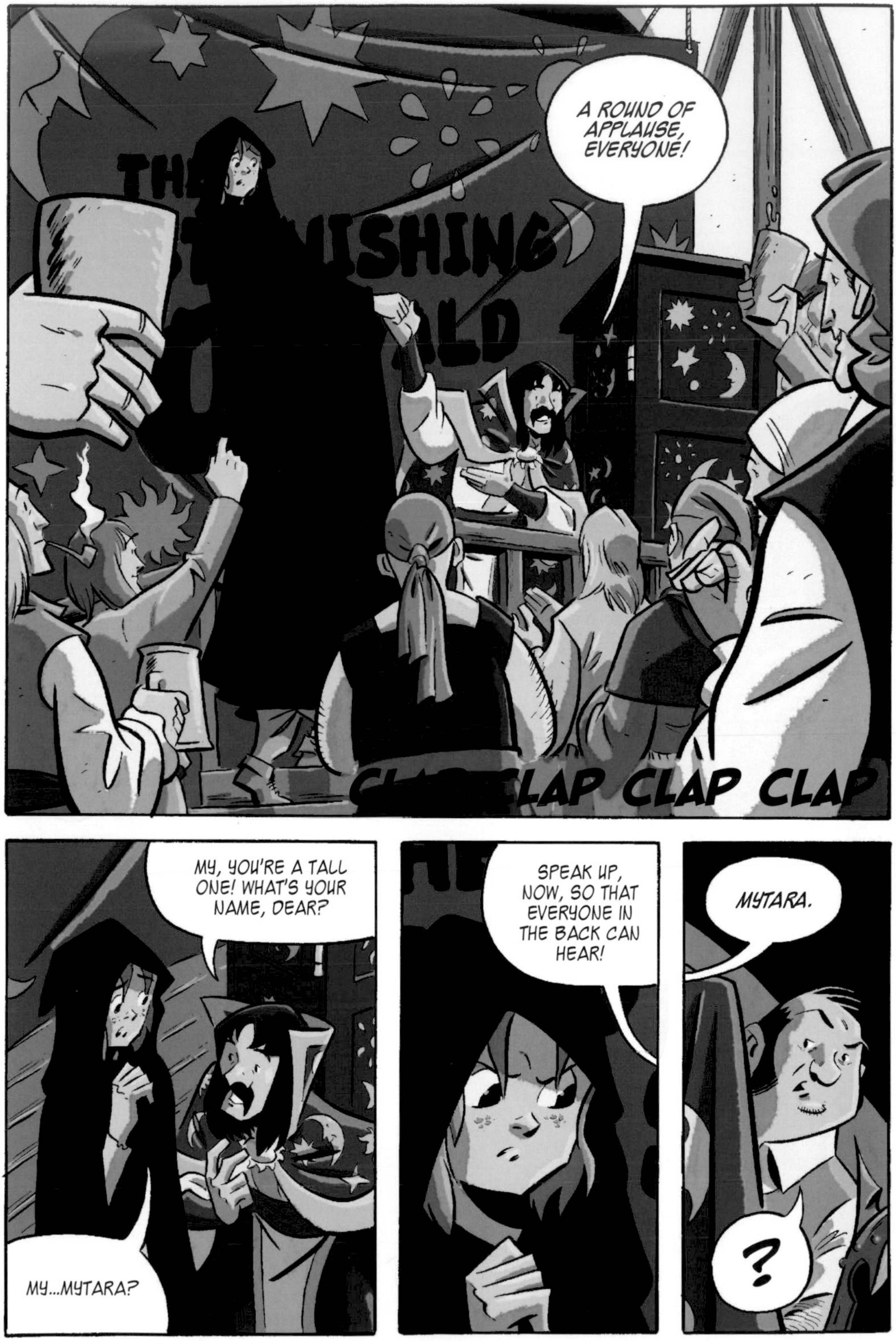
A ROUND OF APPLAUSE, EVERYONE!
CLAP CLAP CLAP
MY, YOU'RE A TALL ONE! WHAT'S YOUR NAME, DEAR?
MY...MYTARA?
SPEAK UP, NOW, SO THAT EVERYONE IN THE BACK CAN HEAR!
MYTARA.
?

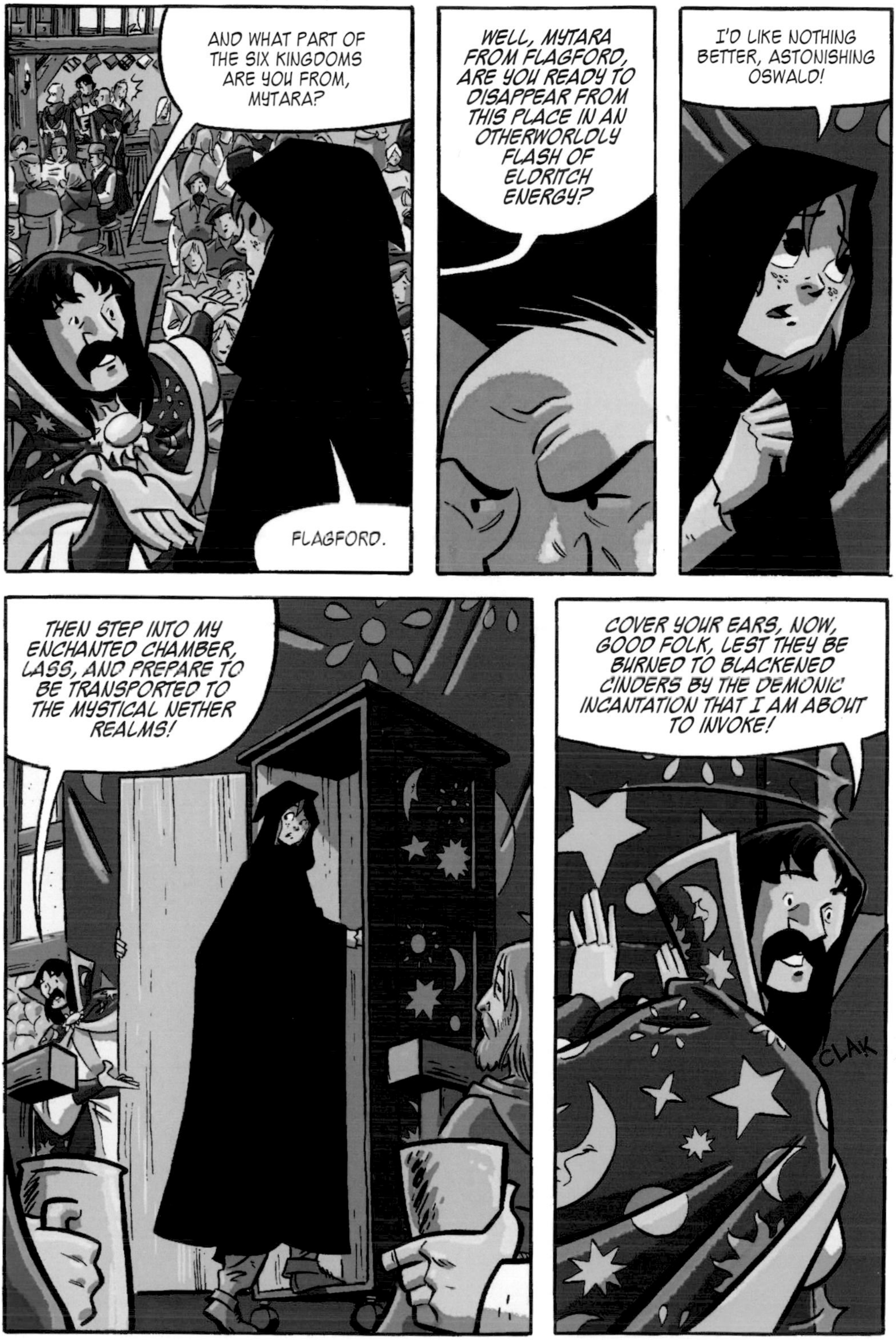
AND WHAT PART OF THE SIX KINGDOMS ARE YOU FROM, MYTARA?
FLAGFORD.
WELL, MYTARA FROM FLAGFORD, ARE YOU READY TO DISAPPEAR FROM THIS PLACE IN AN OTHERWORLDLY FLASH OF ELDRITCH ENERGY?
I'D LIKE NOTHING BETTER, ASTONISHING OSWALD!
THEN STEP INTO MY ENCHANTED CHAMBER, LASS, AND PREPARE TO BE TRANSPORTED TO THE MYSTICAL NETHER REALMS!
COVER YOUR EARS, NOW, GOOD FOLK, LEST THEY BE BURNED TO BLACKENED CINDERS BY THE DEMONIC INCANTATION THAT I AM ABOUT TO INVOKE!
CLAK

ABRA CADABRA ZAPPITY ZONN...
...MYTARA OF FLAGFORD WILL NOW BE...
POOOF
...GONE!
CLAP CLAP CLAP CLAP CLAP CLAP
CLAP CLAP

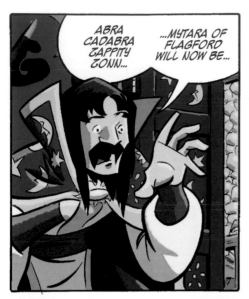

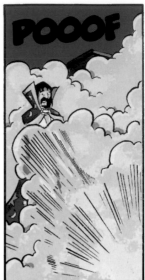

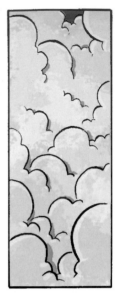

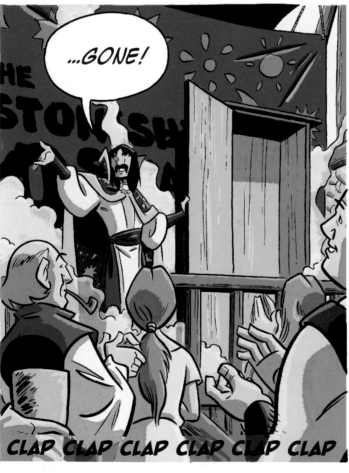

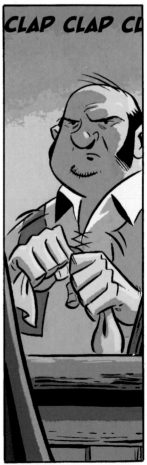

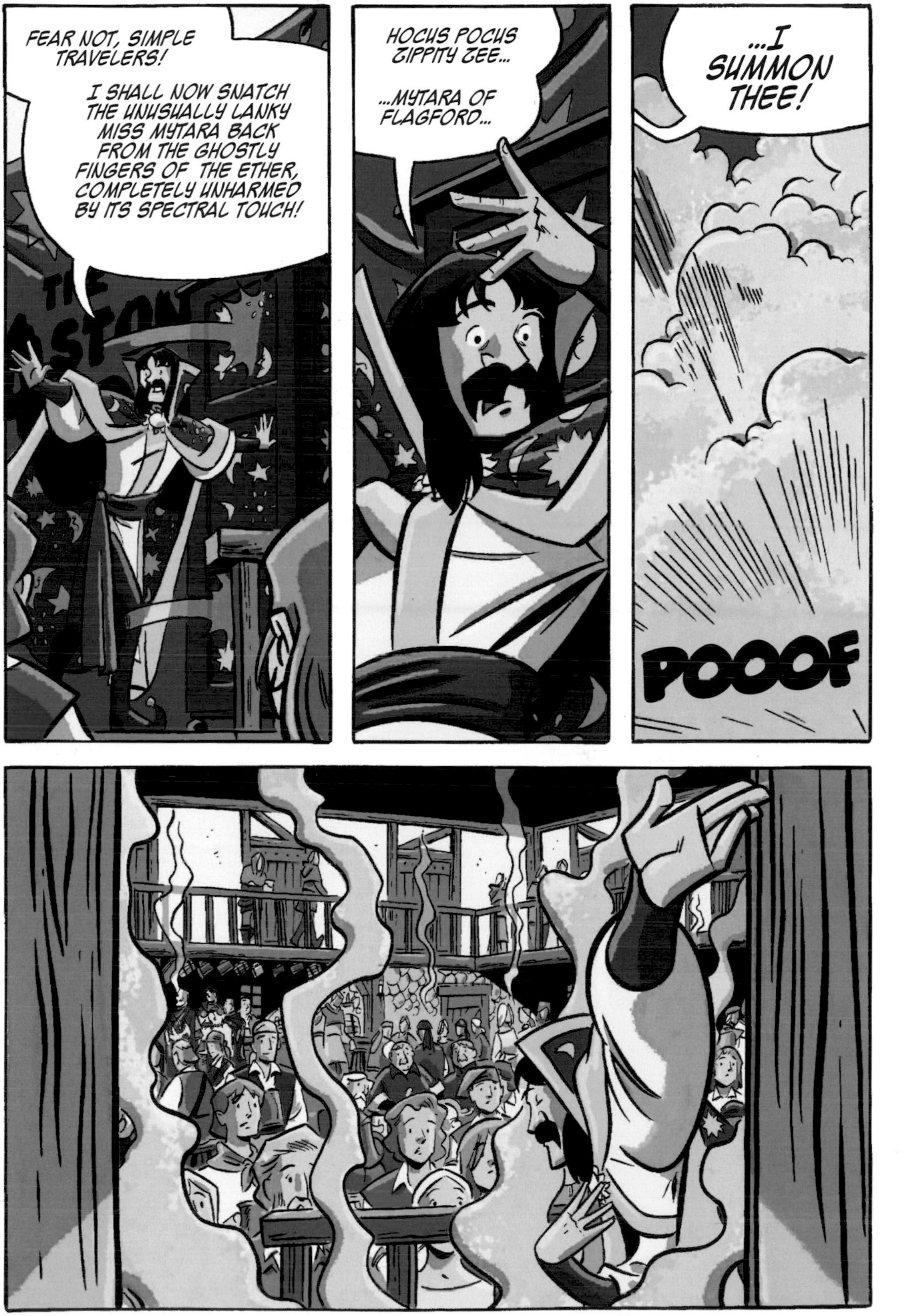
FEAR NOT, SIMPLE TRAVELERS!
I SHALL NOW SNATCH THE UNUSUALLY LANKY MISS MYTARA BACK FROM THE GHOSTLY FINGERS OF THE ETHER, COMPLETELY UNHARMED BY ITS SPECTRAL TOUCH!
HOCUS POCUS ZIPPITY ZEE...
...MYTARA OF FLAGFORD...
...I SUMMON THEE!
POOOF

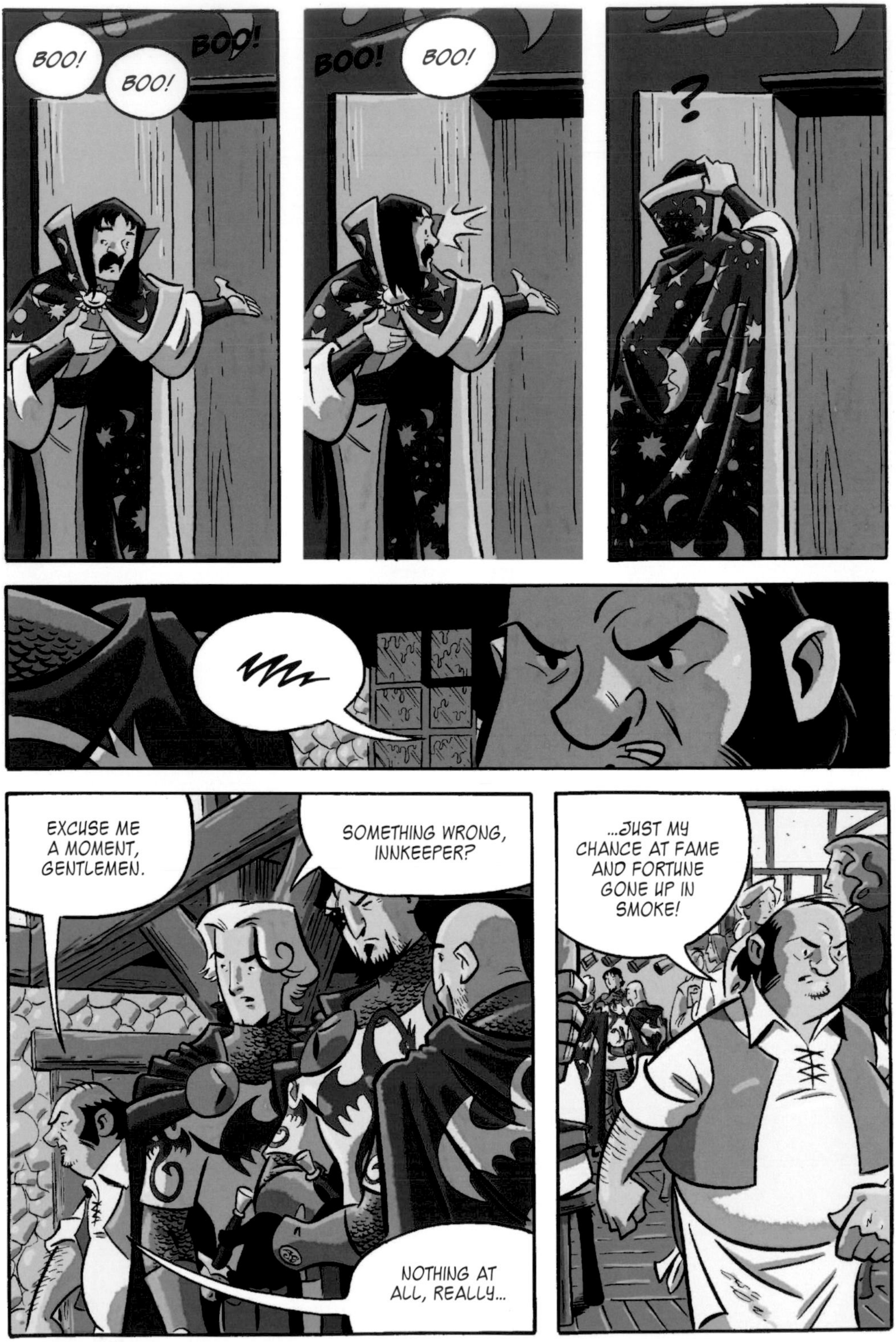
BOO!
BOO!
BOO!
BOO!
BOO!
?
EXCUSE ME A MOMENT, GENTLEMEN.
SOMETHING WRONG, INNKEEPER?
NOTHING AT ALL, REALLY...
...JUST MY CHANCE AT FAME AND FORTUNE GONE UP IN SMOKE!

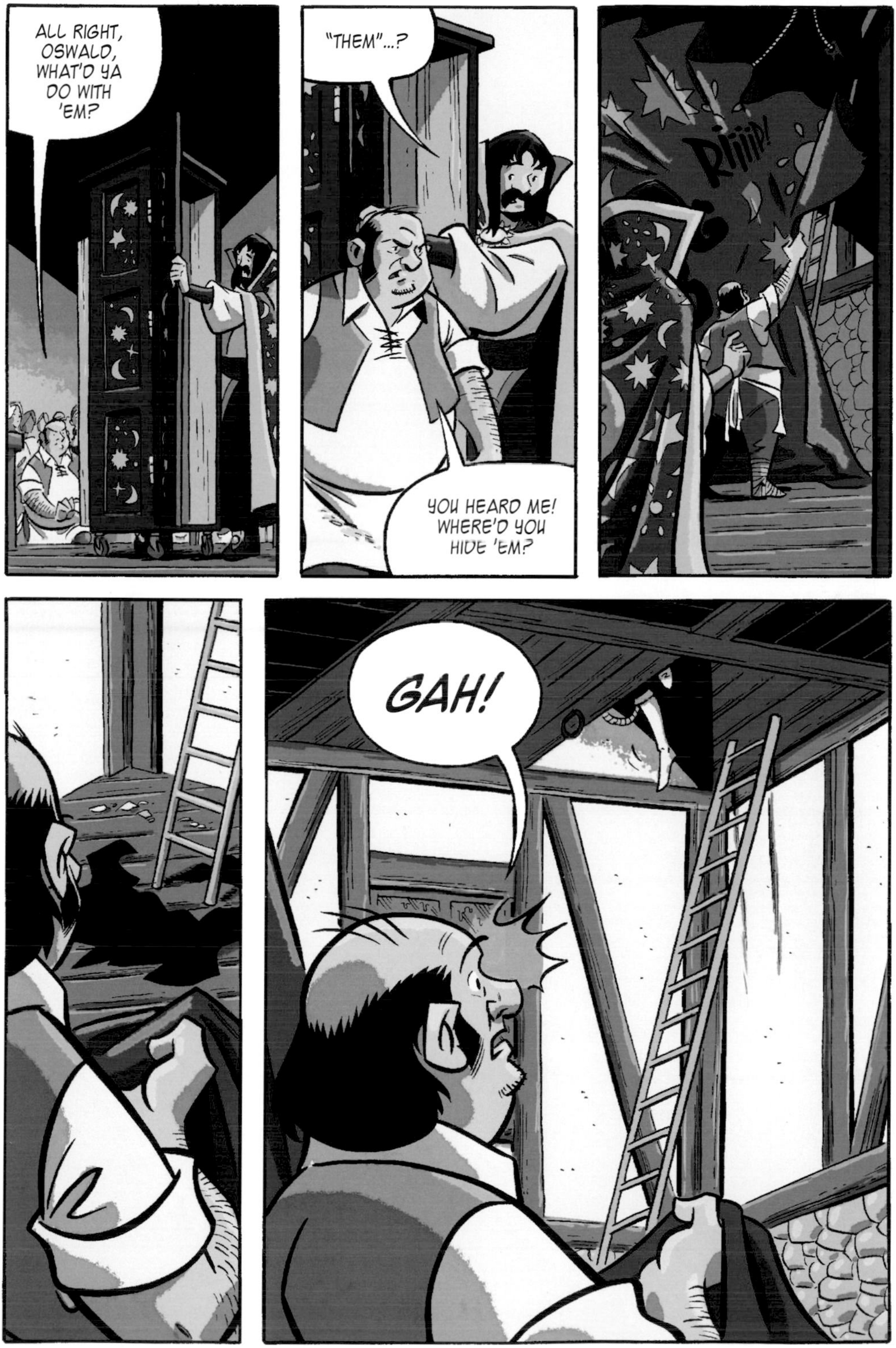
ALL RIGHT, OSWALD, WHAT'D YA DO WITH 'EM?
"THEM"...?
YOU HEARD ME! WHERE'D YOU HIDE 'EM?
RIIIIP!
GAH!

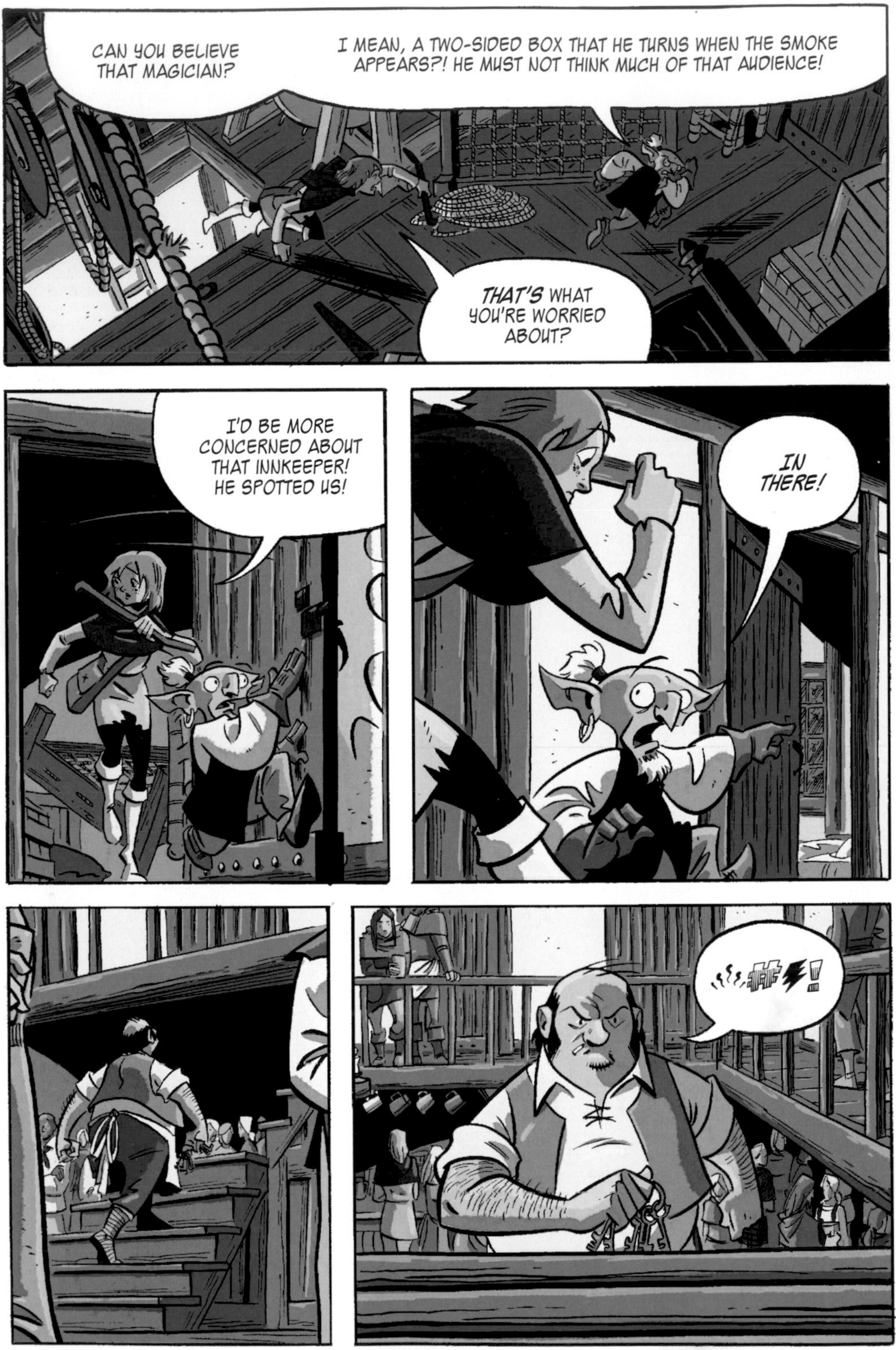
CAN YOU BELIEVE THAT MAGICIAN?
I MEAN, A TWO-SIDED BOX THAT HE TURNS WHEN THE SMOKE APPEARS?! HE MUST NOT THINK MUCH OF THAT AUDIENCE!
THAT'S WHAT YOU'RE WORRIED ABOUT?
I'D BE MORE CONCERNED ABOUT THAT INNKEEPER! HE SPOTTED US!
IN THERE!

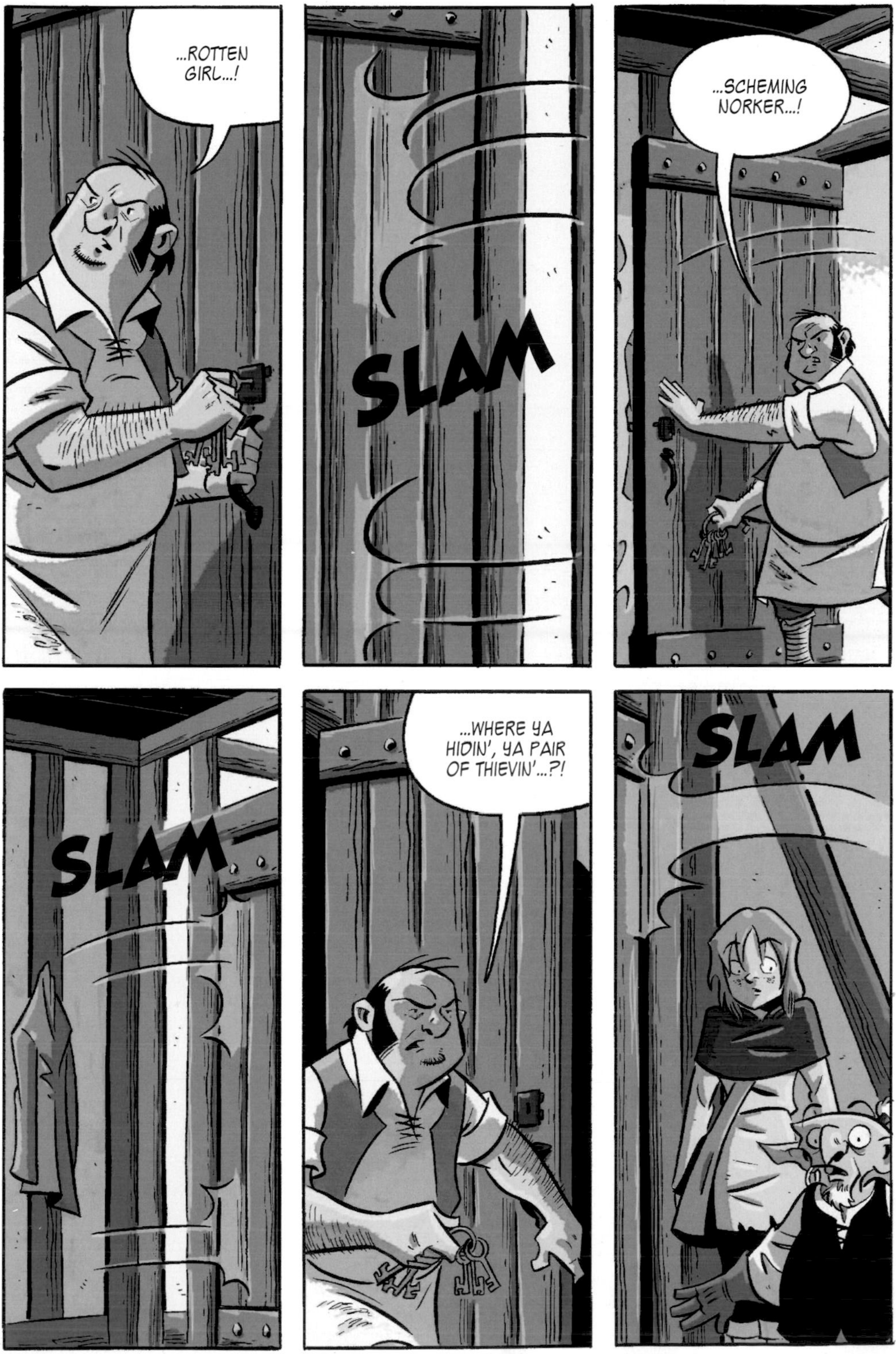
...ROTTEN GIRL...!
SLAM
...SCHEMING NORKER...!
SLAM
...WHERE YA HIDIN', YA PAIR OF THIEVIN'...?!
SLAM

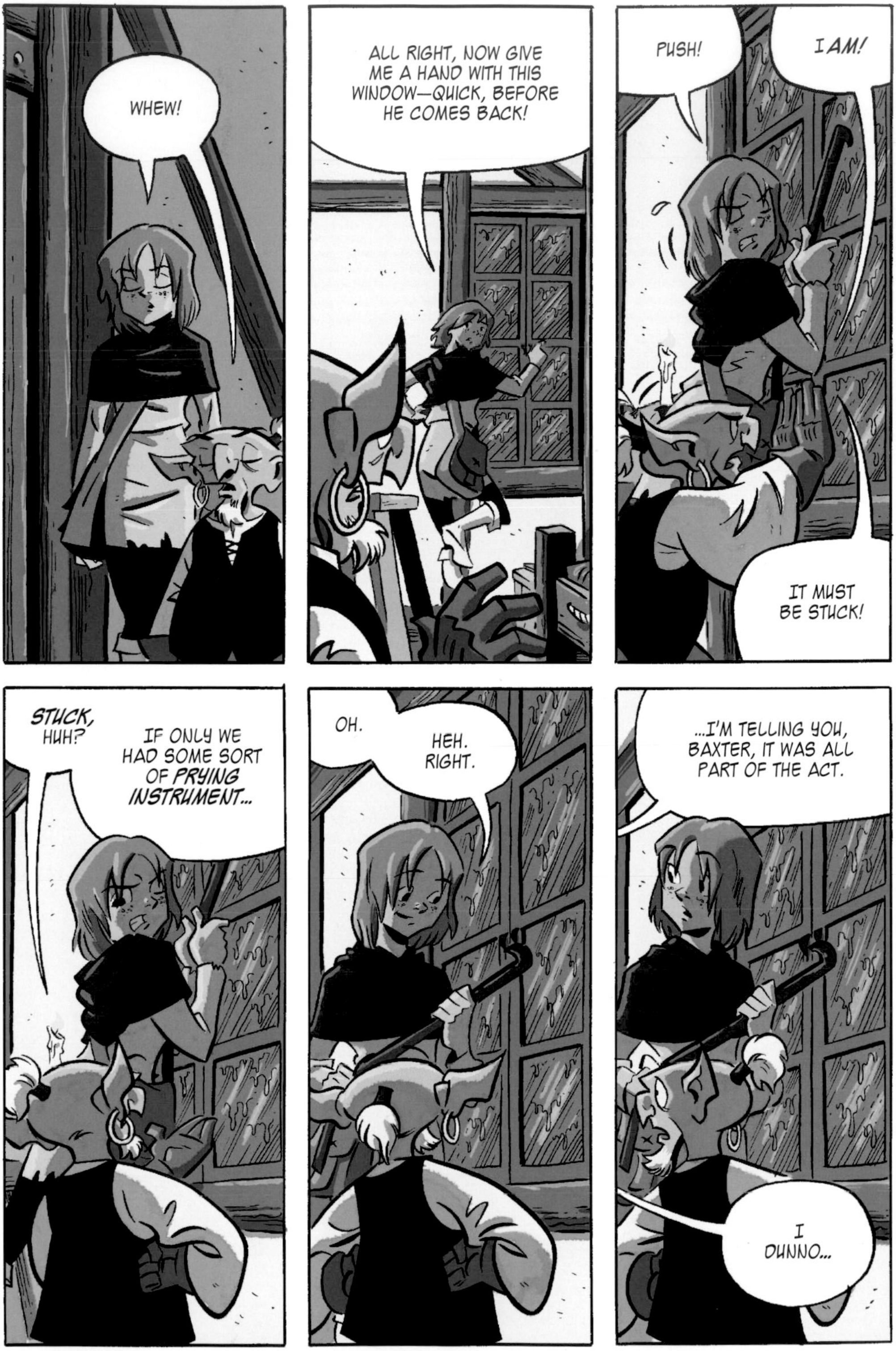
WHEW!
ALL RIGHT, NOW GIVE ME A HAND WITH THIS WINDOW—QUICK, BEFORE HE COMES BACK!
PUSH!
I AM!
IT MUST BE STUCK!
STUCK, HUH?
IF ONLY WE HAD SOME SORT OF PRYING INSTRUMENT...
OH.
HEH. RIGHT.
...I'M TELLING YOU, BAXTER, IT WAS ALL PART OF THE ACT.
I DUNNO...

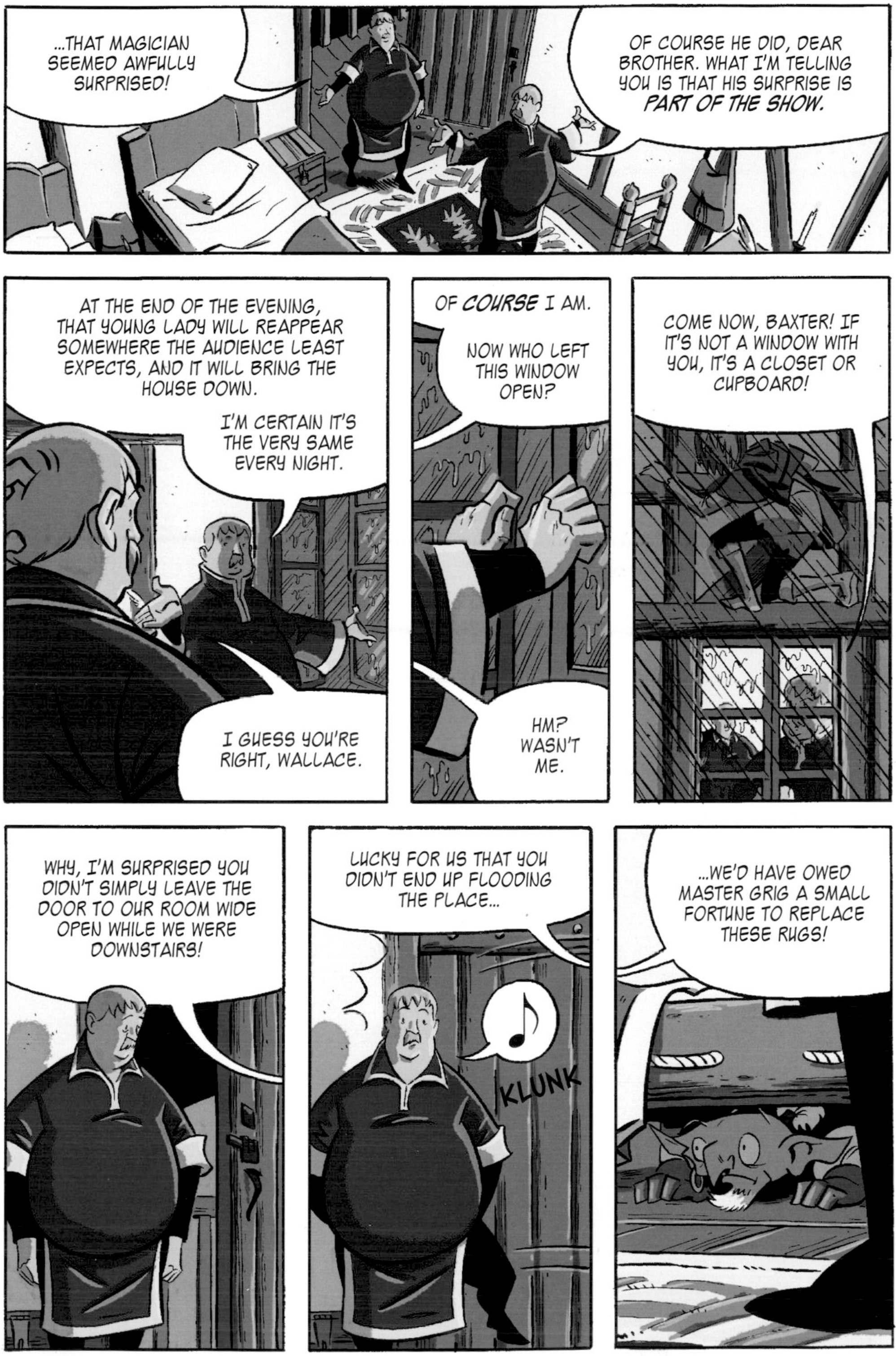
...THAT MAGICIAN SEEMED AWFULLY SURPRISED!
OF COURSE HE DID, DEAR BROTHER. WHAT I'M TELLING YOU IS THAT HIS SURPRISE IS *PART OF THE SHOW.*
AT THE END OF THE EVENING, THAT YOUNG LADY WILL REAPPEAR SOMEWHERE THE AUDIENCE LEAST EXPECTS, AND IT WILL BRING THE HOUSE DOWN.
I'M CERTAIN IT'S THE VERY SAME EVERY NIGHT.
I GUESS YOU'RE RIGHT, WALLACE.
OF *COURSE* I AM.
NOW WHO LEFT THIS WINDOW OPEN?
HM? WASN'T ME.
COME NOW, BAXTER! IF IT'S NOT A WINDOW WITH YOU, IT'S A CLOSET OR CUPBOARD!
WHY, I'M SURPRISED YOU DIDN'T SIMPLY LEAVE THE DOOR TO OUR ROOM WIDE OPEN WHILE WE WERE DOWNSTAIRS!
LUCKY FOR US THAT YOU DIDN'T END UP FLOODING THE PLACE...
♪
KLUNK
...WE'D HAVE OWED MASTER GRIG A SMALL FORTUNE TO REPLACE THESE RUGS!

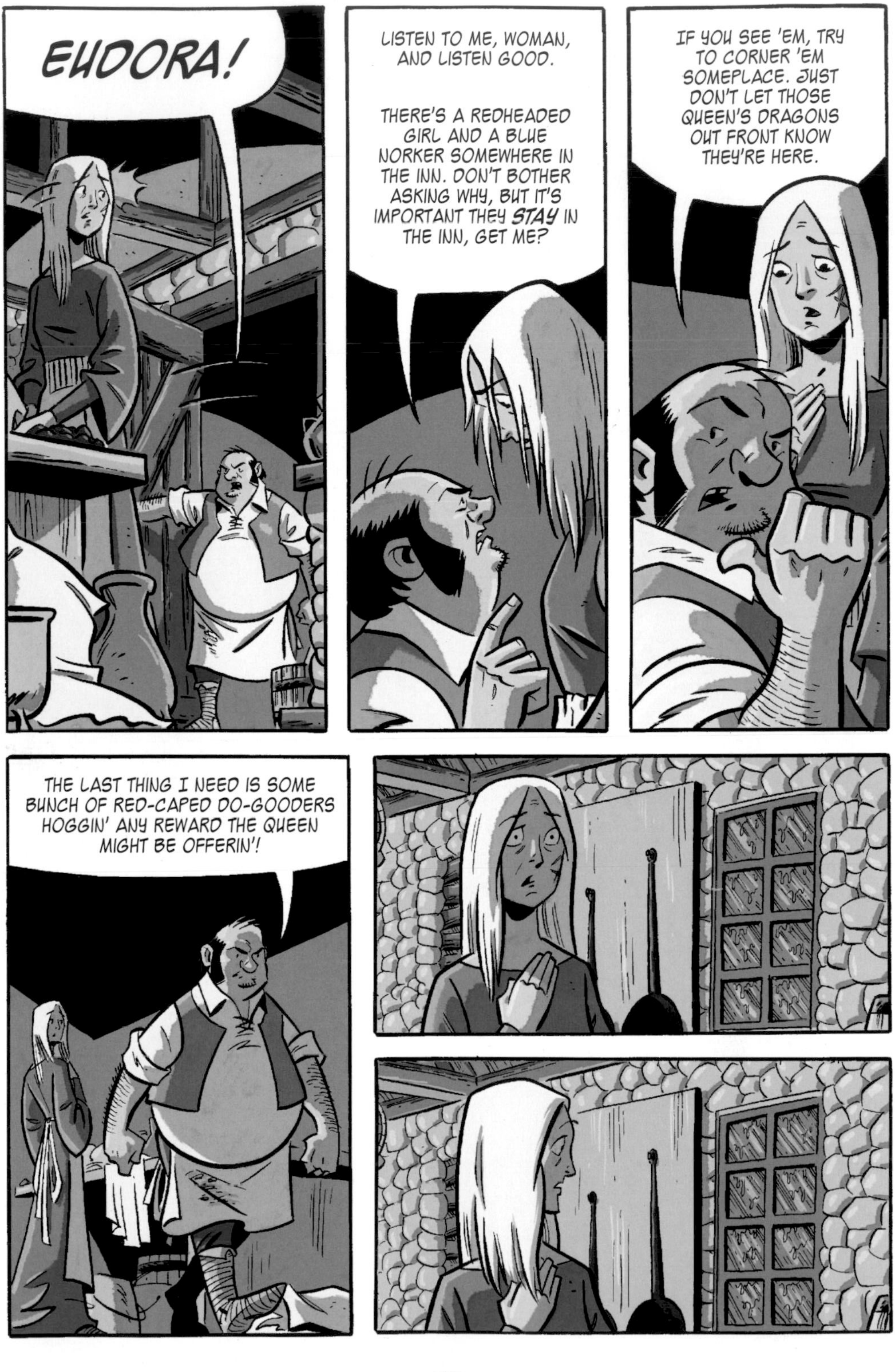
EUDORA!
LISTEN TO ME, WOMAN, AND LISTEN GOOD.
THERE'S A REDHEADED GIRL AND A BLUE NORKER SOMEWHERE IN THE INN. DON'T BOTHER ASKING WHY, BUT IT'S IMPORTANT THEY STAY IN THE INN, GET ME?
IF YOU SEE 'EM, TRY TO CORNER 'EM SOMEPLACE. JUST DON'T LET THOSE QUEEN'S DRAGONS OUT FRONT KNOW THEY'RE HERE.
THE LAST THING I NEED IS SOME BUNCH OF RED-CAPED DO-GOODERS HOGGIN' ANY REWARD THE QUEEN MIGHT BE OFFERIN'!

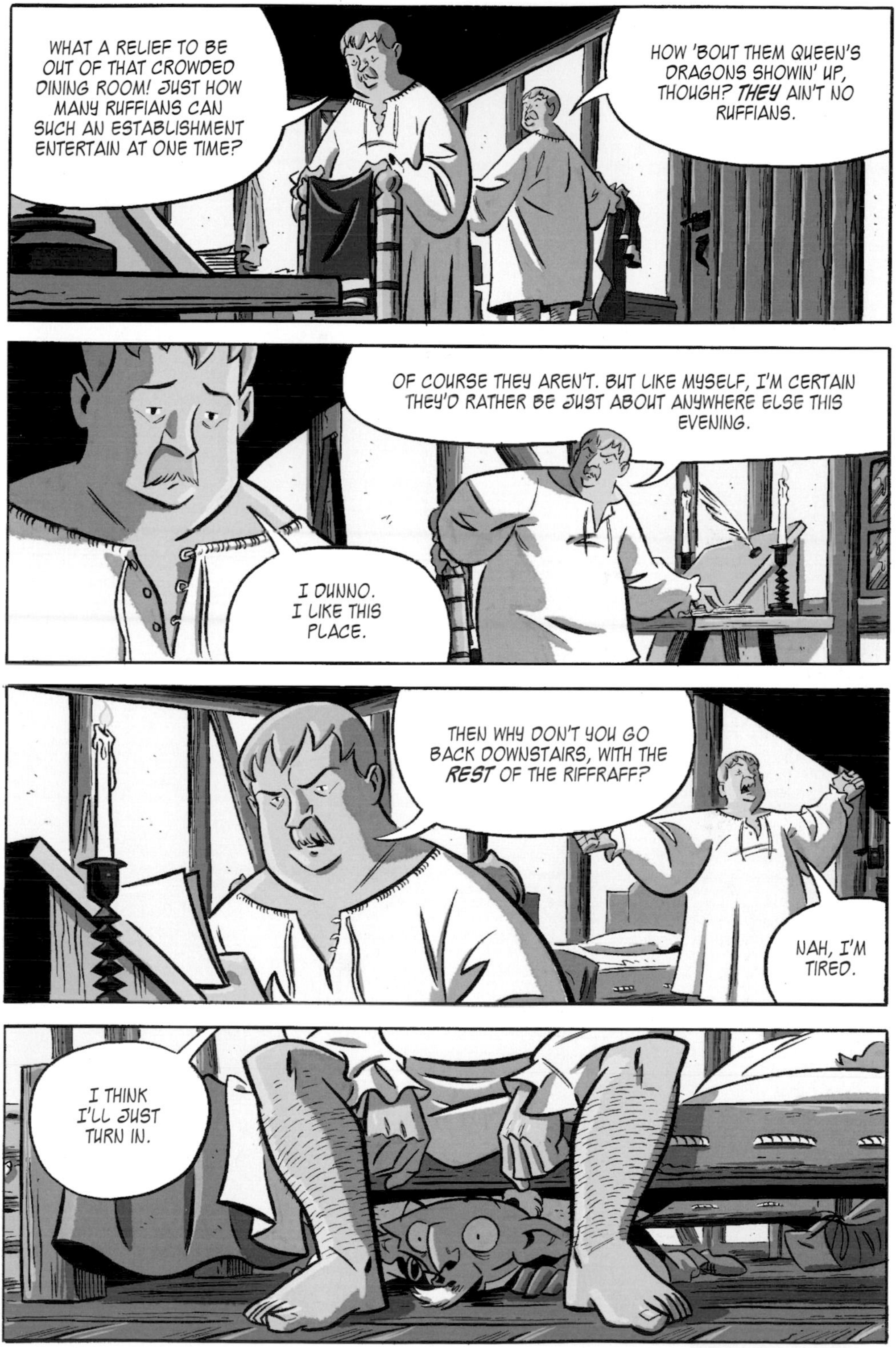
WHAT A RELIEF TO BE OUT OF THAT CROWDED DINING ROOM! JUST HOW MANY RUFFIANS CAN SUCH AN ESTABLISHMENT ENTERTAIN AT ONE TIME?
HOW 'BOUT THEM QUEEN'S DRAGONS SHOWIN' UP, THOUGH? THEY AIN'T NO RUFFIANS.
OF COURSE THEY AREN'T. BUT LIKE MYSELF, I'M CERTAIN THEY'D RATHER BE JUST ABOUT ANYWHERE ELSE THIS EVENING.
I DUNNO. I LIKE THIS PLACE.
THEN WHY DON'T YOU GO BACK DOWNSTAIRS, WITH THE REST OF THE RIFFRAFF?
NAH, I'M TIRED.
I THINK I'LL JUST TURN IN.

FINE WITH ME, THOUGH HOW YOU CAN SLEEP WITH THE RACKET GOING ON DOWNSTAIRS IS BEYOND ME!

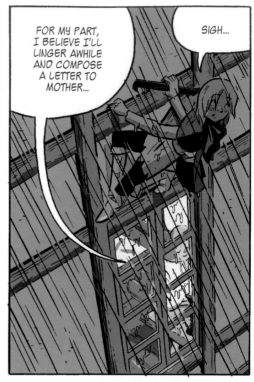

FOR MY PART, I BELIEVE I'LL LINGER AWHILE AND COMPOSE A LETTER TO MOTHER...

SIGH...

"DEAR MOTHER..."

NO, THAT WON'T DO.

"DEAREST MOTHER..."

HM...NO, THAT'S NOT QUITE RIGHT, EITHER...

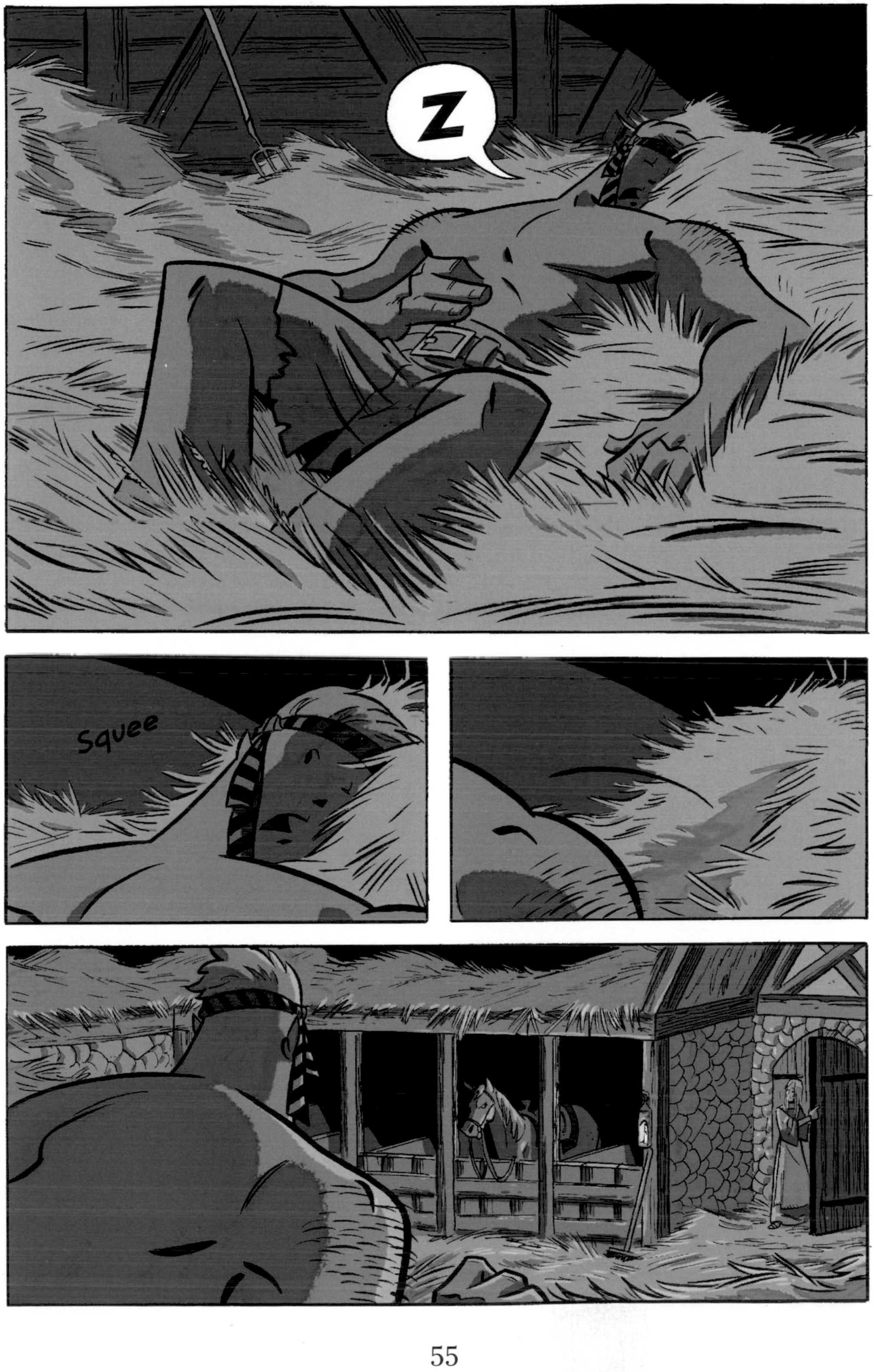
Z
Squee

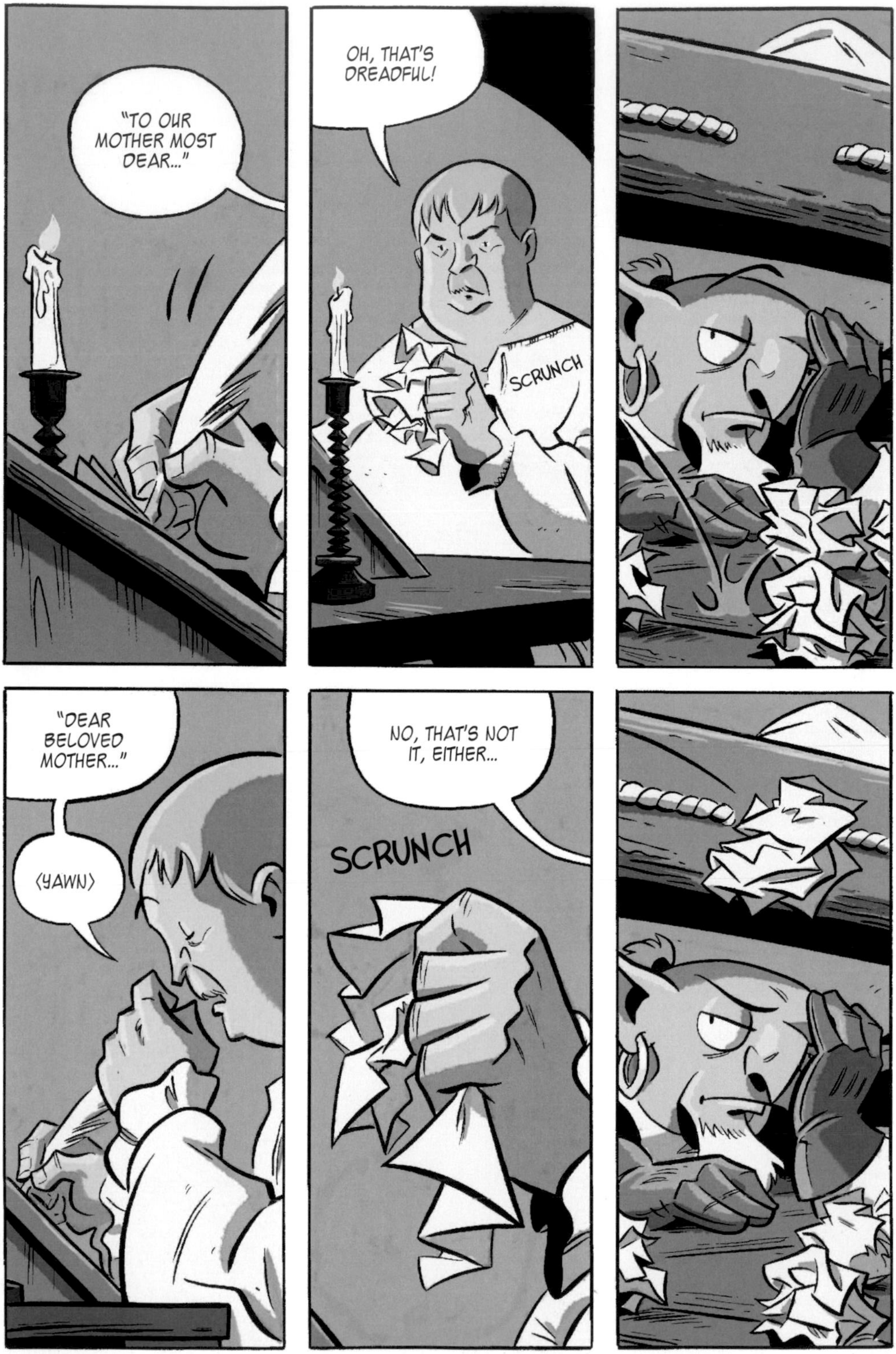
"TO OUR MOTHER MOST DEAR..."
OH, THAT'S DREADFUL!
SCRUNCH
"DEAR BELOVED MOTHER..."
⟨YAWN⟩
NO, THAT'S NOT IT, EITHER...
SCRUNCH

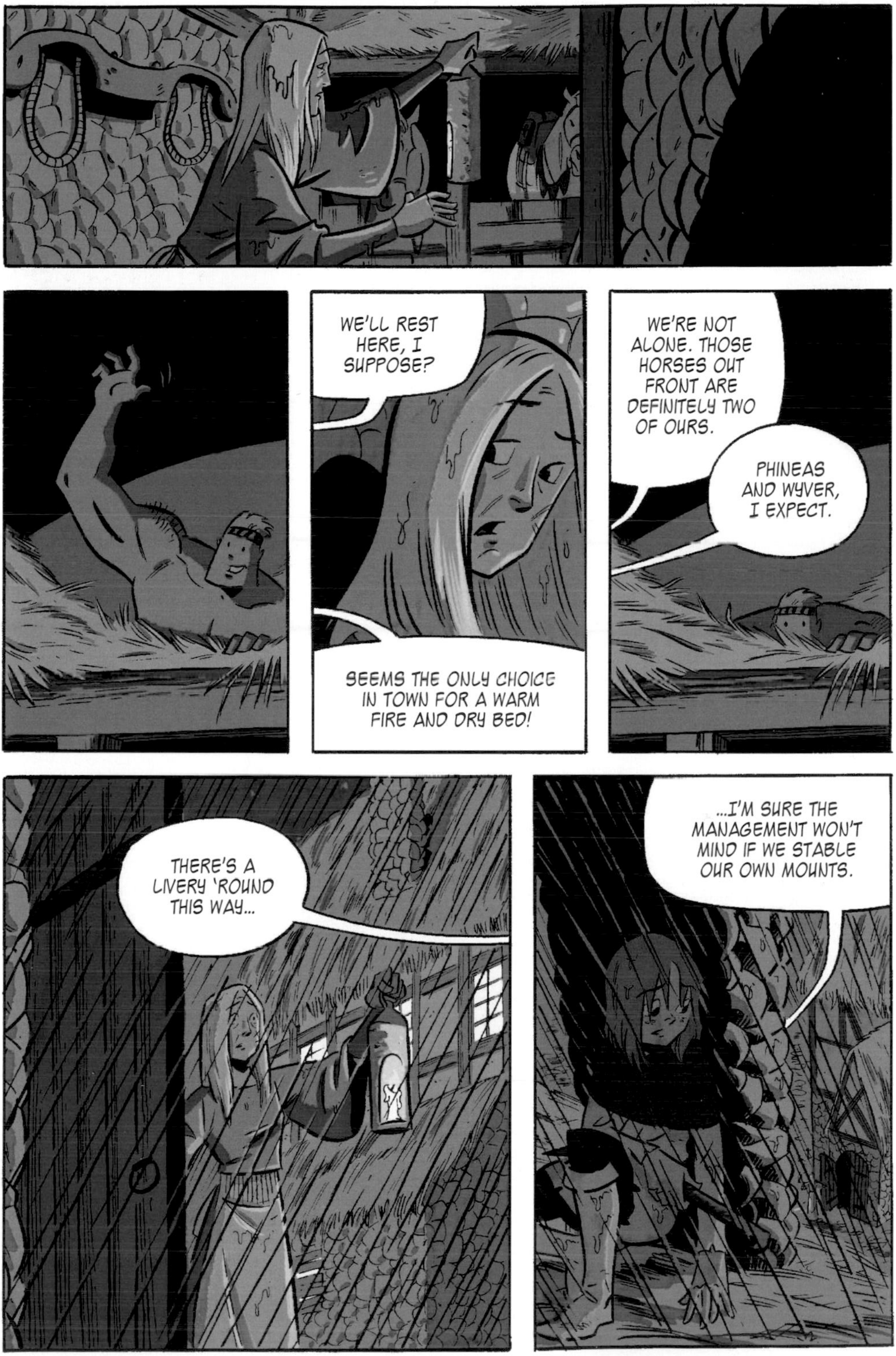
WE'LL REST HERE, I SUPPOSE?
SEEMS THE ONLY CHOICE IN TOWN FOR A WARM FIRE AND DRY BED!
WE'RE NOT ALONE. THOSE HORSES OUT FRONT ARE DEFINITELY TWO OF OURS.
PHINEAS AND WYVER, I EXPECT.
THERE'S A LIVERY 'ROUND THIS WAY...
...I'M SURE THE MANAGEMENT WON'T MIND IF WE STABLE OUR OWN MOUNTS.

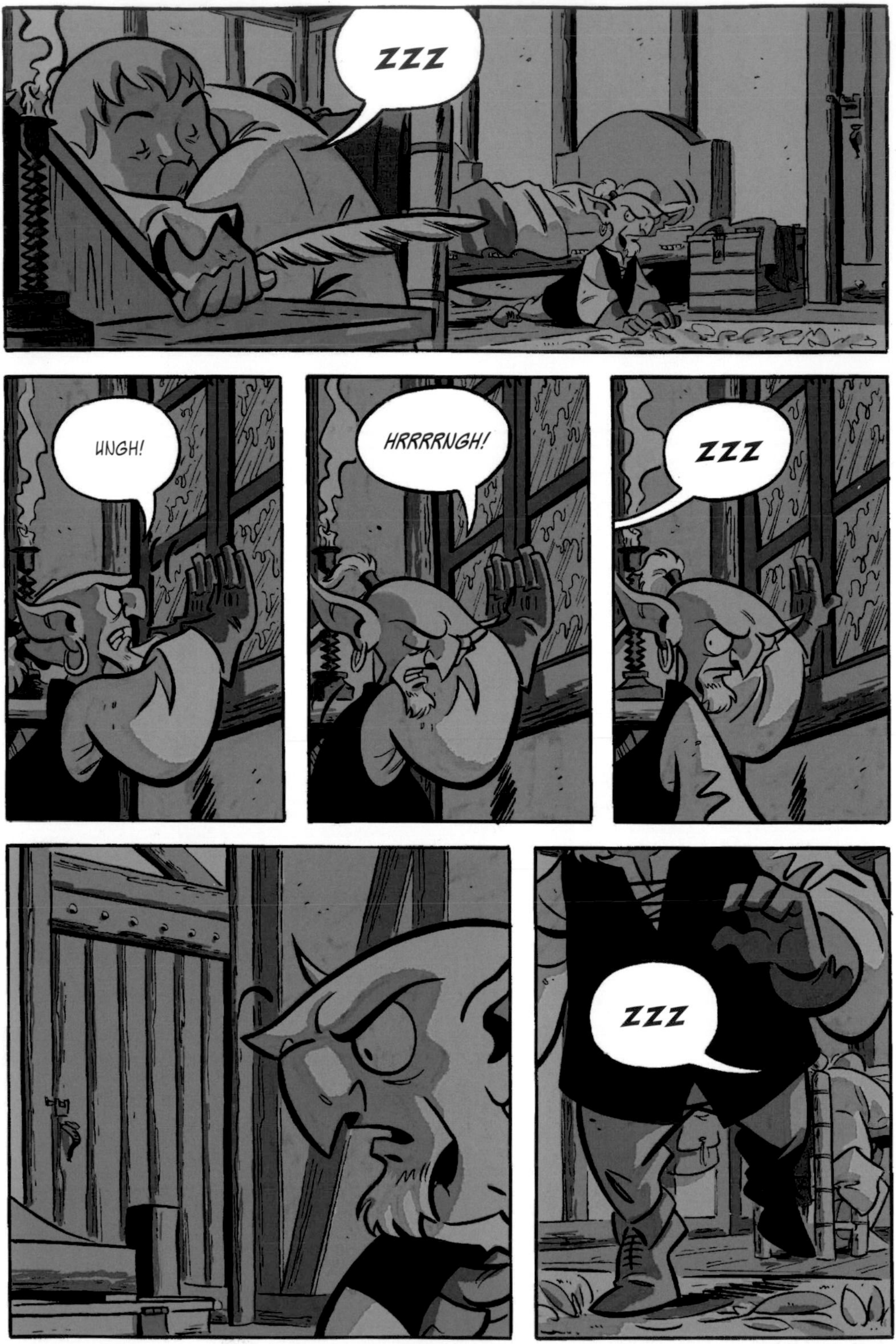
ZZZ
UNGH!
HRRRRNGH!
ZZZ
ZZZ

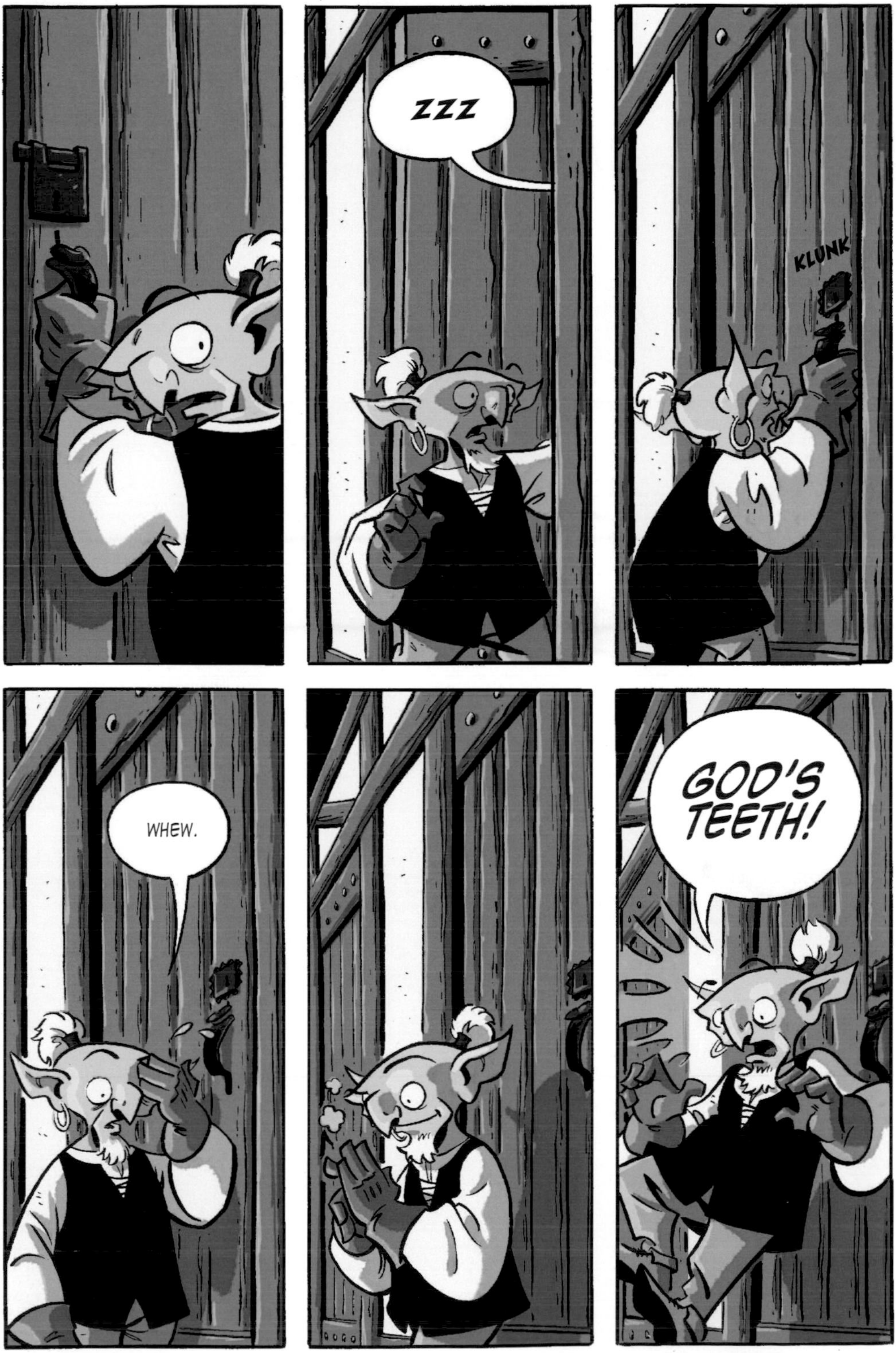
ZZZ
KLUNK
WHEW.
GOD'S TEETH!

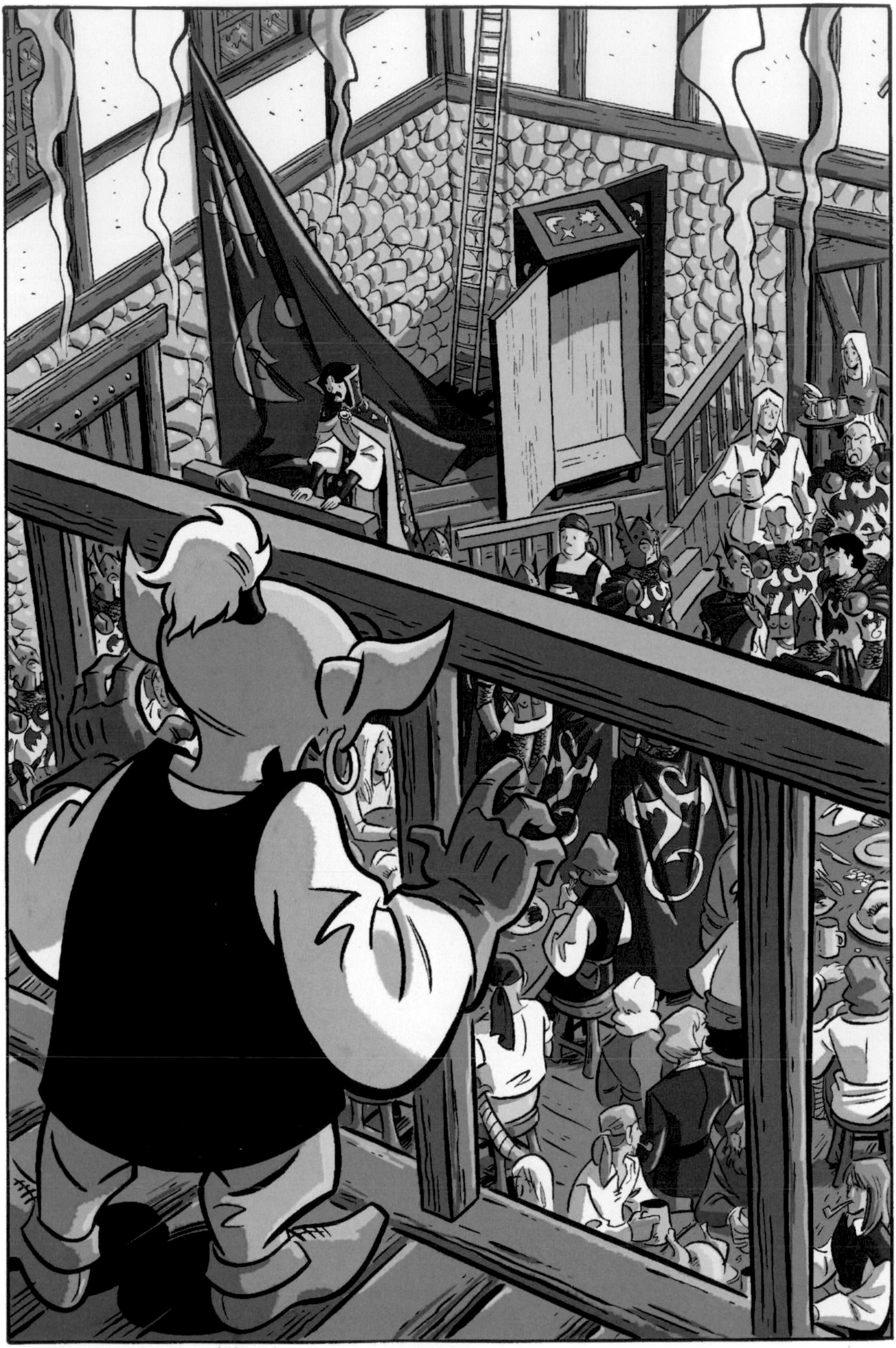

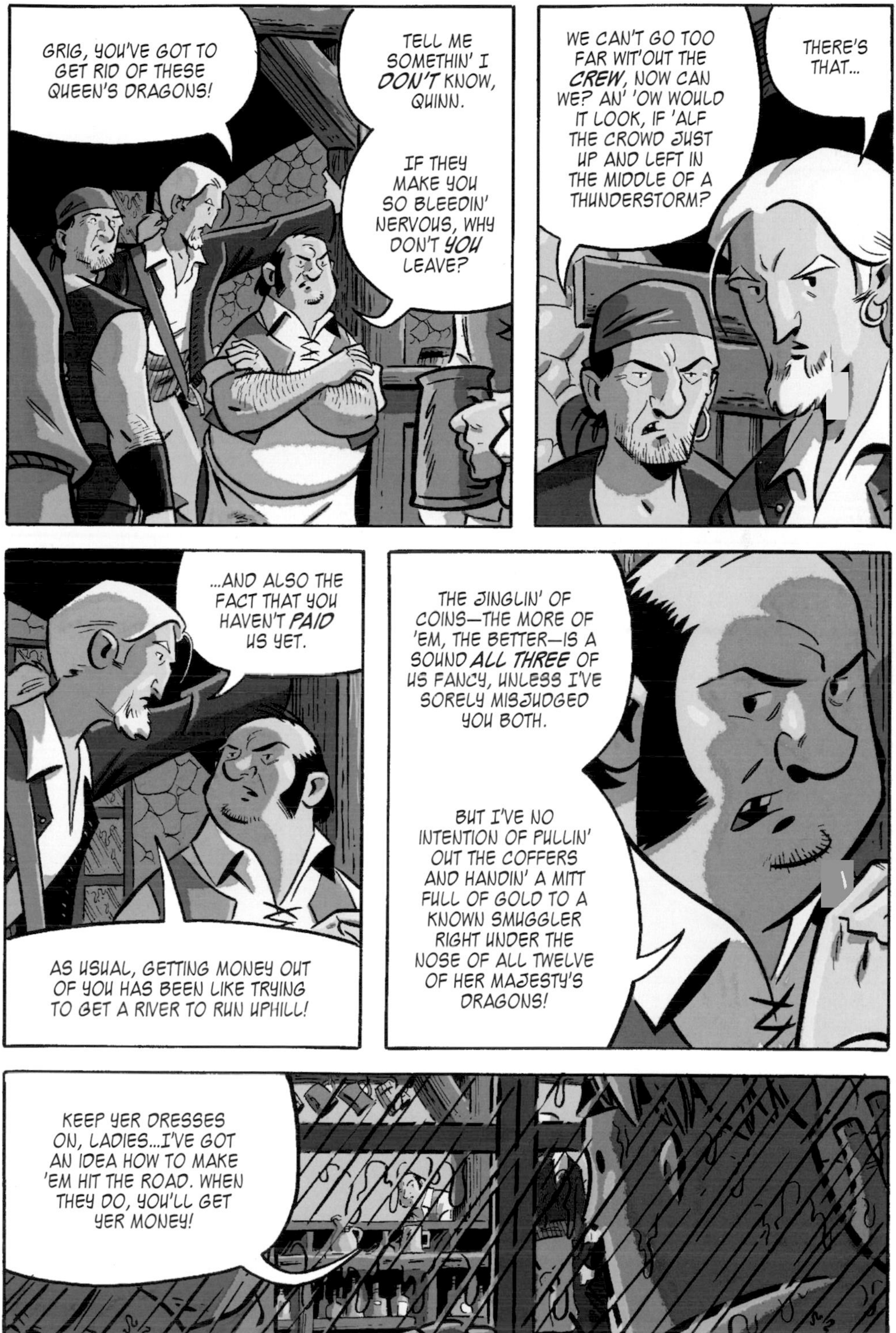
GRIG, YOU'VE GOT TO GET RID OF THESE QUEEN'S DRAGONS!
TELL ME SOMETHIN' I *DON'T* KNOW, QUINN.
IF THEY MAKE YOU SO BLEEDIN' NERVOUS, WHY DON'T *YOU* LEAVE?
WE CAN'T GO TOO FAR WIT'OUT THE *CREW*, NOW CAN WE? AN' 'OW WOULD IT LOOK, IF 'ALF THE CROWD JUST UP AND LEFT IN THE MIDDLE OF A THUNDERSTORM?
THERE'S THAT...
...AND ALSO THE FACT THAT YOU HAVEN'T *PAID* US YET.
AS USUAL, GETTING MONEY OUT OF YOU HAS BEEN LIKE TRYING TO GET A RIVER TO RUN UPHILL!
THE JINGLIN' OF COINS—THE MORE OF 'EM, THE BETTER—IS A SOUND *ALL THREE* OF US FANCY, UNLESS I'VE SORELY MISJUDGED YOU BOTH.
BUT I'VE NO INTENTION OF PULLIN' OUT THE COFFERS AND HANDIN' A MITT FULL OF GOLD TO A KNOWN SMUGGLER RIGHT UNDER THE NOSE OF ALL TWELVE OF HER MAJESTY'S DRAGONS!
KEEP YER DRESSES ON, LADIES...I'VE GOT AN IDEA HOW TO MAKE 'EM HIT THE ROAD. WHEN THEY DO, YOU'LL GET YER MONEY!

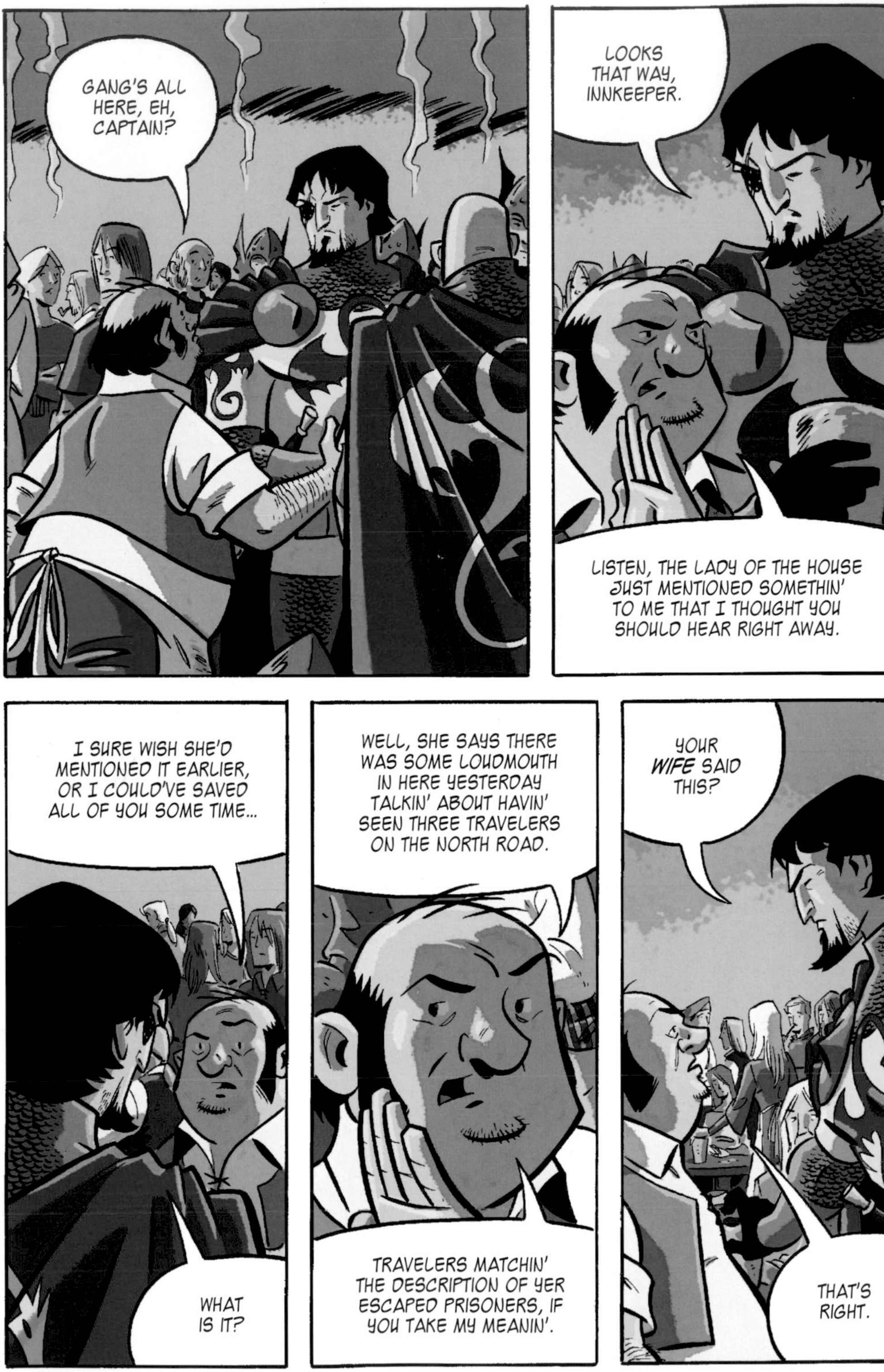
GANG'S ALL HERE, EH, CAPTAIN?
LOOKS THAT WAY, INNKEEPER.
LISTEN, THE LADY OF THE HOUSE JUST MENTIONED SOMETHIN' TO ME THAT I THOUGHT YOU SHOULD HEAR RIGHT AWAY.
I SURE WISH SHE'D MENTIONED IT EARLIER, OR I COULD'VE SAVED ALL OF YOU SOME TIME...
WHAT IS IT?
WELL, SHE SAYS THERE WAS SOME LOUDMOUTH IN HERE YESTERDAY TALKIN' ABOUT HAVIN' SEEN THREE TRAVELERS ON THE NORTH ROAD.
TRAVELERS MATCHIN' THE DESCRIPTION OF YER ESCAPED PRISONERS, IF YOU TAKE MY MEANIN'.
YOUR WIFE SAID THIS?
THAT'S RIGHT.

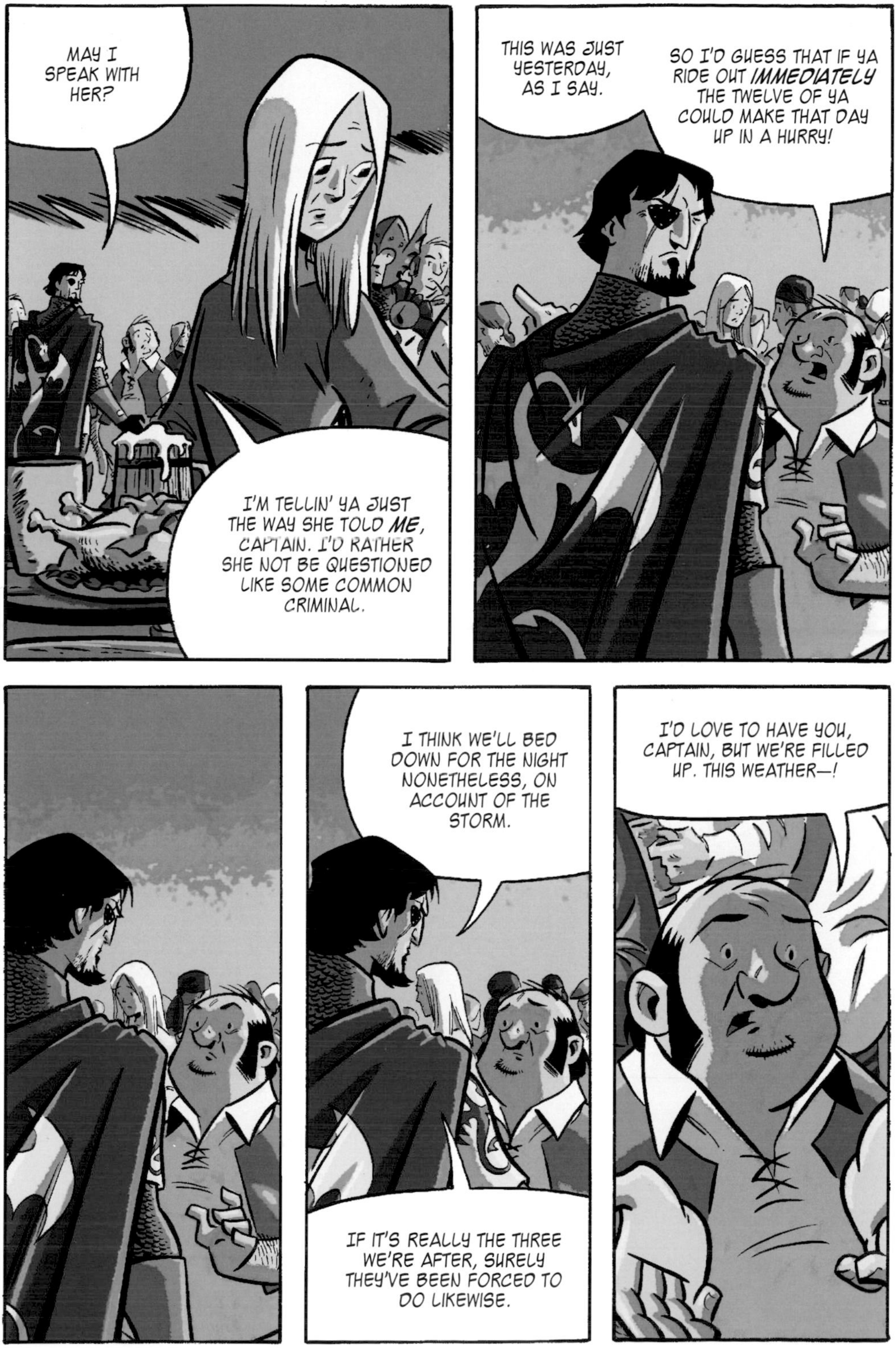
MAY I SPEAK WITH HER?
I'M TELLIN' YA JUST THE WAY SHE TOLD ME, CAPTAIN. I'D RATHER SHE NOT BE QUESTIONED LIKE SOME COMMON CRIMINAL.
THIS WAS JUST YESTERDAY, AS I SAY.
SO I'D GUESS THAT IF YA RIDE OUT IMMEDIATELY THE TWELVE OF YA COULD MAKE THAT DAY UP IN A HURRY!
I THINK WE'LL BED DOWN FOR THE NIGHT NONETHELESS, ON ACCOUNT OF THE STORM.
IF IT'S REALLY THE THREE WE'RE AFTER, SURELY THEY'VE BEEN FORCED TO DO LIKEWISE.
I'D LOVE TO HAVE YOU, CAPTAIN, BUT WE'RE FILLED UP. THIS WEATHER—!

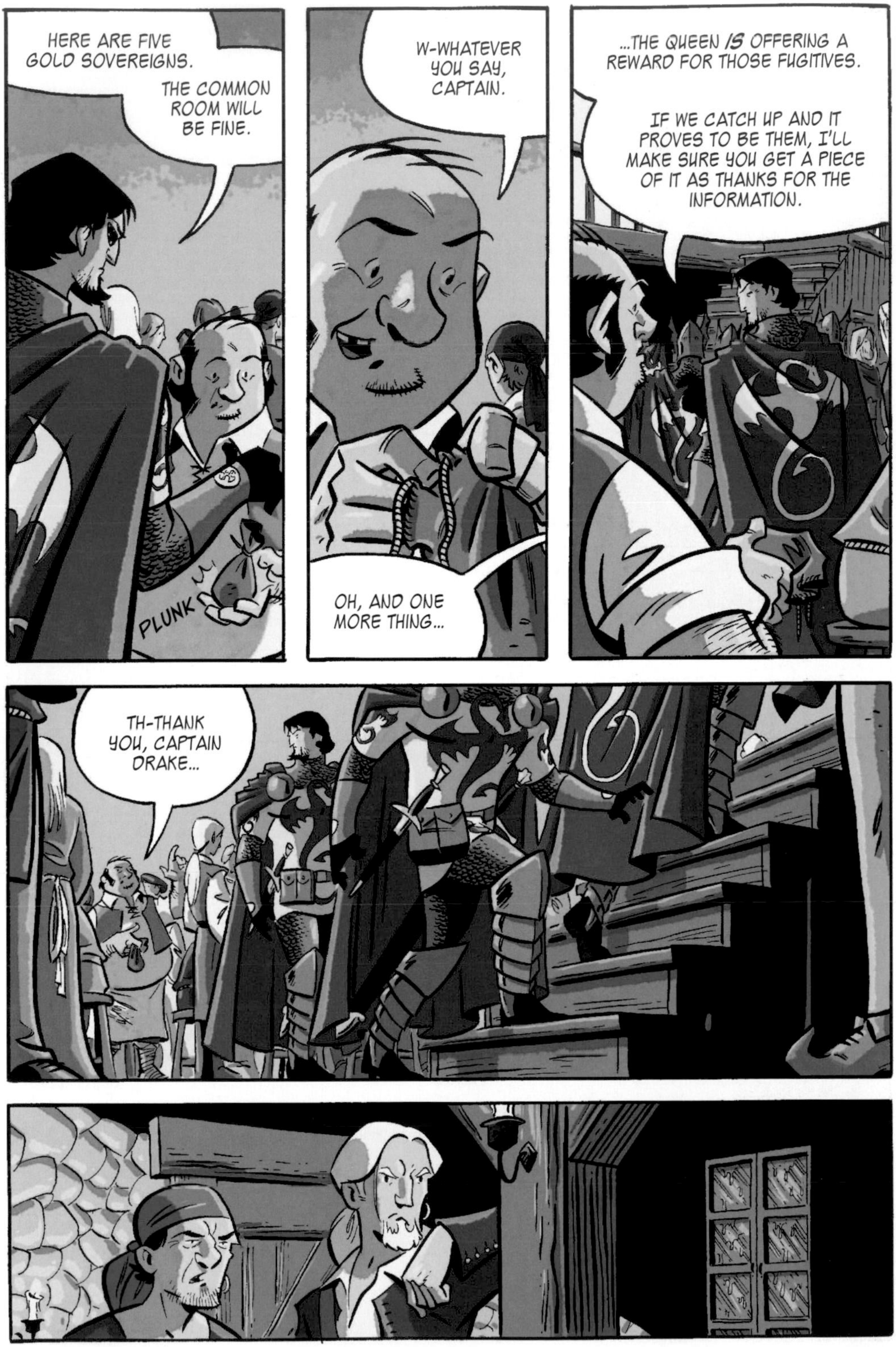
HERE ARE FIVE GOLD SOVEREIGNS.
THE COMMON ROOM WILL BE FINE.
PLUNK
W-WHATEVER YOU SAY, CAPTAIN.
OH, AND ONE MORE THING...
...THE QUEEN *IS* OFFERING A REWARD FOR THOSE FUGITIVES.
IF WE CATCH UP AND IT PROVES TO BE THEM, I'LL MAKE SURE YOU GET A PIECE OF IT AS THANKS FOR THE INFORMATION.
TH-THANK YOU, CAPTAIN DRAKE...

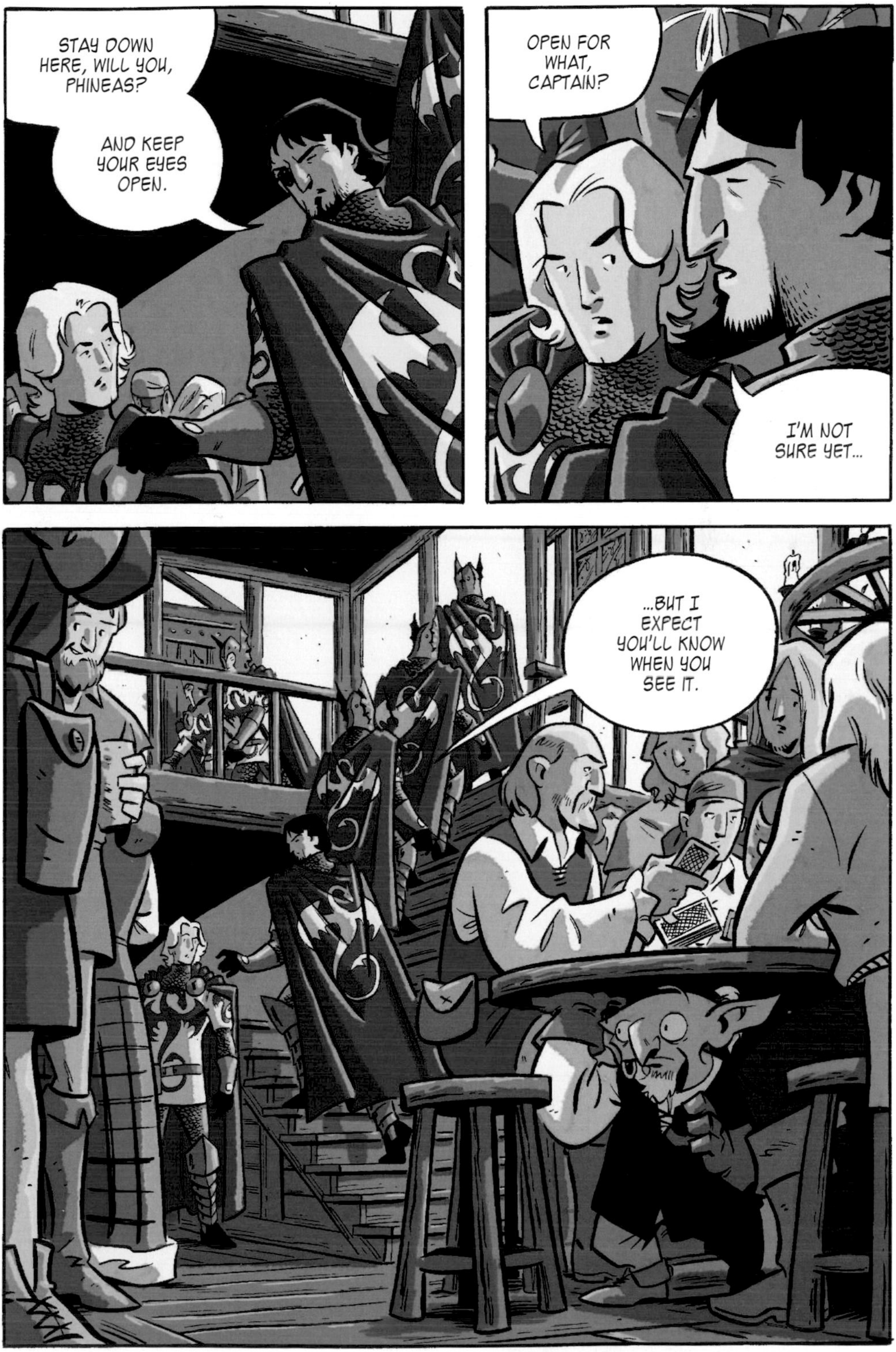
STAY DOWN HERE, WILL YOU, PHINEAS?
AND KEEP YOUR EYES OPEN.
OPEN FOR WHAT, CAPTAIN?
I'M NOT SURE YET...
...BUT I EXPECT YOU'LL KNOW WHEN YOU SEE IT.

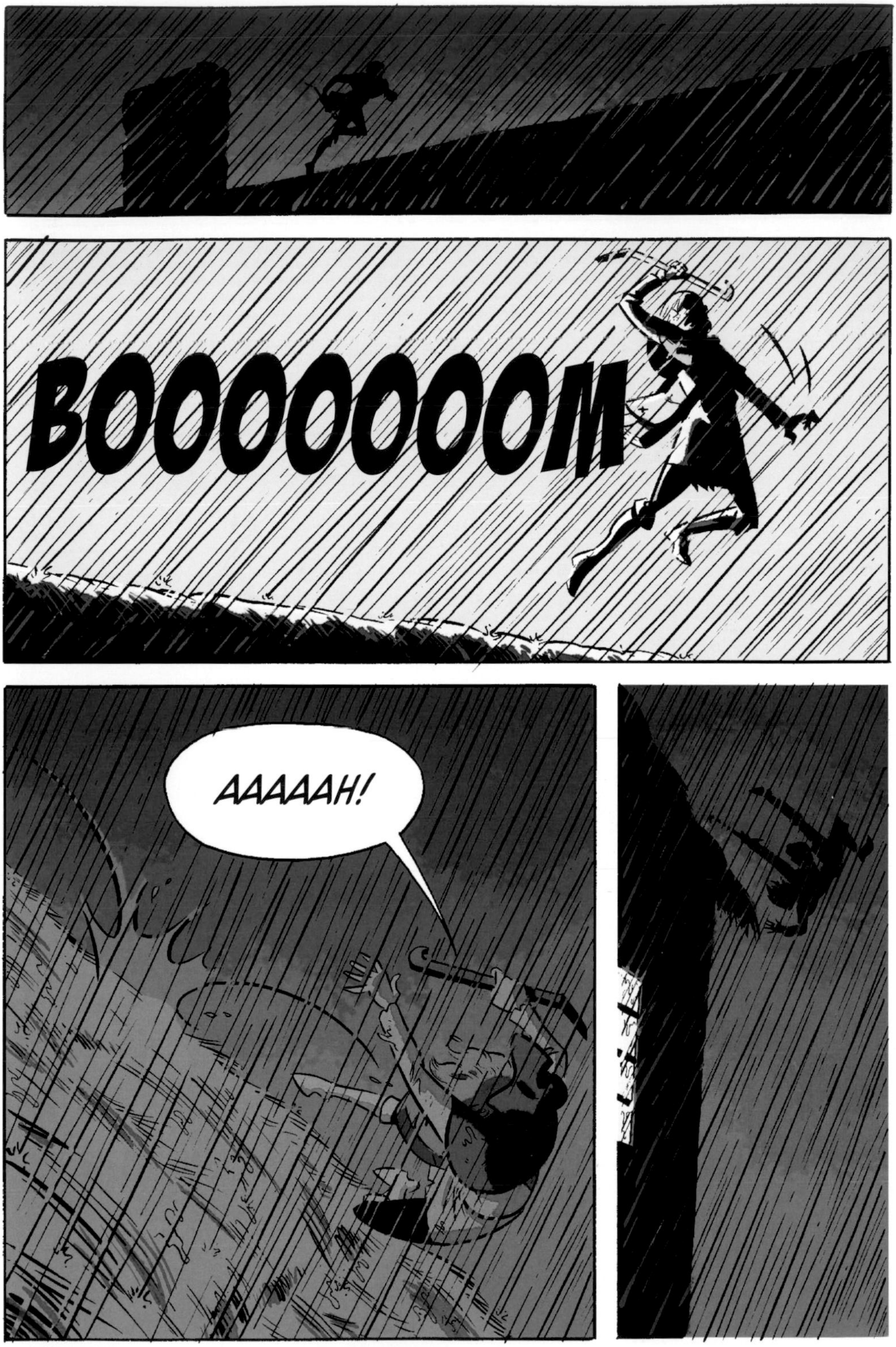
BOOOOOOOM
AAAAAH!

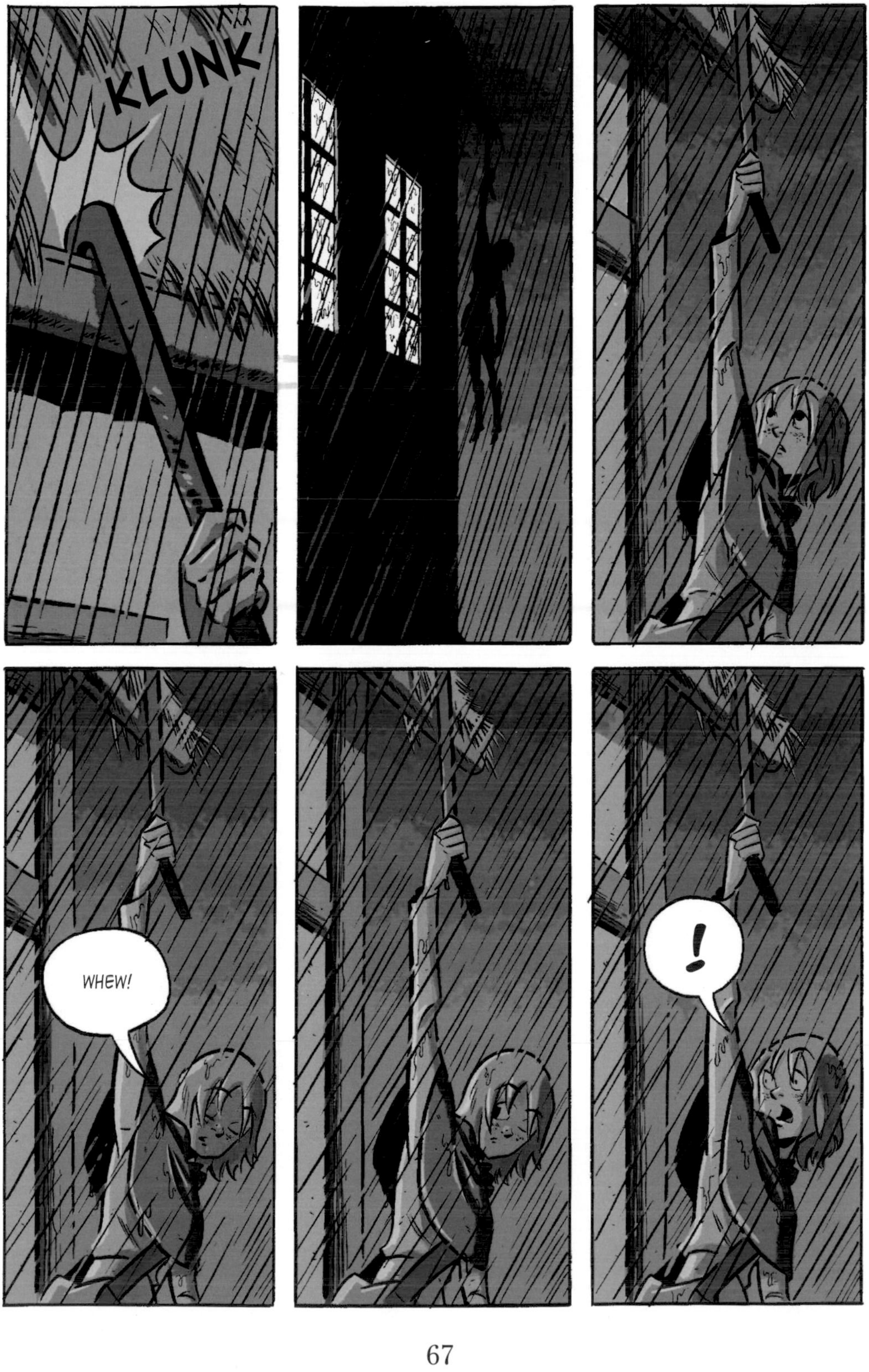
KLUNK
WHEW!
!

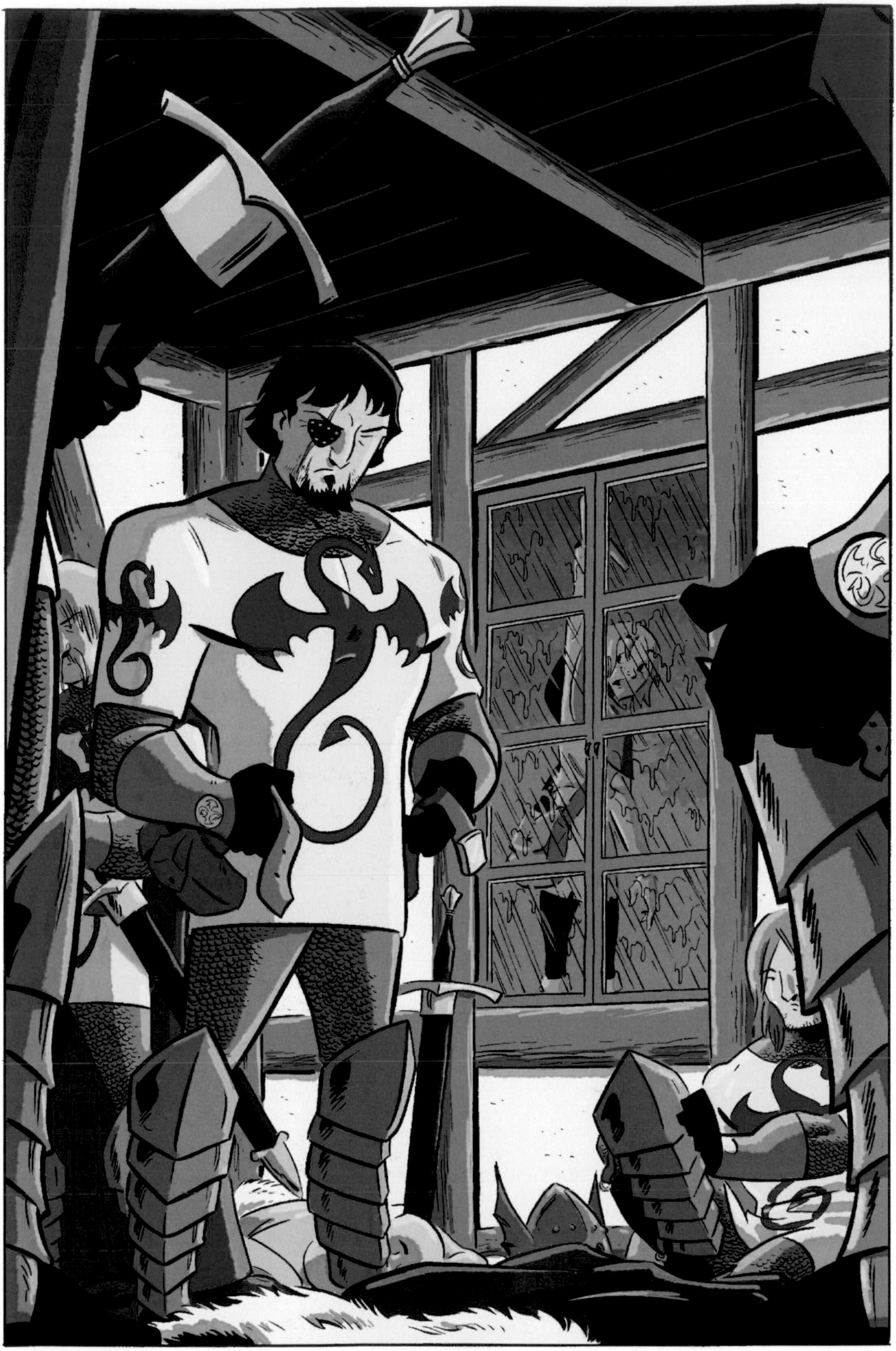

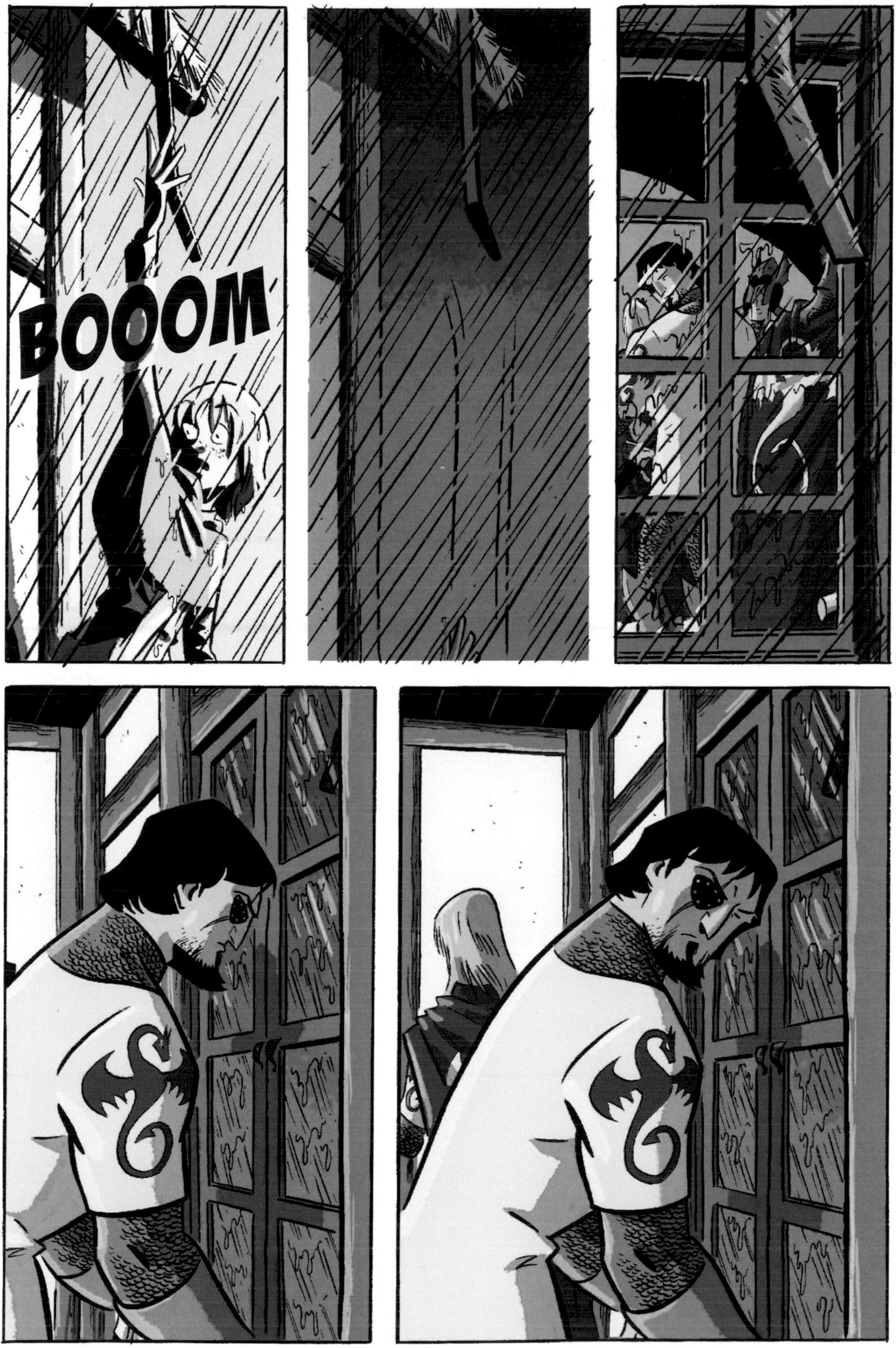
BOOOM

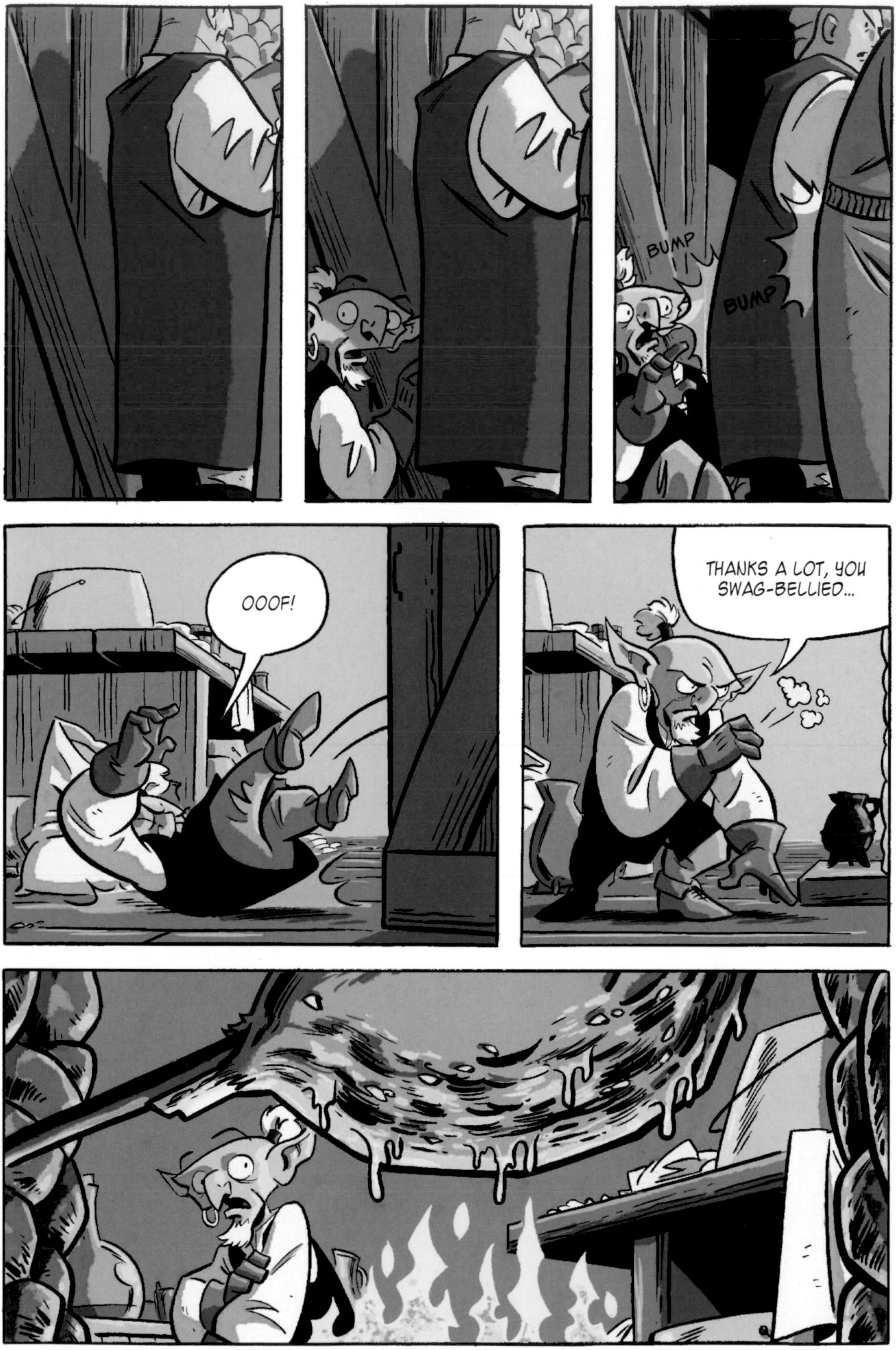
BUMP
BUMP
OOOF!
THANKS A LOT, YOU SWAG-BELLIED...

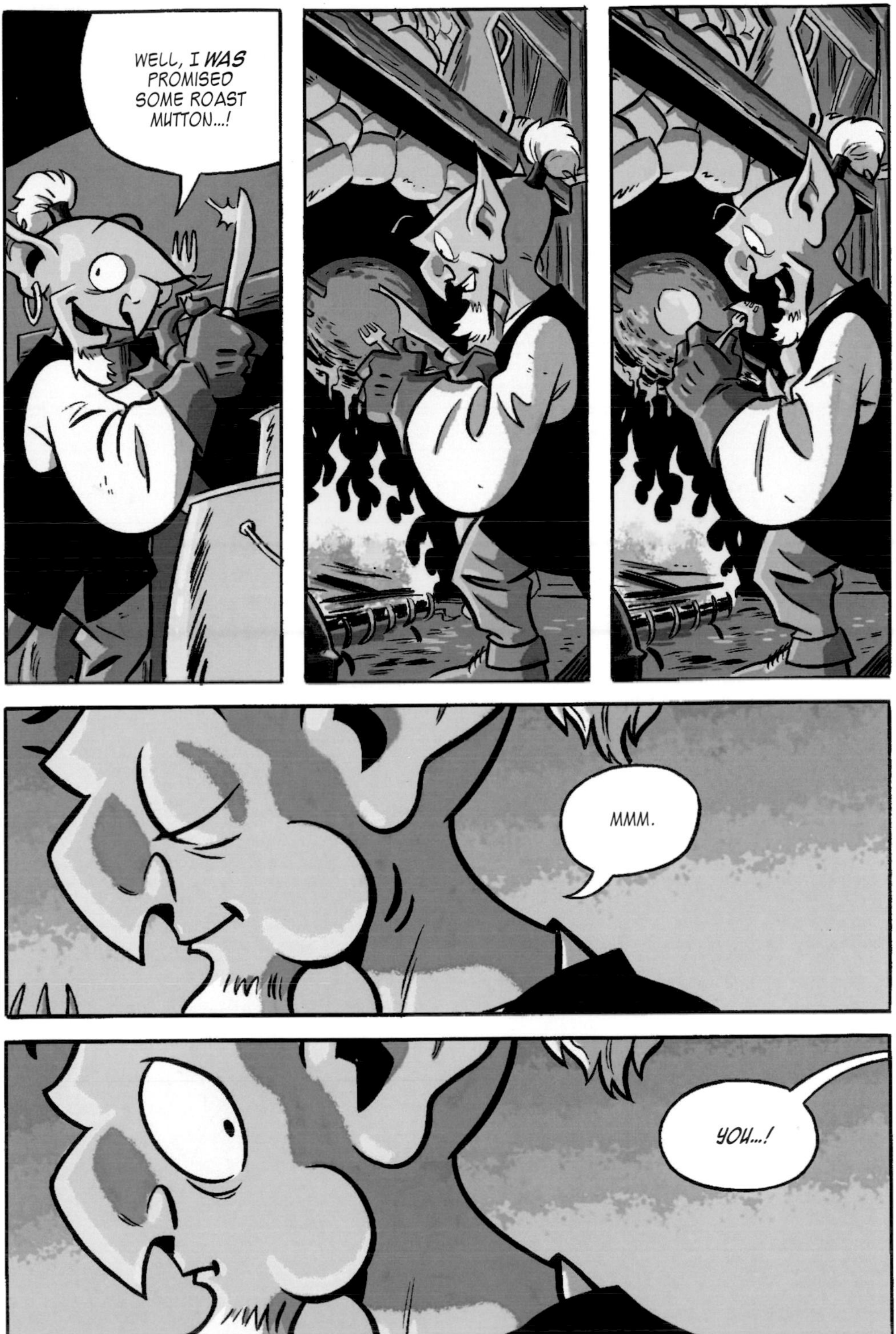
WELL, I *WAS* PROMISED SOME ROAST MUTTON...!
MMM.
YOU...!

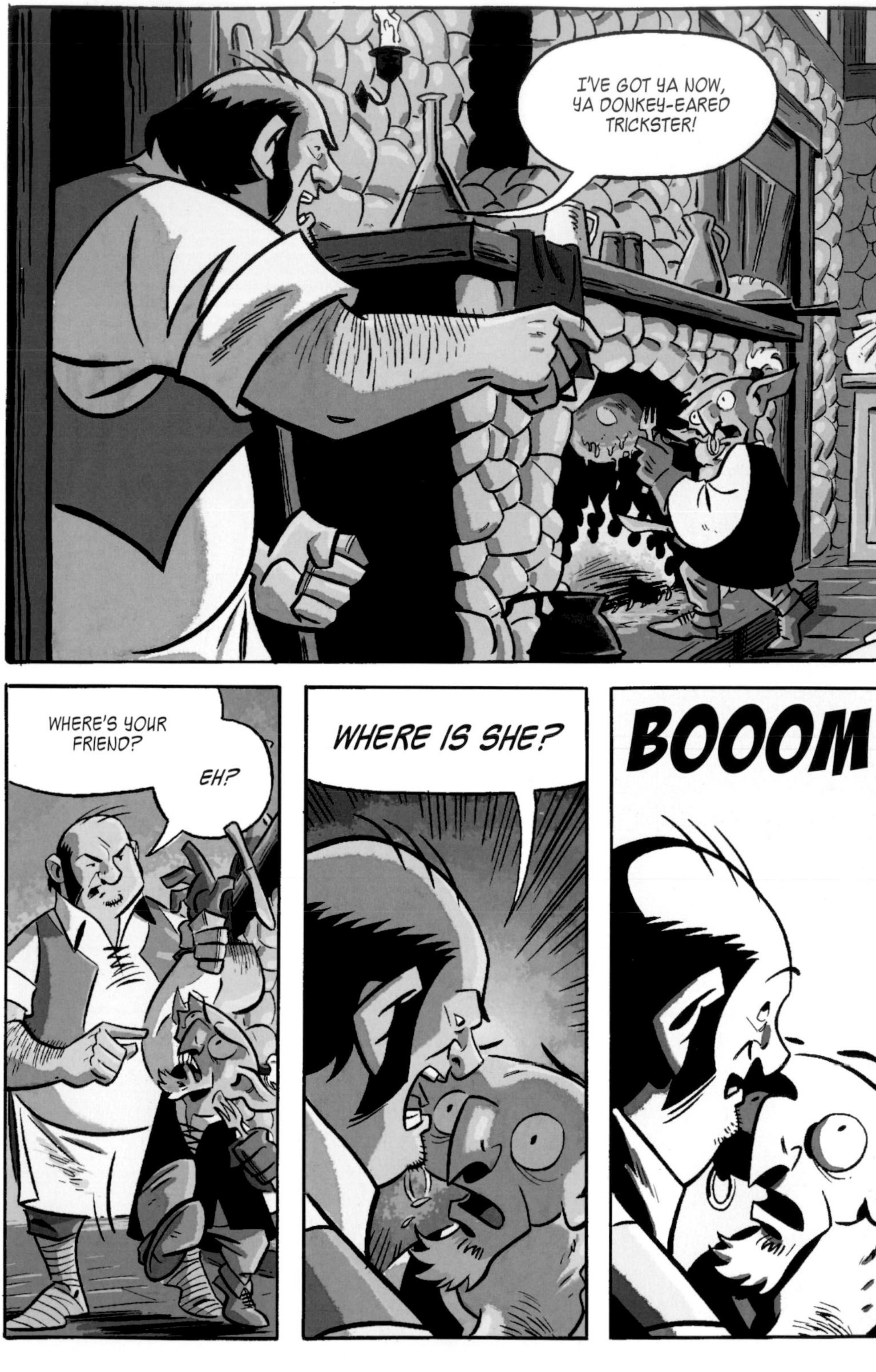
I'VE GOT YA NOW, YA DONKEY-EARED TRICKSTER!
WHERE'S YOUR FRIEND?
EH?
WHERE IS SHE?
BOOOM

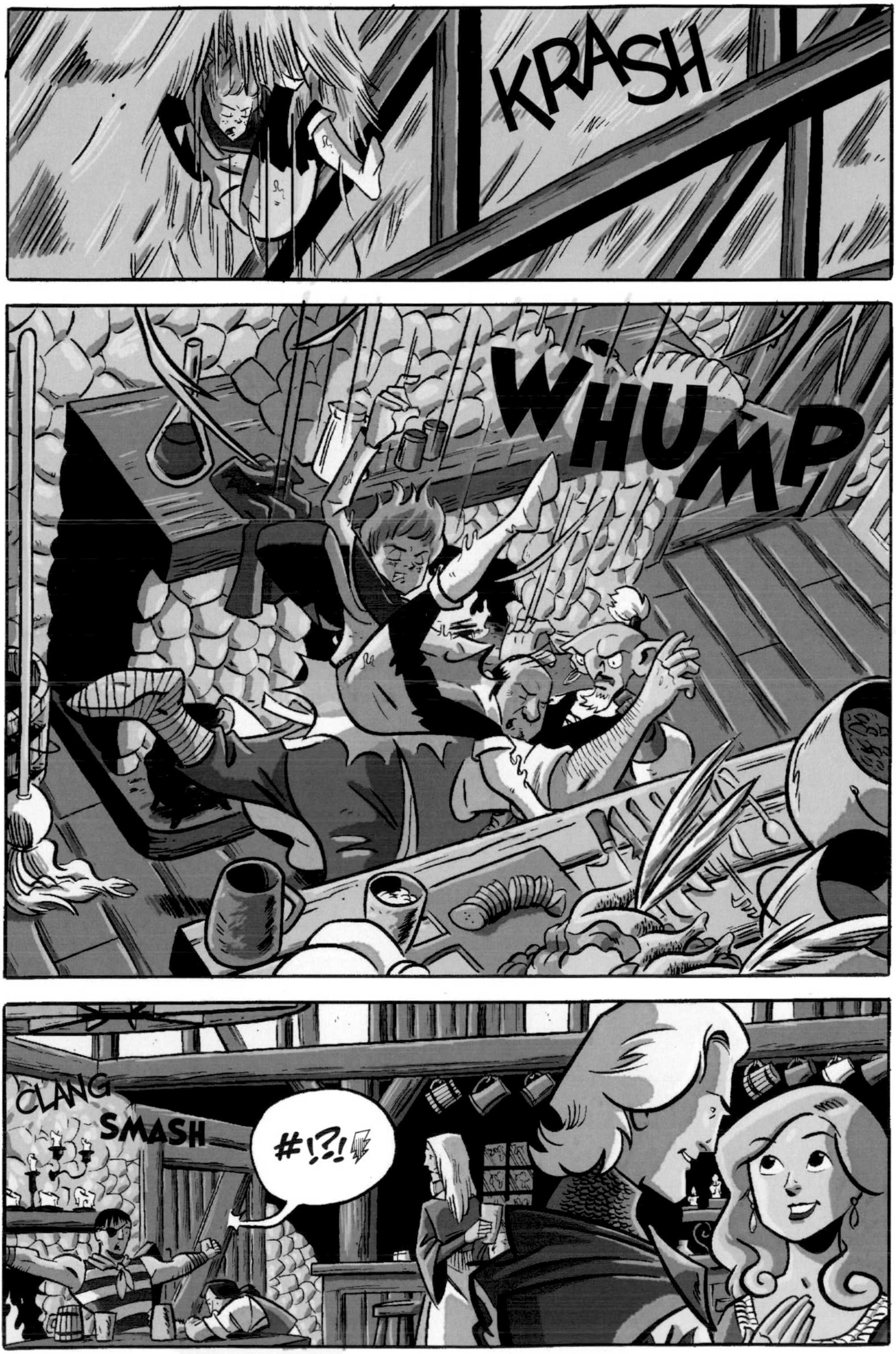
KRASH
WHUMP
CLANG
SMASH
#!?!

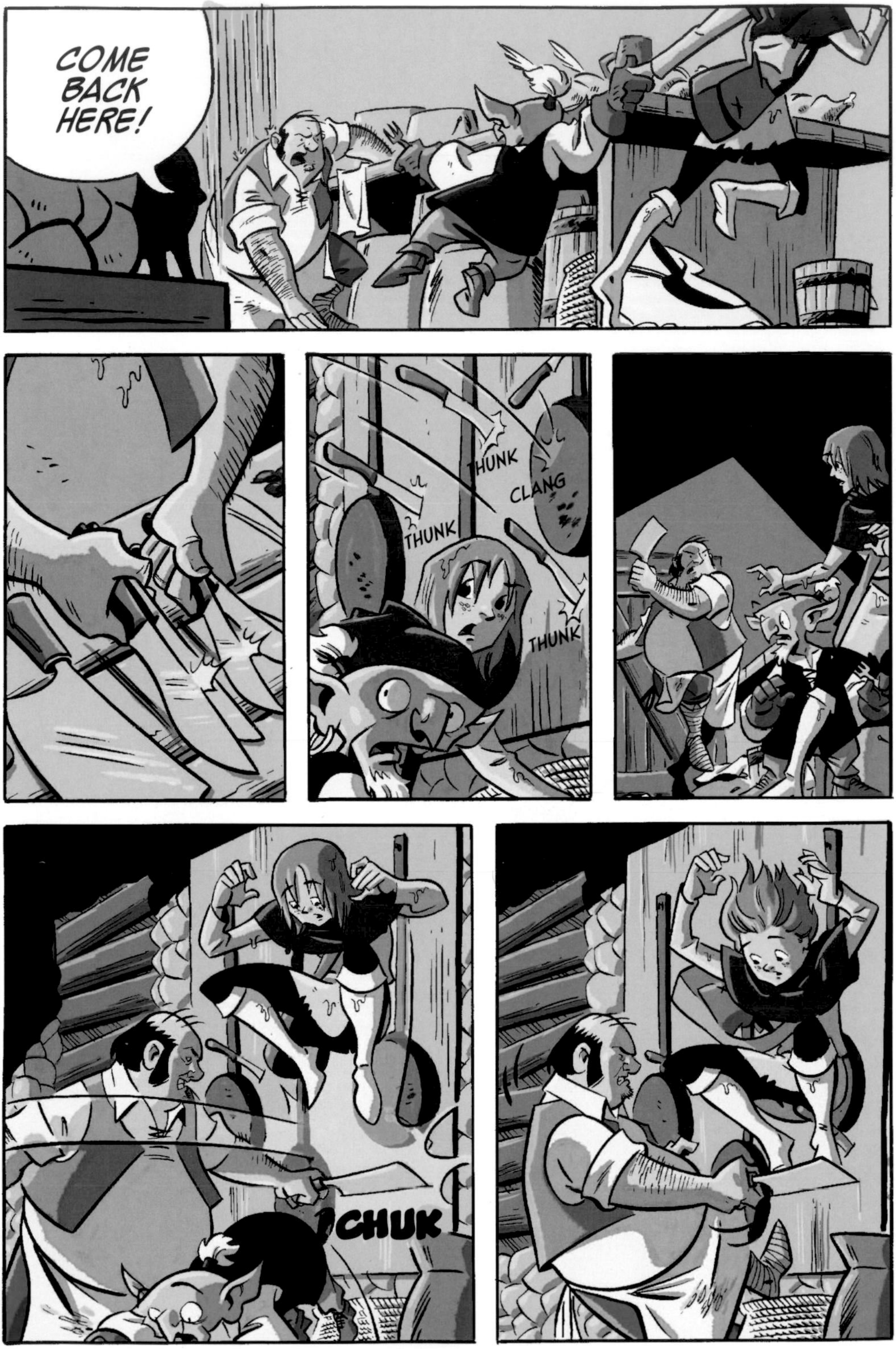
COME BACK HERE!
THUNK
CLANG
THUNK
THUNK
CHUK

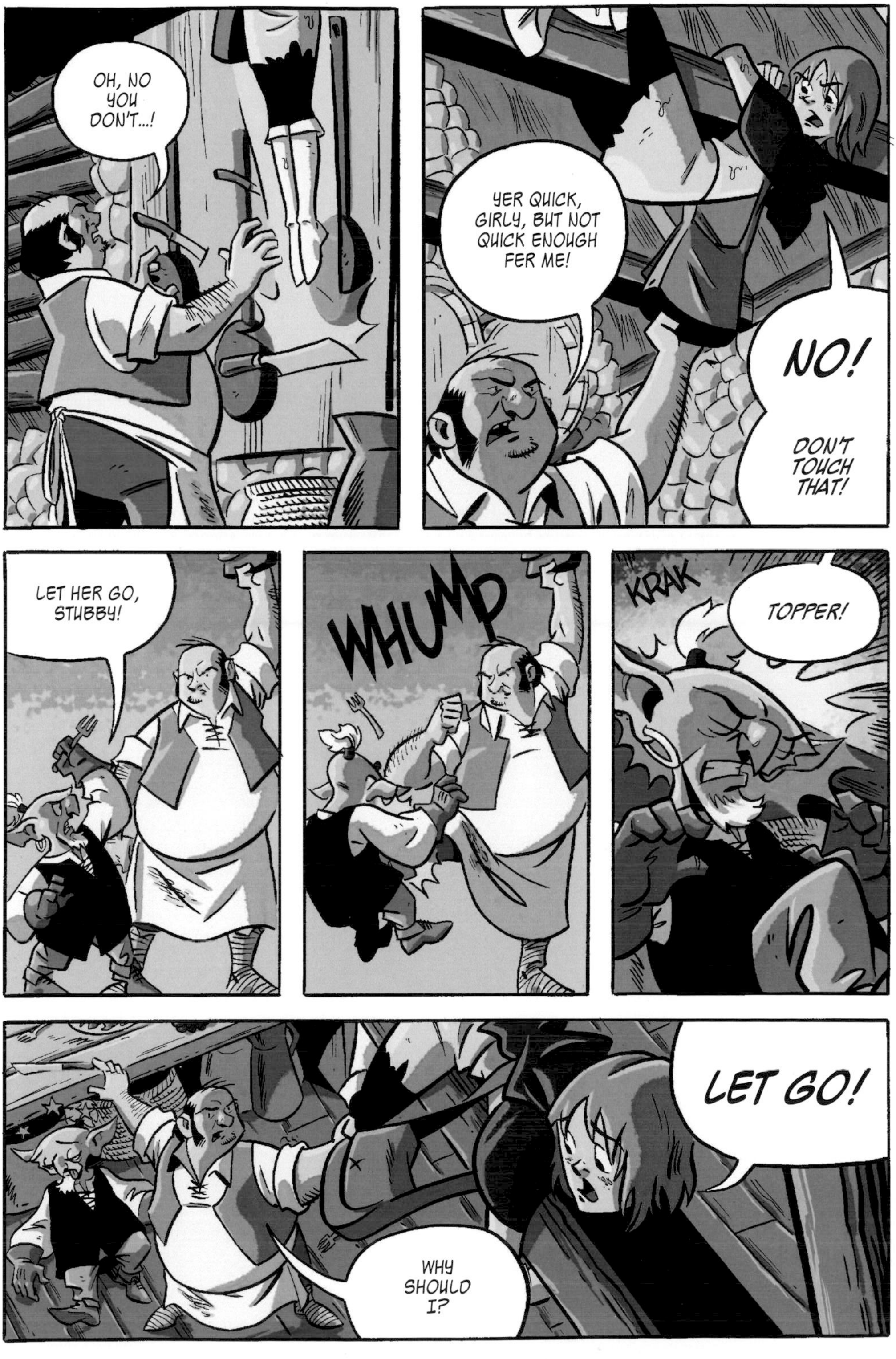
OH, NO YOU DON'T...!
YER QUICK, GIRLY, BUT NOT QUICK ENOUGH FER ME!
NO!
DON'T TOUCH THAT!
LET HER GO, STUBBY!
WHUMP
KRAK
TOPPER!
LET GO!
WHY SHOULD I?

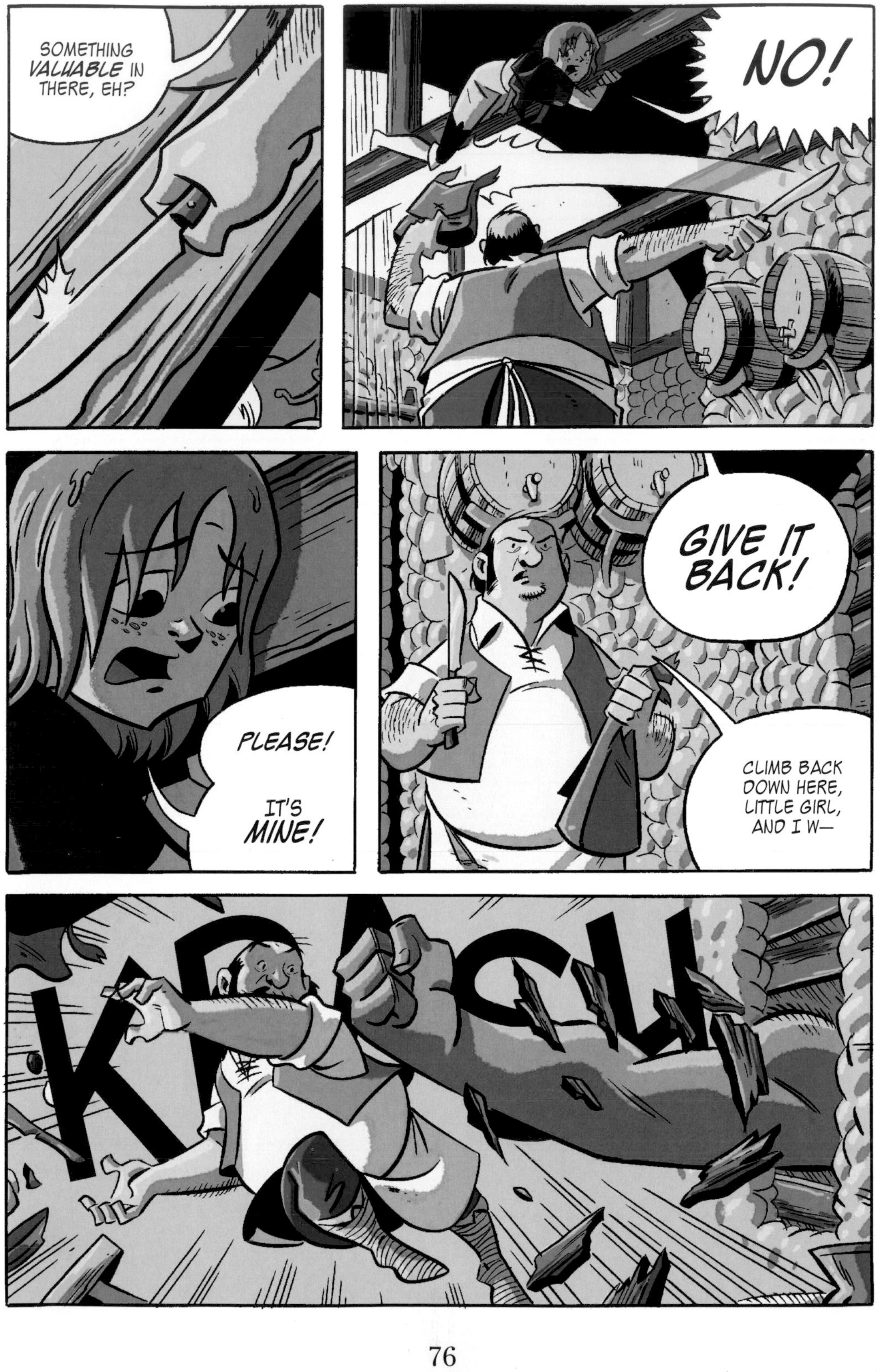
SOMETHING VALUABLE IN THERE, EH?
NO!
PLEASE!
IT'S MINE!
GIVE IT BACK!
CLIMB BACK DOWN HERE, LITTLE GIRL, AND I W—

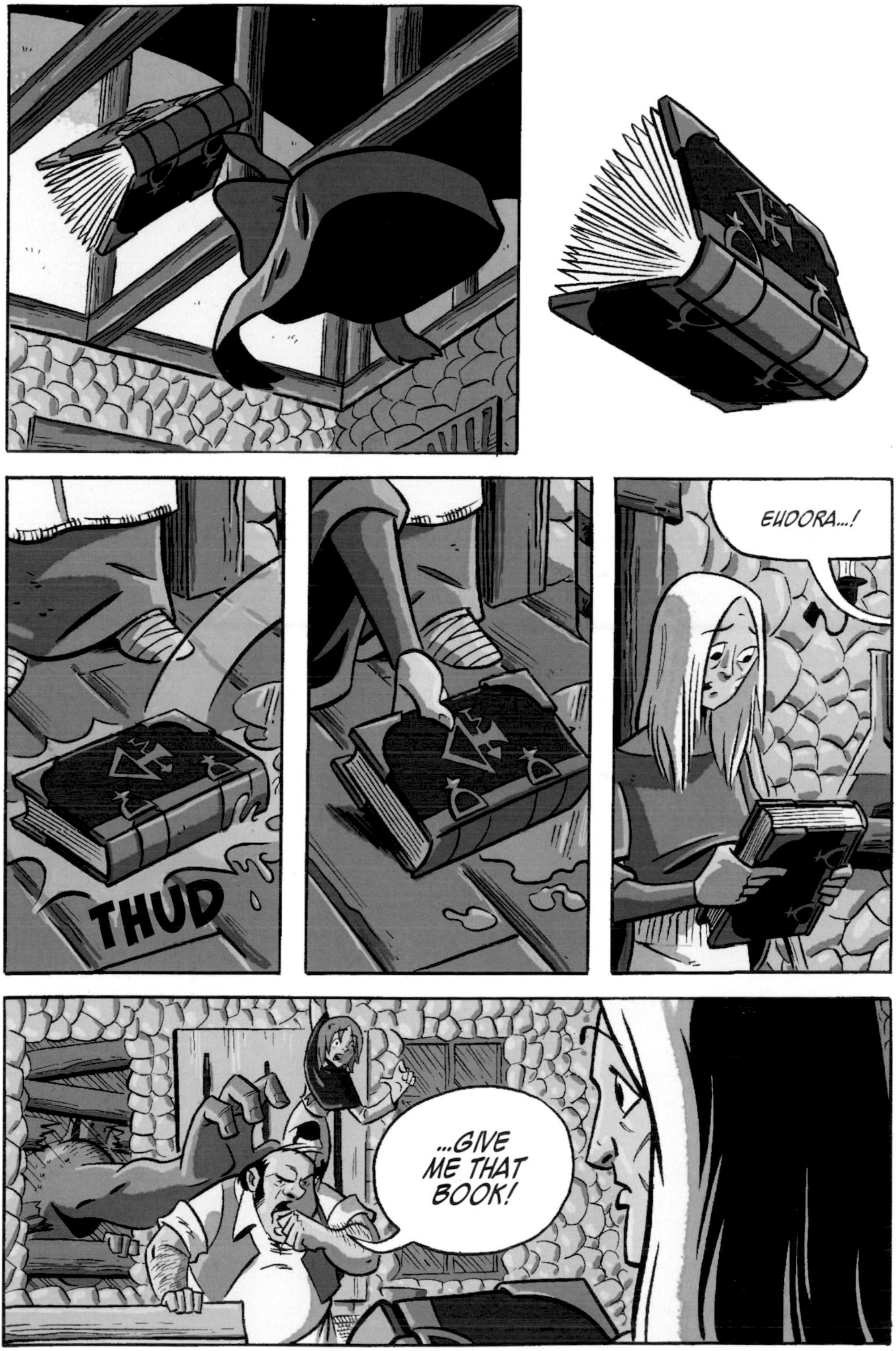
THUD
EUDORA...!
...GIVE ME THAT BOOK!

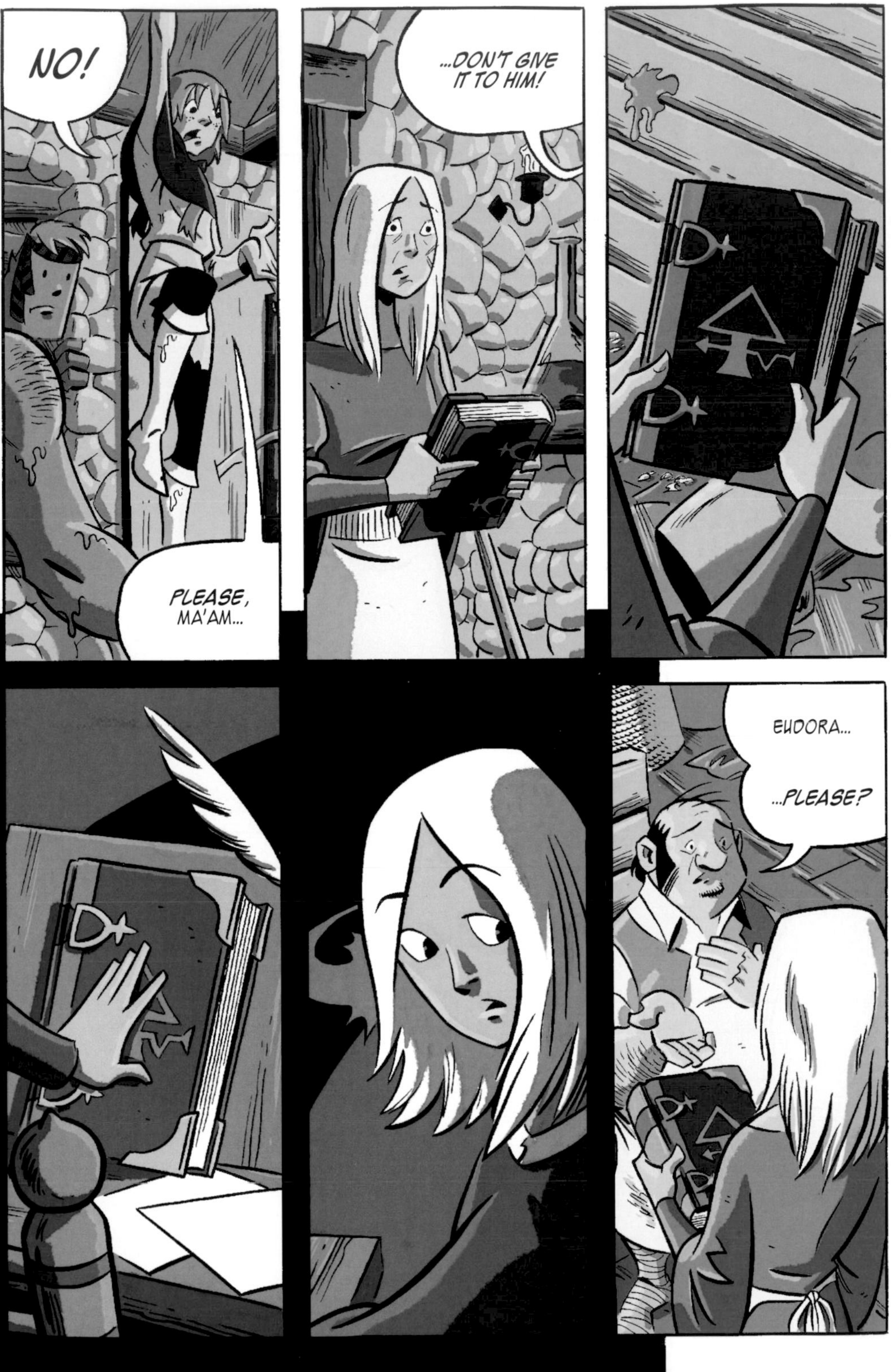
NO!
PLEASE, MA'AM...
...DON'T GIVE IT TO HIM!
EUDORA...
...PLEASE?

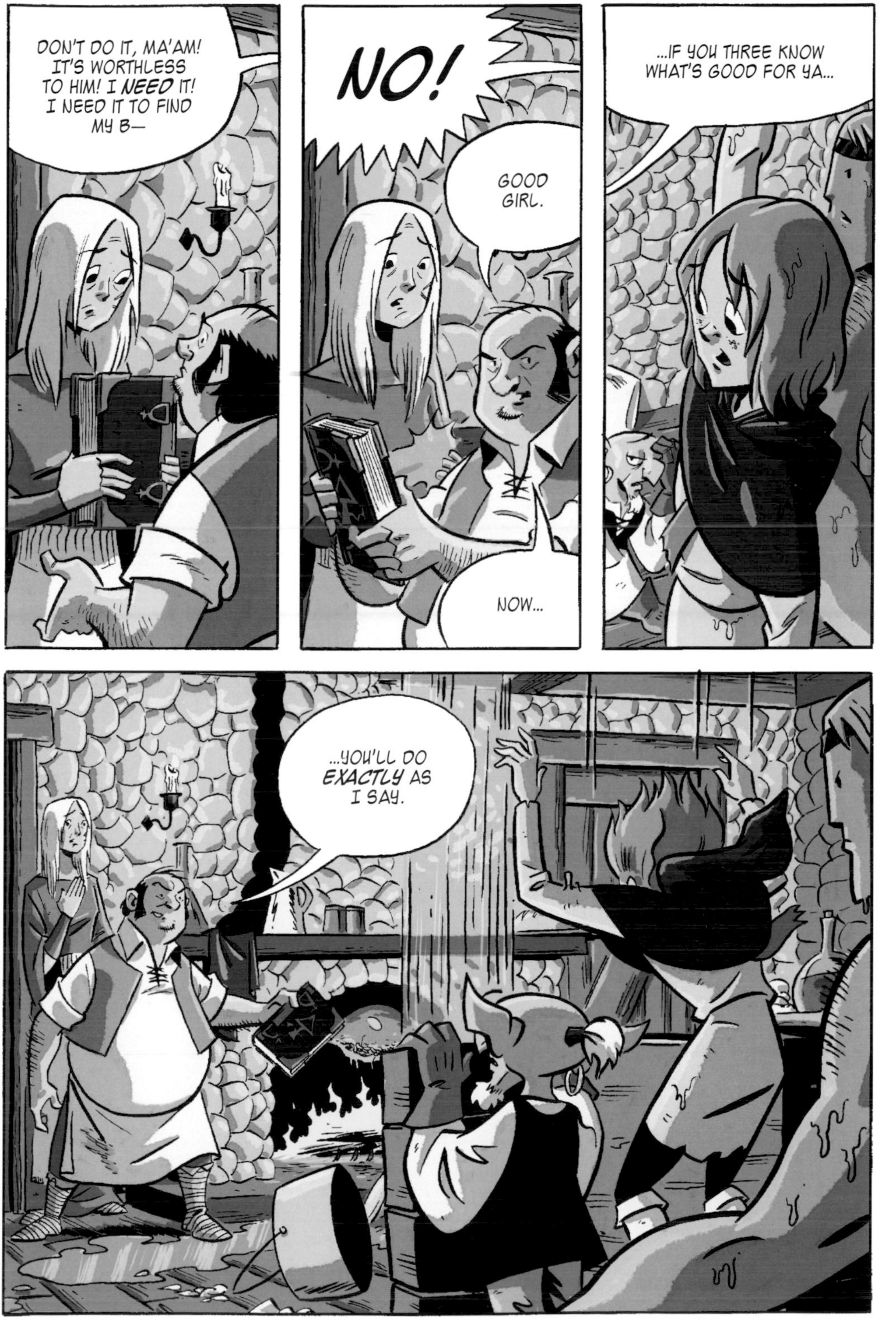
DON'T DO IT, MA'AM! IT'S WORTHLESS TO HIM! I NEED IT! I NEED IT TO FIND MY B—
NO!
GOOD GIRL.
NOW...
...IF YOU THREE KNOW WHAT'S GOOD FOR YA...
...YOU'LL DO EXACTLY AS I SAY.

ACT THREE
SCARS

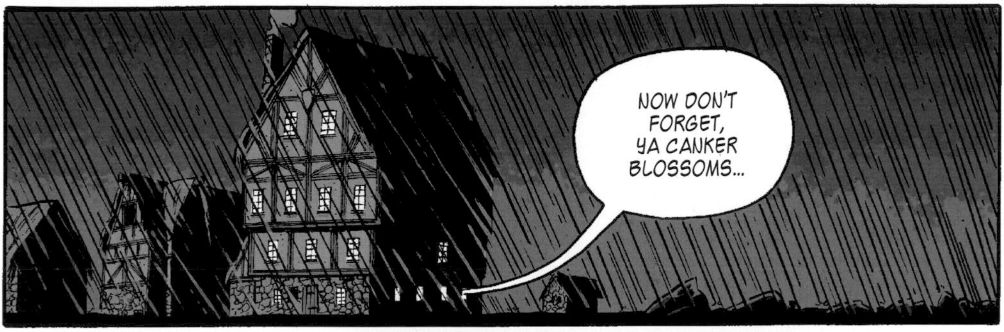
NOW DON'T FORGET, YA CANKER BLOSSOMS...

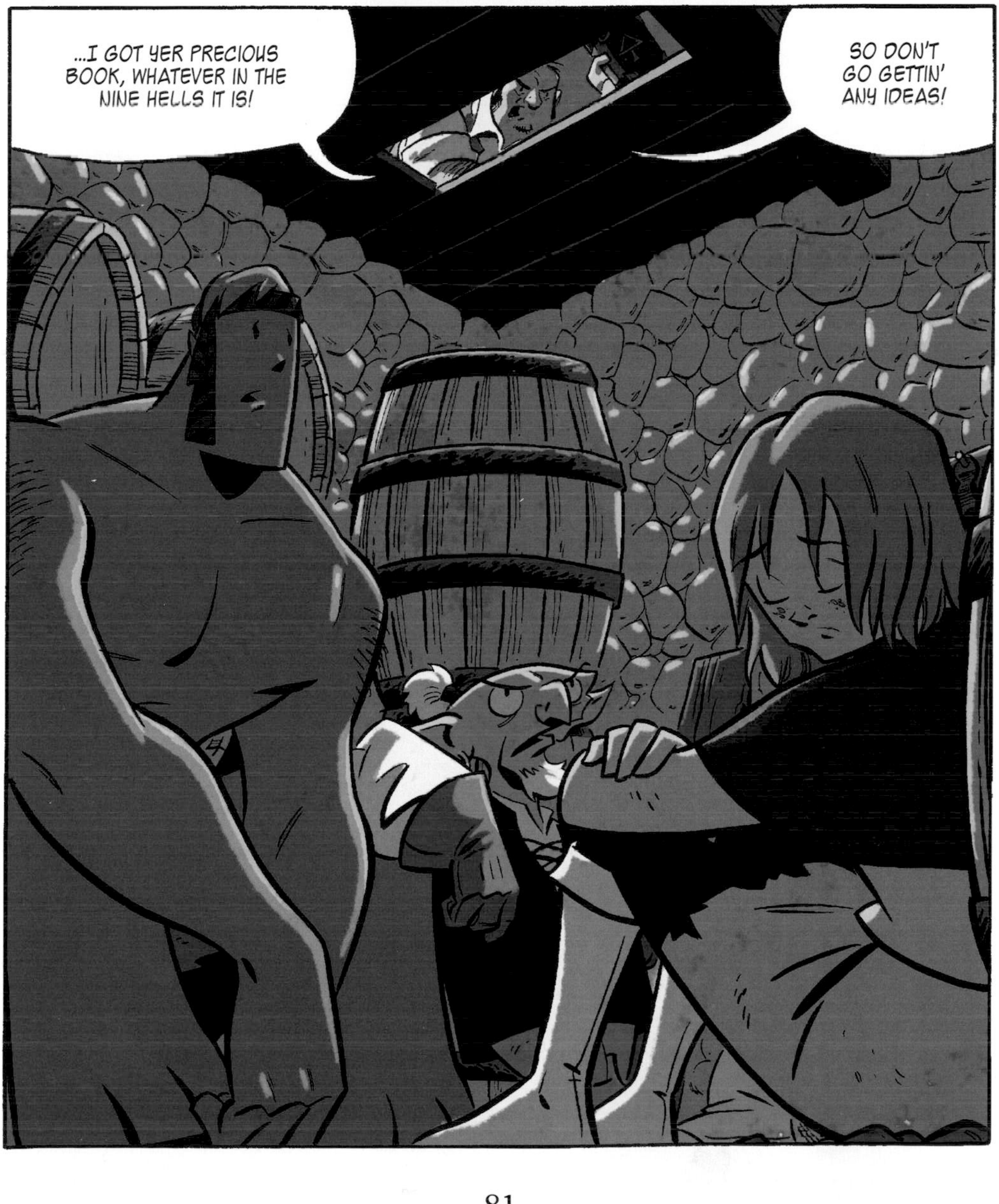
...I GOT YER PRECIOUS BOOK, WHATEVER IN THE NINE HELLS IT IS!
SO DON'T GO GETTIN' ANY IDEAS!

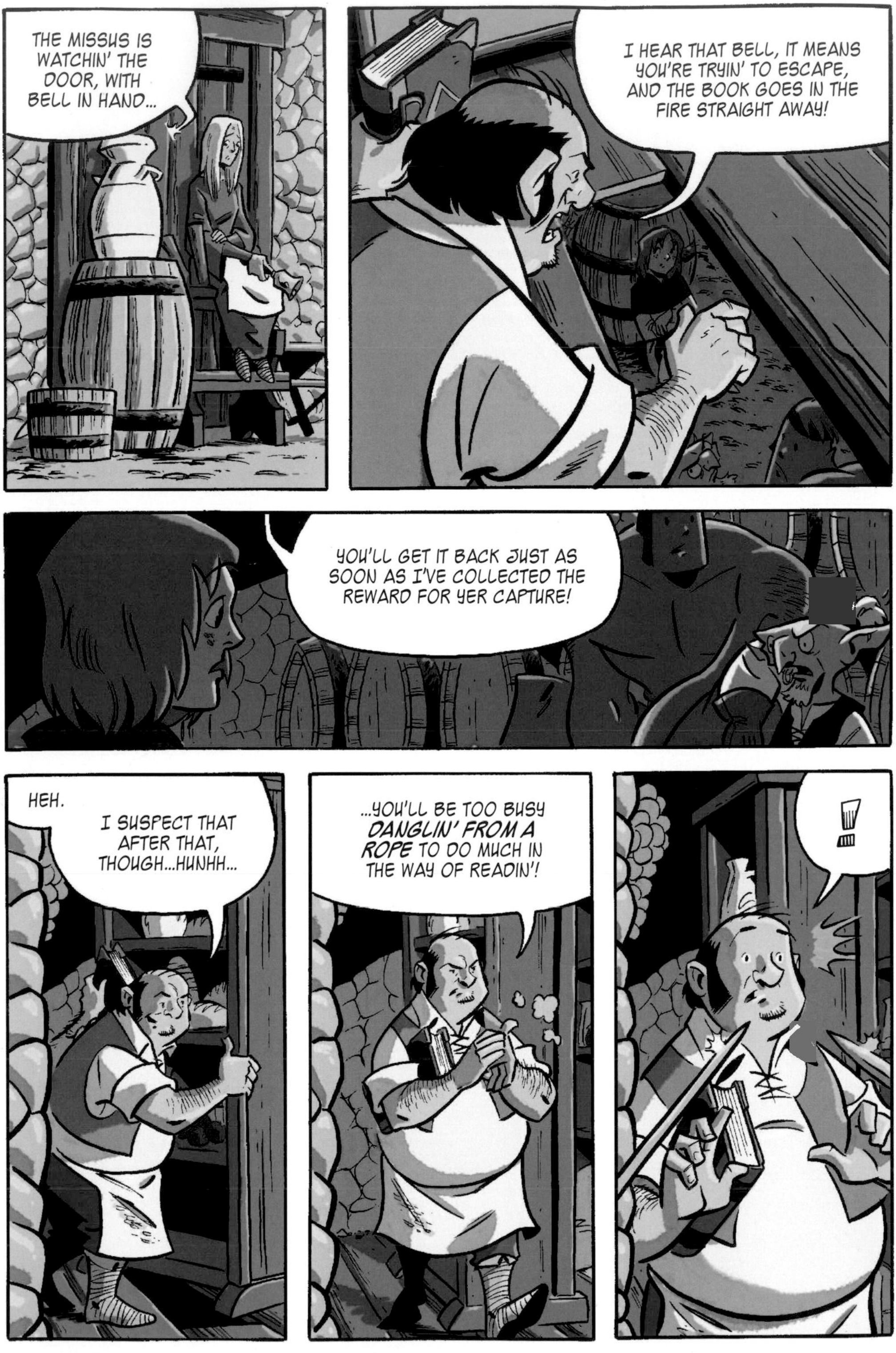
THE MISSUS IS WATCHIN' THE DOOR, WITH BELL IN HAND...
I HEAR THAT BELL, IT MEANS YOU'RE TRYIN' TO ESCAPE, AND THE BOOK GOES IN THE FIRE STRAIGHT AWAY!
YOU'LL GET IT BACK JUST AS SOON AS I'VE COLLECTED THE REWARD FOR YER CAPTURE!
HEH.
I SUSPECT THAT AFTER THAT, THOUGH...HUNHH...
...YOU'LL BE TOO BUSY DANGLIN' FROM A ROPE TO DO MUCH IN THE WAY OF READIN'!
!

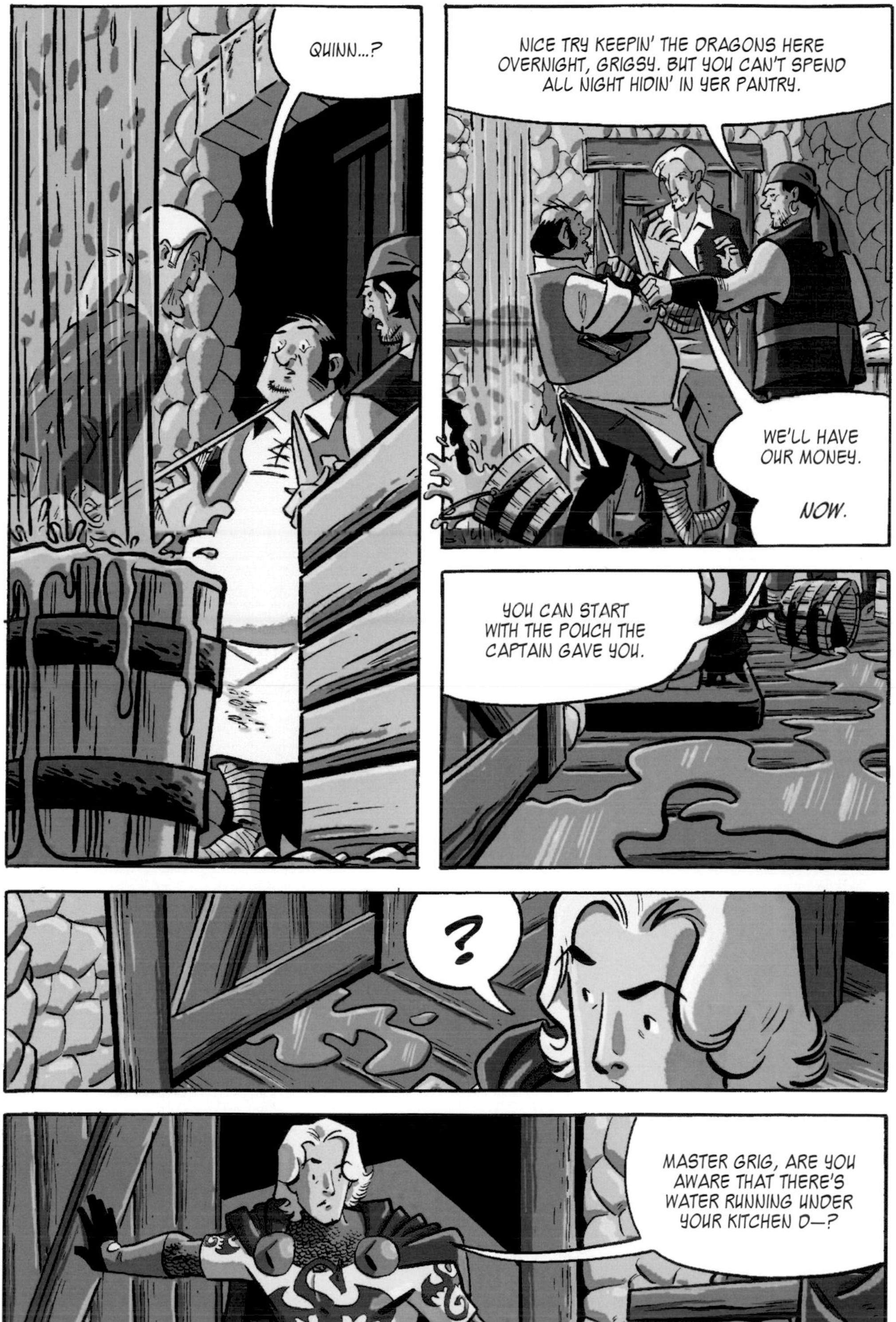
QUINN...?
NICE TRY KEEPIN' THE DRAGONS HERE OVERNIGHT, GRIGSY. BUT YOU CAN'T SPEND ALL NIGHT HIDIN' IN YER PANTRY.
WE'LL HAVE OUR MONEY.
NOW.
YOU CAN START WITH THE POUCH THE CAPTAIN GAVE YOU.
?
MASTER GRIG, ARE YOU AWARE THAT THERE'S WATER RUNNING UNDER YOUR KITCHEN D—?

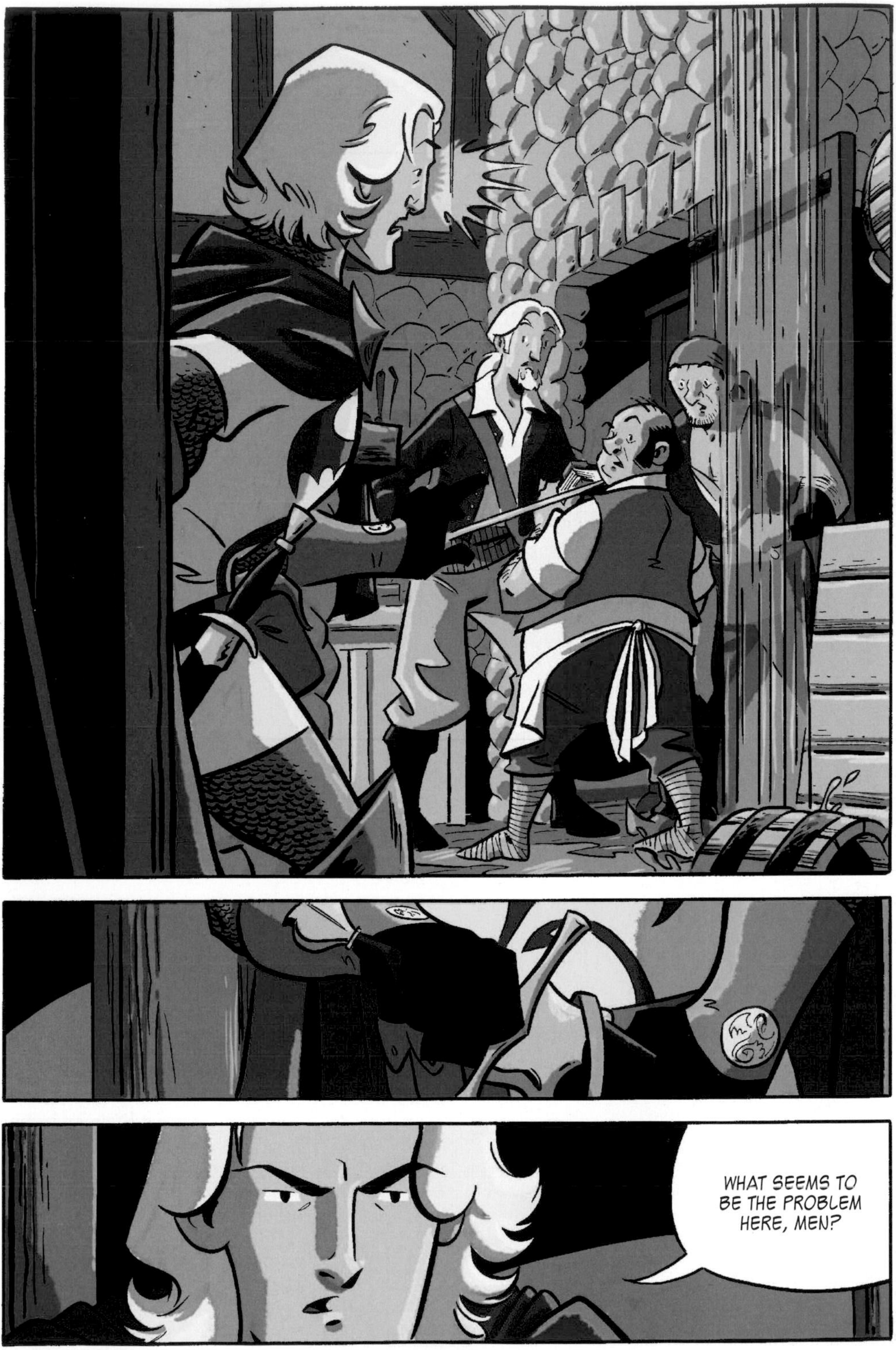
WHAT SEEMS TO BE THE PROBLEM HERE, MEN?

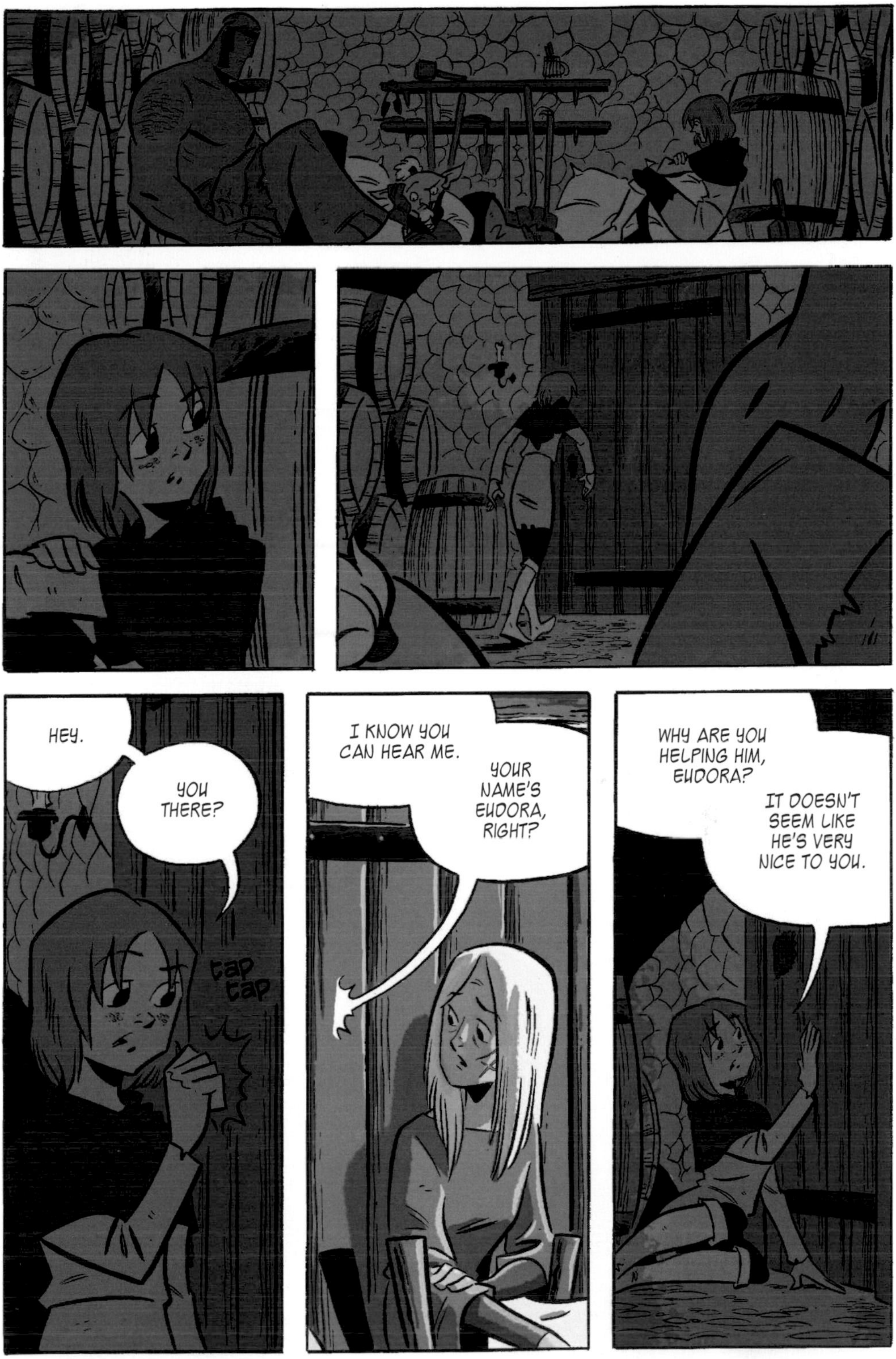
HEY.
YOU THERE?
tap tap
I KNOW YOU CAN HEAR ME.
YOUR NAME'S EUDORA, RIGHT?
WHY ARE YOU HELPING HIM, EUDORA?
IT DOESN'T SEEM LIKE HE'S VERY NICE TO YOU.

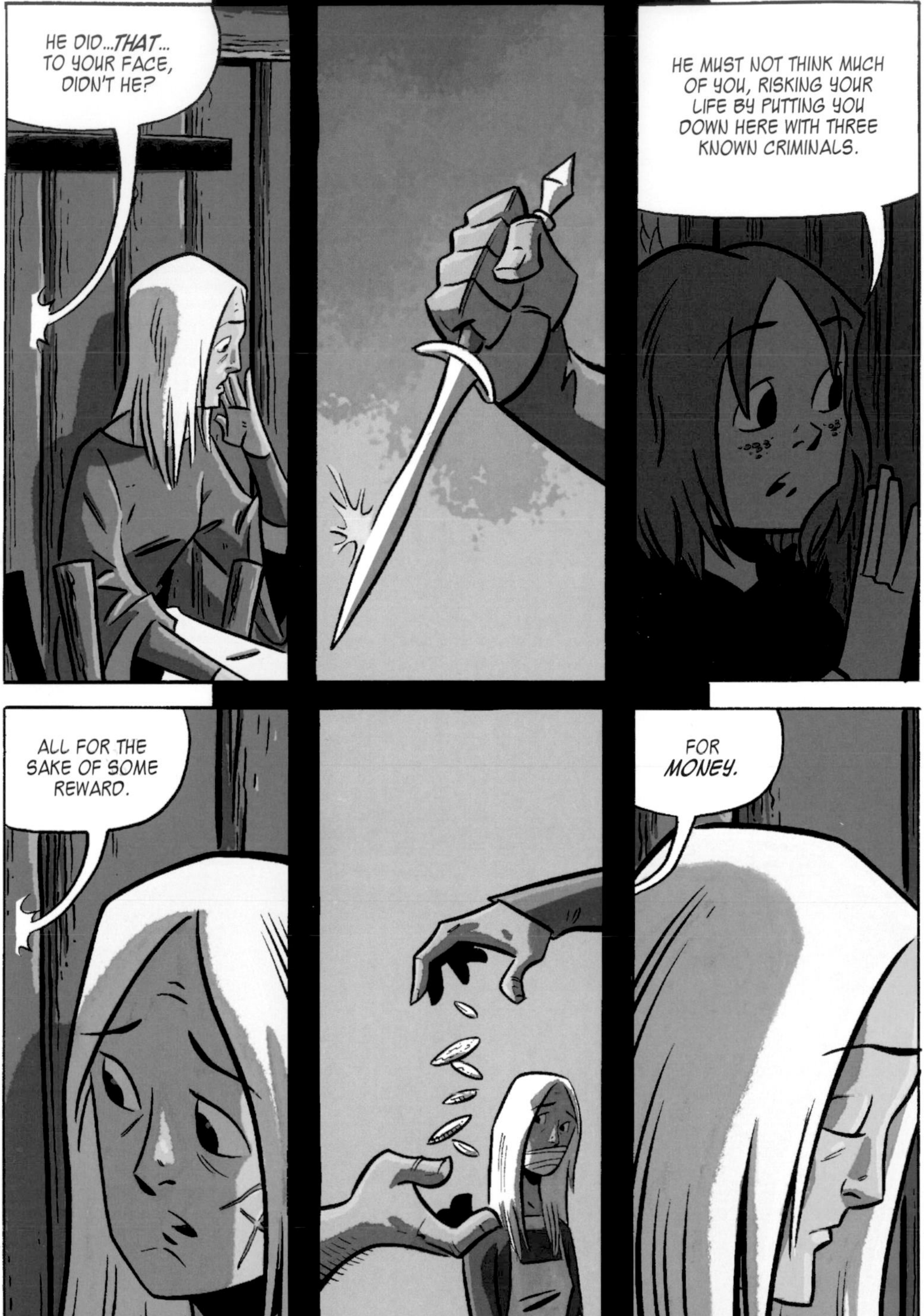
HE DID...*THAT*... TO YOUR FACE, DIDN'T HE?
HE MUST NOT THINK MUCH OF YOU, RISKING YOUR LIFE BY PUTTING YOU DOWN HERE WITH THREE KNOWN CRIMINALS.
ALL FOR THE SAKE OF SOME REWARD.
FOR *MONEY*.

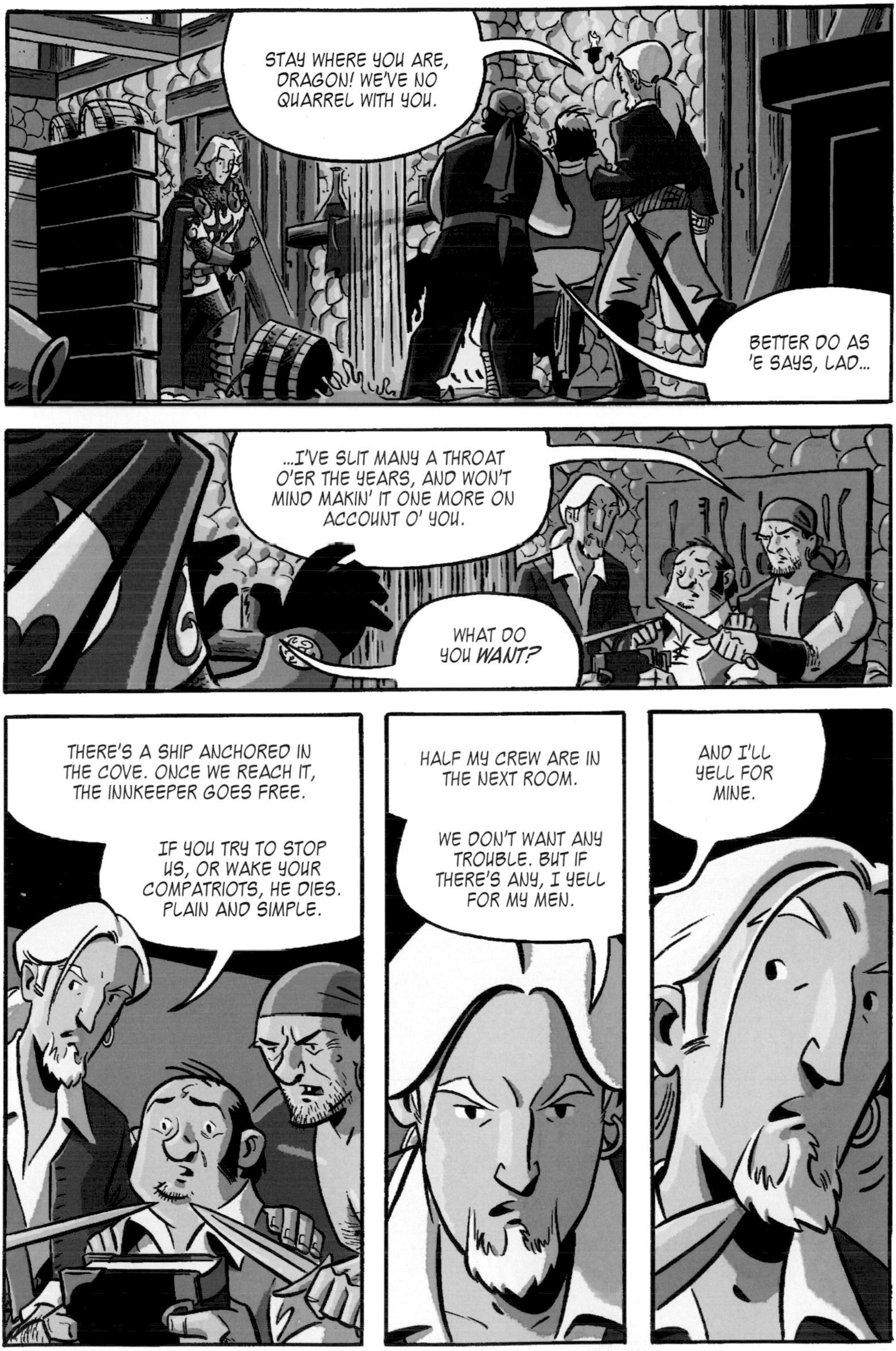
STAY WHERE YOU ARE, DRAGON! WE'VE NO QUARREL WITH YOU.
BETTER DO AS 'E SAYS, LAD...
...I'VE SLIT MANY A THROAT O'ER THE YEARS, AND WON'T MIND MAKIN' IT ONE MORE ON ACCOUNT O' YOU.
WHAT DO YOU *WANT?*
THERE'S A SHIP ANCHORED IN THE COVE. ONCE WE REACH IT, THE INNKEEPER GOES FREE.
IF YOU TRY TO STOP US, OR WAKE YOUR COMPATRIOTS, HE DIES. PLAIN AND SIMPLE.
HALF MY CREW ARE IN THE NEXT ROOM.
WE DON'T WANT ANY TROUBLE. BUT IF THERE'S ANY, I YELL FOR MY MEN.
AND I'LL YELL FOR MINE.

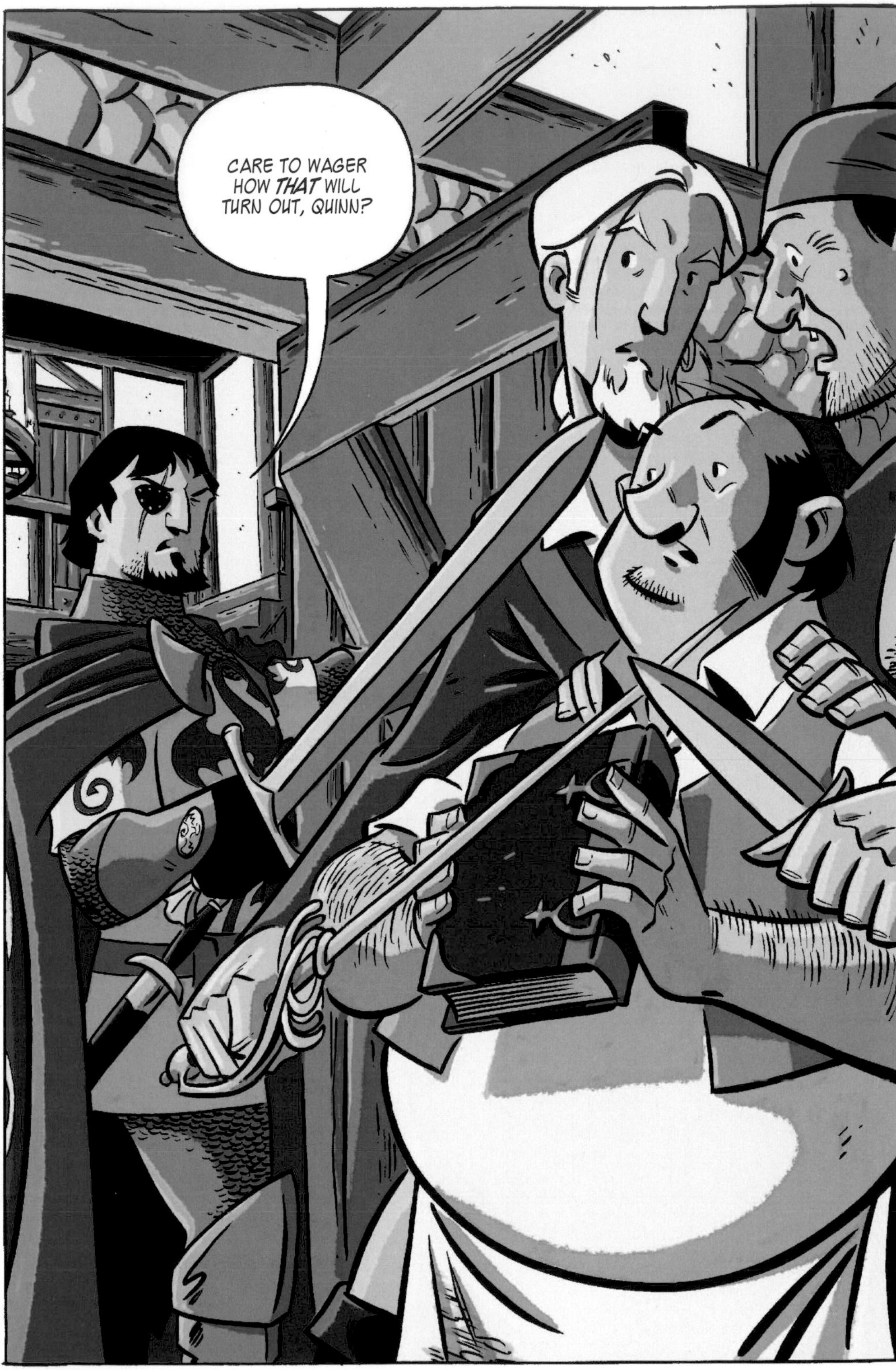
CARE TO WAGER HOW *THAT* WILL TURN OUT, QUINN?

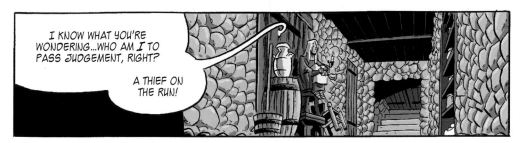

I KNOW WHAT YOU'RE WONDERING...WHO AM *I* TO PASS JUDGEMENT, RIGHT?

A THIEF ON THE RUN!

MAYBE YOU EVEN KNOW WHAT WE DID.

I WON'T INSULT YOU BY CLAIMING THAT THE THREE OF US ARE INNOCENT.

Drip

BUT IF YOU COULD SEE THE AMOUNT OF GOLD THE QUEEN IS HOARDING WHILE HER PEOPLE STARVE IN THE STREETS, YOU'D HAVE DONE THE SAME THING WE DID.

Drip

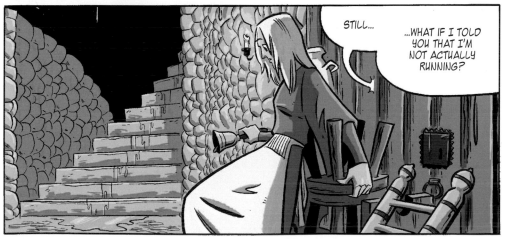

STILL...

...WHAT IF I TOLD YOU THAT I'M NOT ACTUALLY RUNNING?

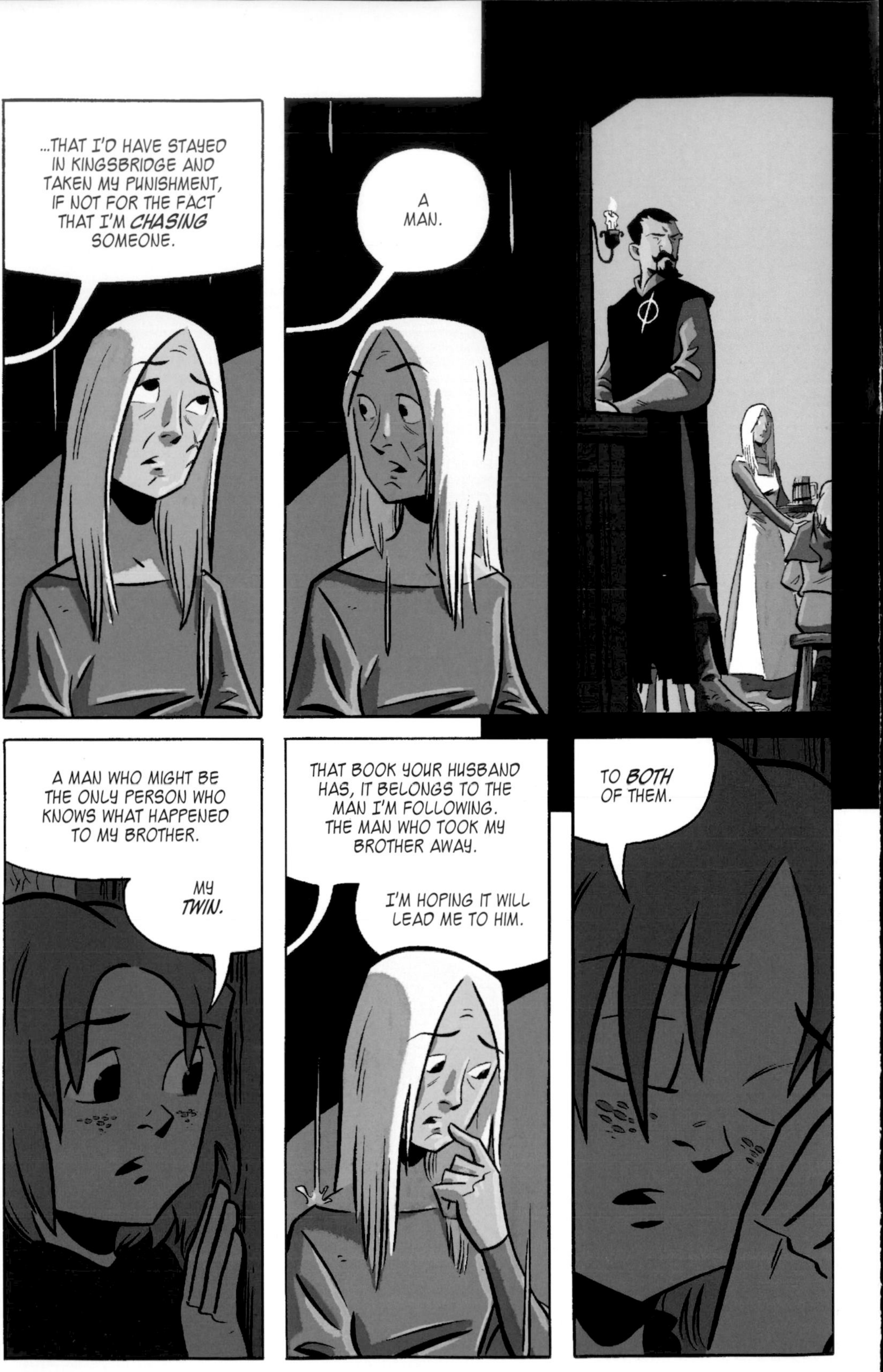
...THAT I'D HAVE STAYED IN KINGSBRIDGE AND TAKEN MY PUNISHMENT, IF NOT FOR THE FACT THAT I'M CHASING SOMEONE.
A MAN.
A MAN WHO MIGHT BE THE ONLY PERSON WHO KNOWS WHAT HAPPENED TO MY BROTHER.
MY TWIN.
THAT BOOK YOUR HUSBAND HAS, IT BELONGS TO THE MAN I'M FOLLOWING. THE MAN WHO TOOK MY BROTHER AWAY.
I'M HOPING IT WILL LEAD ME TO HIM.
TO BOTH OF THEM.

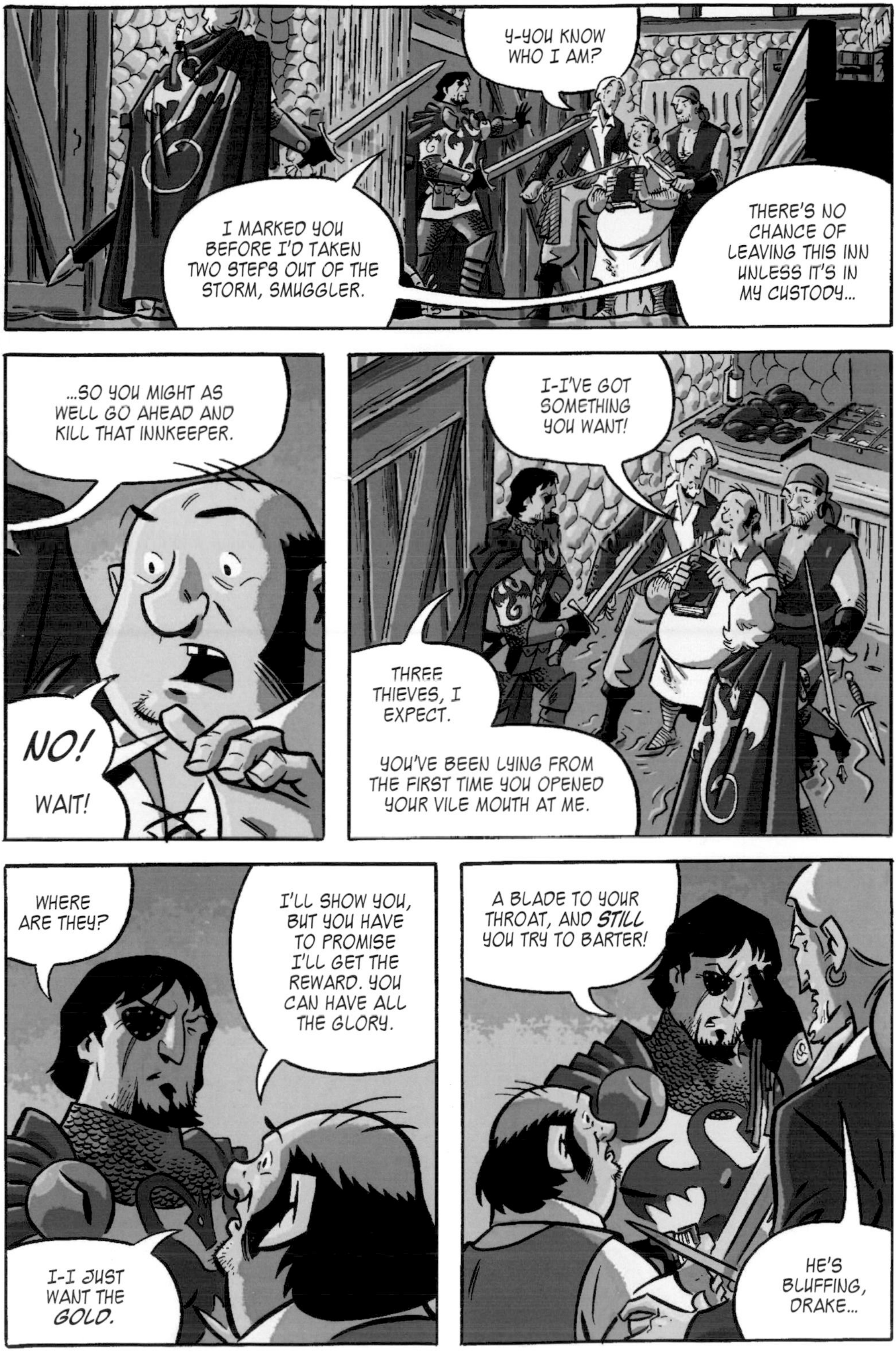
Y-YOU KNOW WHO I AM?
I MARKED YOU BEFORE I'D TAKEN TWO STEPS OUT OF THE STORM, SMUGGLER.
THERE'S NO CHANCE OF LEAVING THIS INN UNLESS IT'S IN MY CUSTODY...
...SO YOU MIGHT AS WELL GO AHEAD AND KILL THAT INNKEEPER.
NO!
WAIT!
I-I'VE GOT SOMETHING YOU WANT!
THREE THIEVES, I EXPECT.
YOU'VE BEEN LYING FROM THE FIRST TIME YOU OPENED YOUR VILE MOUTH AT ME.
WHERE ARE THEY?
I'LL SHOW YOU, BUT YOU HAVE TO PROMISE I'LL GET THE REWARD. YOU CAN HAVE ALL THE GLORY.
I-I JUST WANT THE GOLD.
A BLADE TO YOUR THROAT, AND STILL YOU TRY TO BARTER!
HE'S BLUFFING, DRAKE...

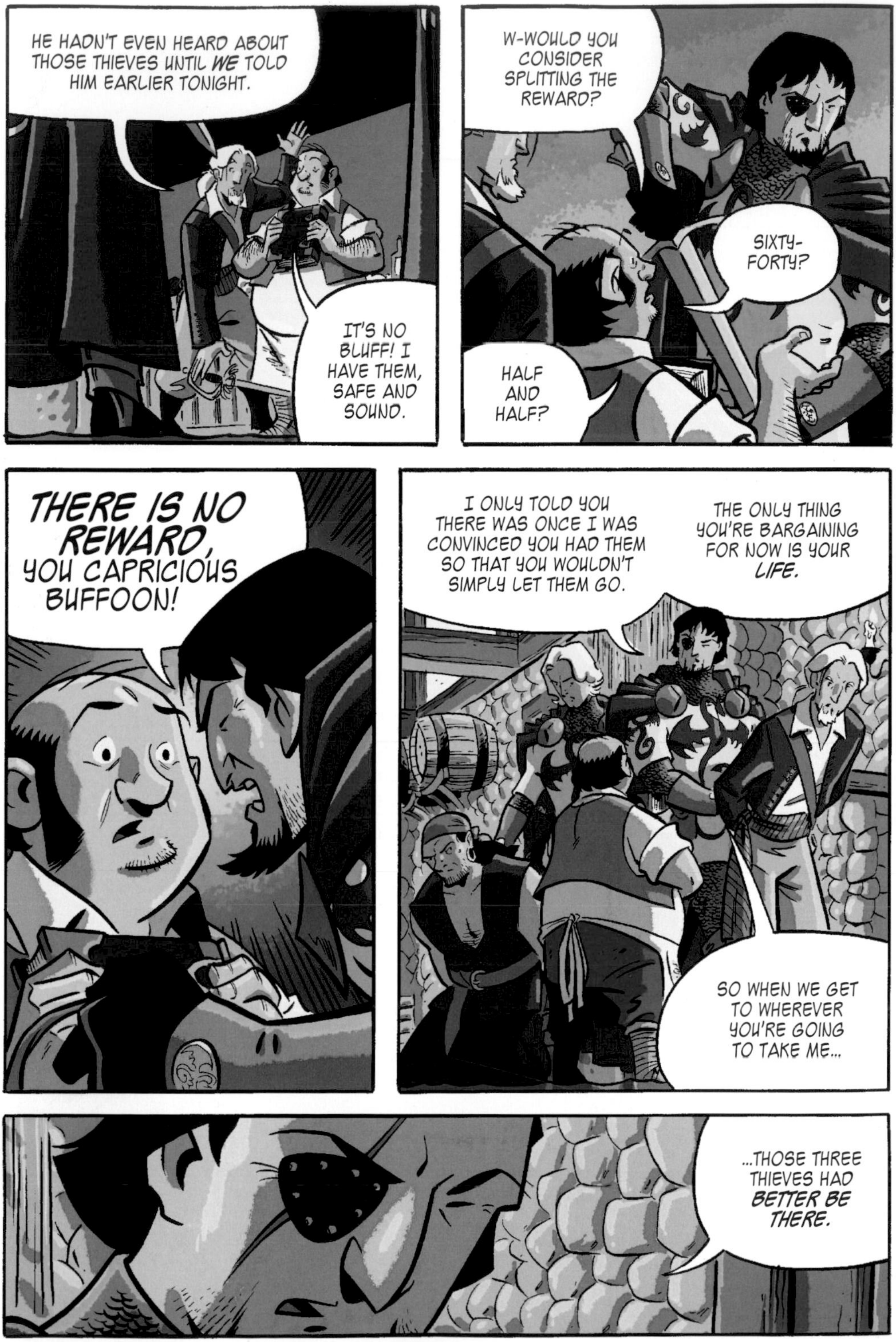

HE HADN'T EVEN HEARD ABOUT THOSE THIEVES UNTIL WE TOLD HIM EARLIER TONIGHT.
IT'S NO BLUFF! I HAVE THEM, SAFE AND SOUND.
W-WOULD YOU CONSIDER SPLITTING THE REWARD?
HALF AND HALF?
SIXTY-FORTY?
THERE IS NO REWARD, YOU CAPRICIOUS BUFFOON!
I ONLY TOLD YOU THERE WAS ONCE I WAS CONVINCED YOU HAD THEM SO THAT YOU WOULDN'T SIMPLY LET THEM GO.
THE ONLY THING YOU'RE BARGAINING FOR NOW IS YOUR LIFE.
SO WHEN WE GET TO WHEREVER YOU'RE GOING TO TAKE ME...
...THOSE THREE THIEVES HAD BETTER BE THERE.

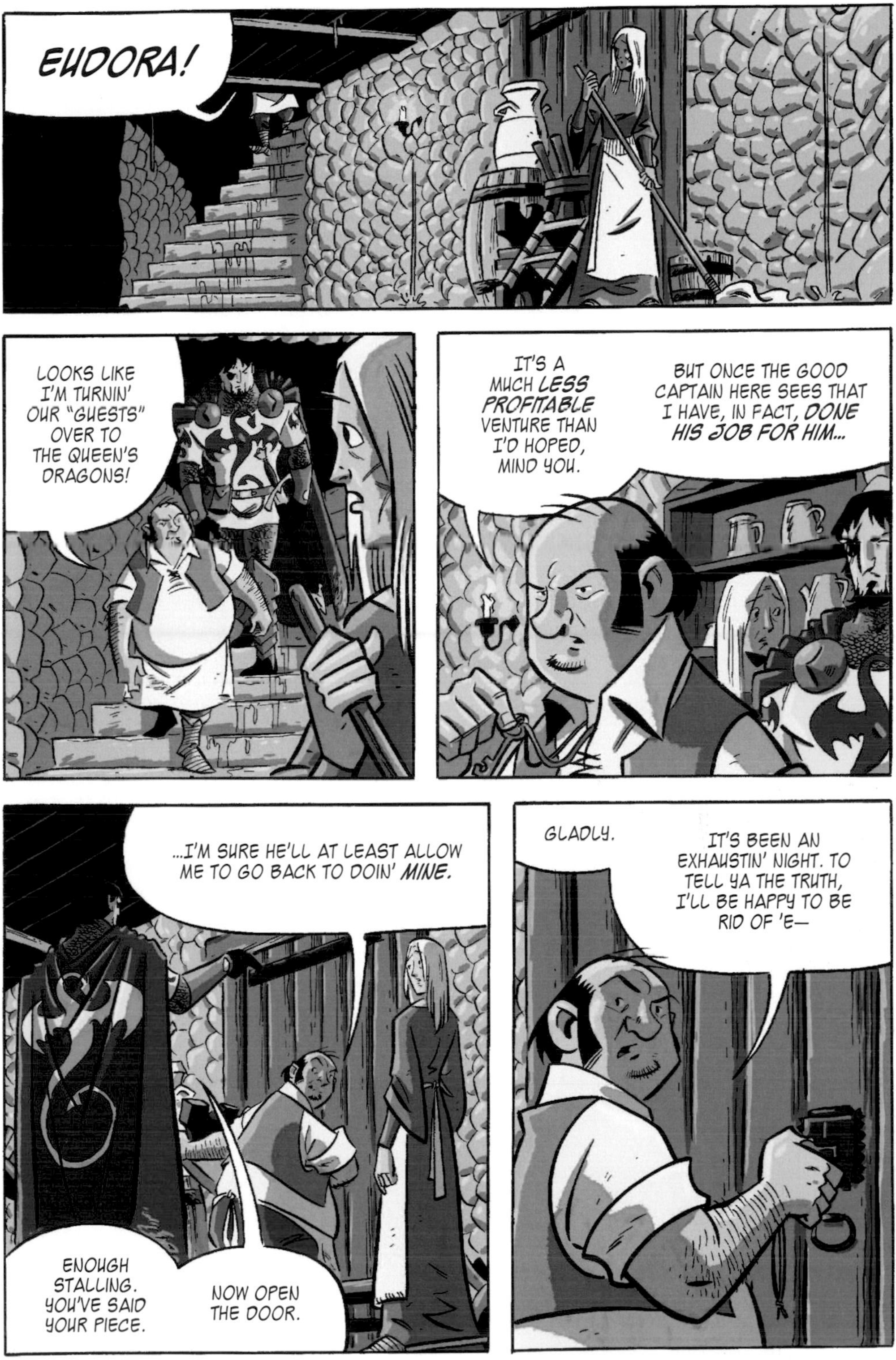
EUDORA!
LOOKS LIKE I'M TURNIN' OUR "GUESTS" OVER TO THE QUEEN'S DRAGONS!
IT'S A MUCH LESS PROFITABLE VENTURE THAN I'D HOPED, MIND YOU.
BUT ONCE THE GOOD CAPTAIN HERE SEES THAT I HAVE, IN FACT, DONE HIS JOB FOR HIM...
...I'M SURE HE'LL AT LEAST ALLOW ME TO GO BACK TO DOIN' MINE.
ENOUGH STALLING. YOU'VE SAID YOUR PIECE.
NOW OPEN THE DOOR.
GLADLY.
IT'S BEEN AN EXHAUSTIN' NIGHT. TO TELL YA THE TRUTH, I'LL BE HAPPY TO BE RID OF 'E—

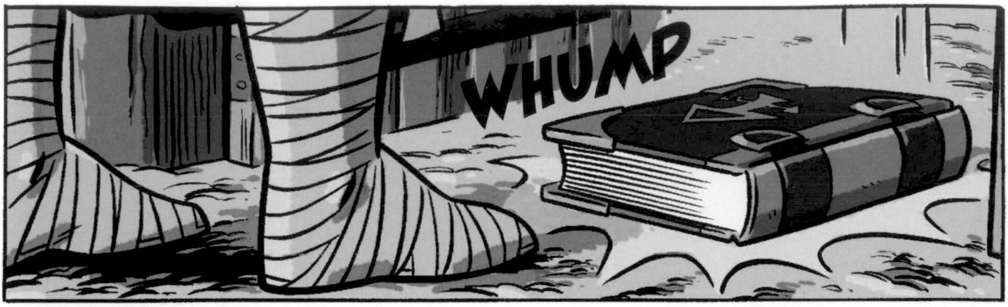
WHUMP

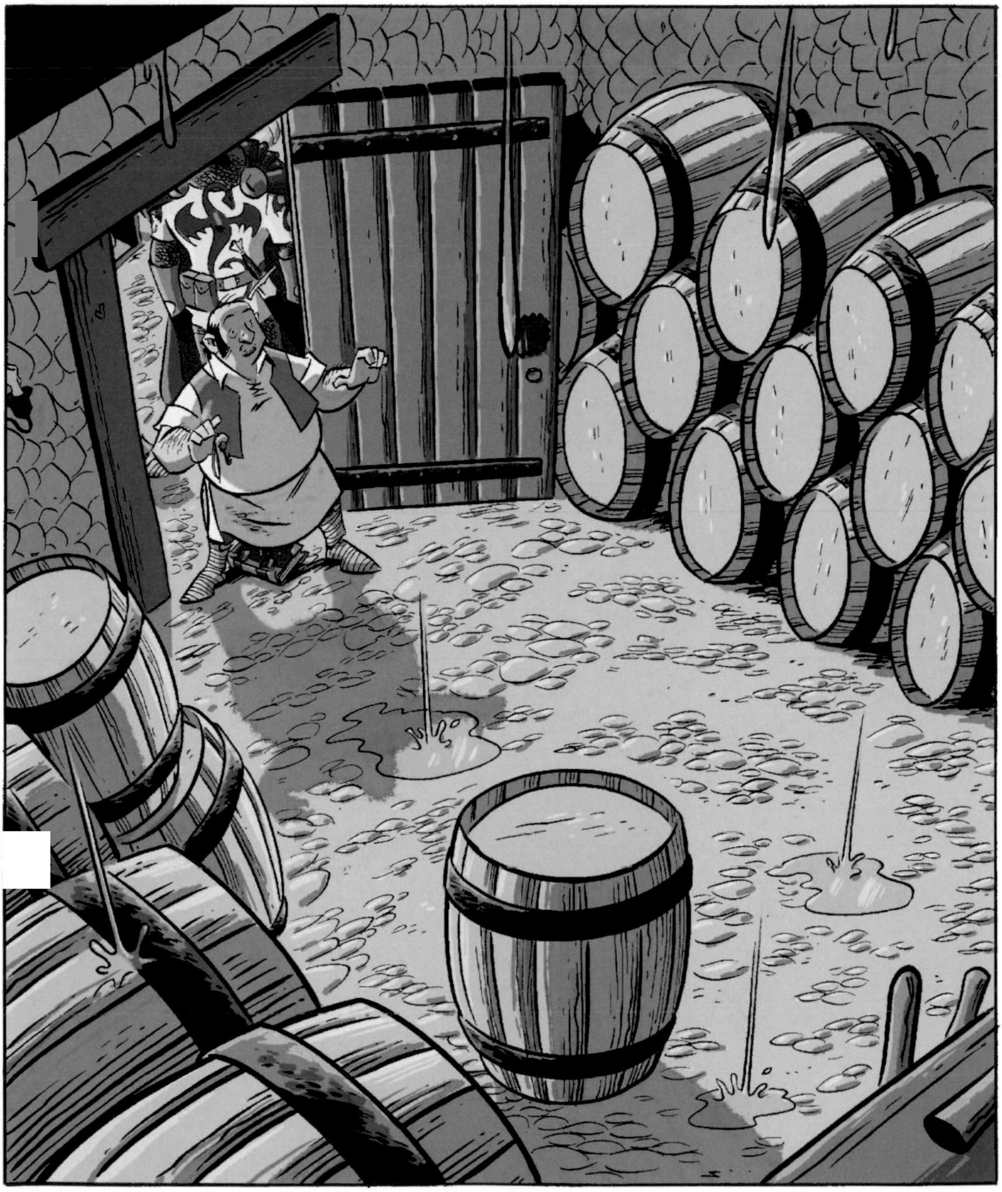

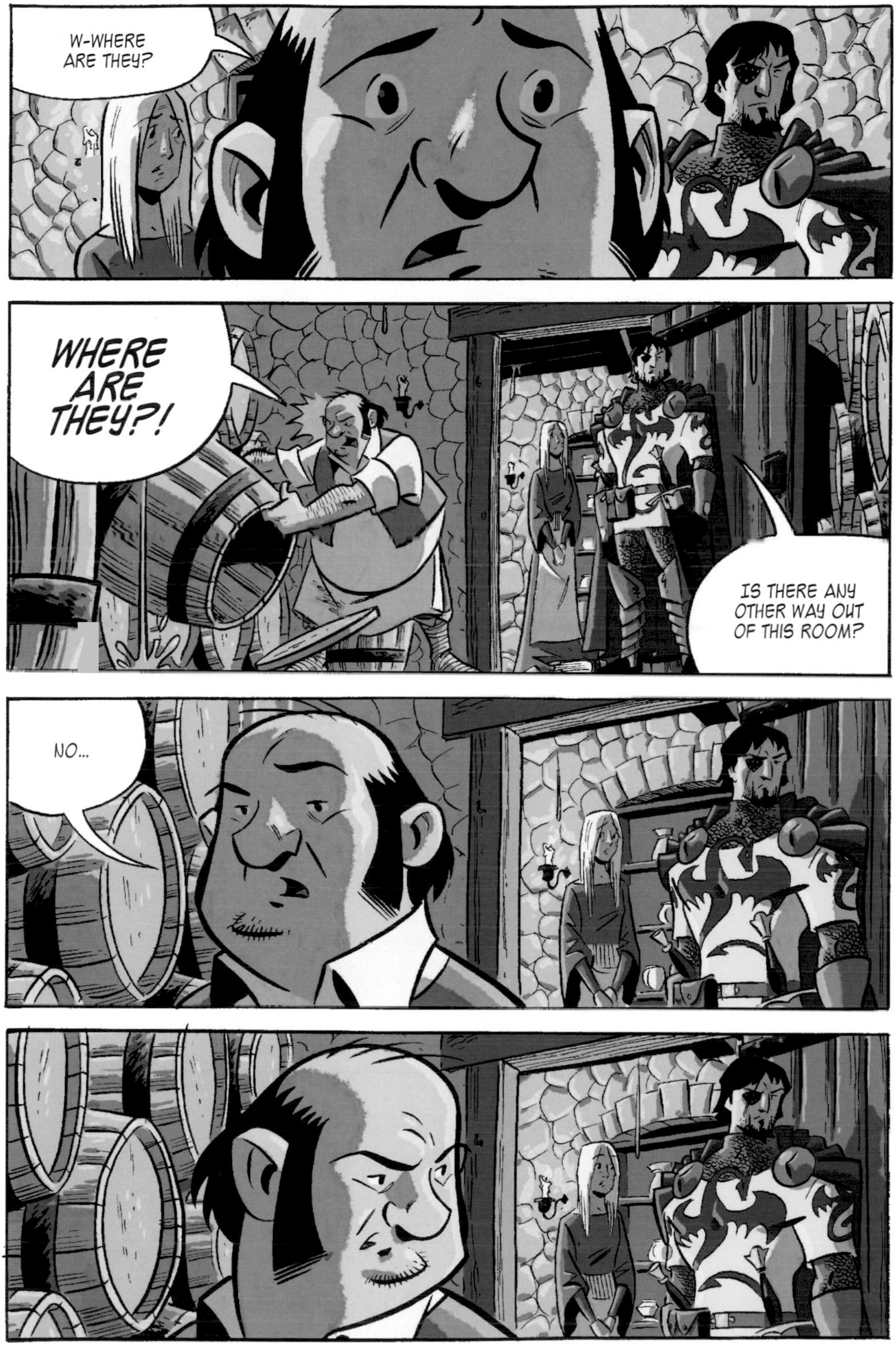
W-WHERE ARE THEY?
WHERE ARE THEY?!
IS THERE ANY OTHER WAY OUT OF THIS ROOM?
NO...

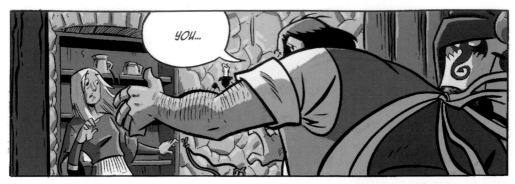

YOU...

...YOU *LET* THEM ESCAPE, DIDN'T YOU?

DIDN'T YOU?!

TELL ME, BEFORE I MAKE THE GOOD SIDE OF YER FACE MATCH THE BAD SIDE!

WHY DIDN'T YOU RING THAT BELL?!

ENOUGH.

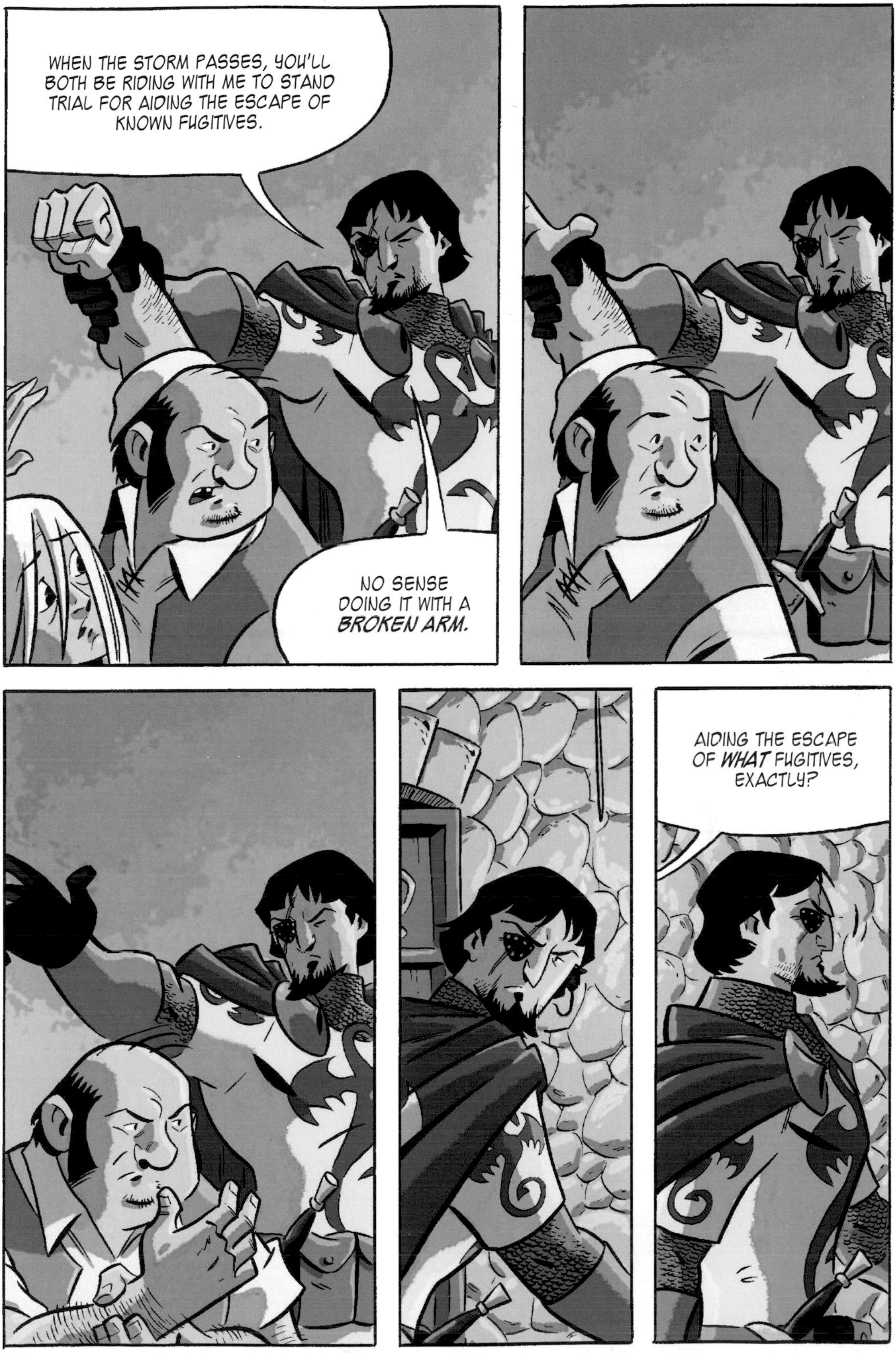
WHEN THE STORM PASSES, YOU'LL BOTH BE RIDING WITH ME TO STAND TRIAL FOR AIDING THE ESCAPE OF KNOWN FUGITIVES.
NO SENSE DOING IT WITH A *BROKEN ARM.*
AIDING THE ESCAPE OF *WHAT* FUGITIVES, EXACTLY?

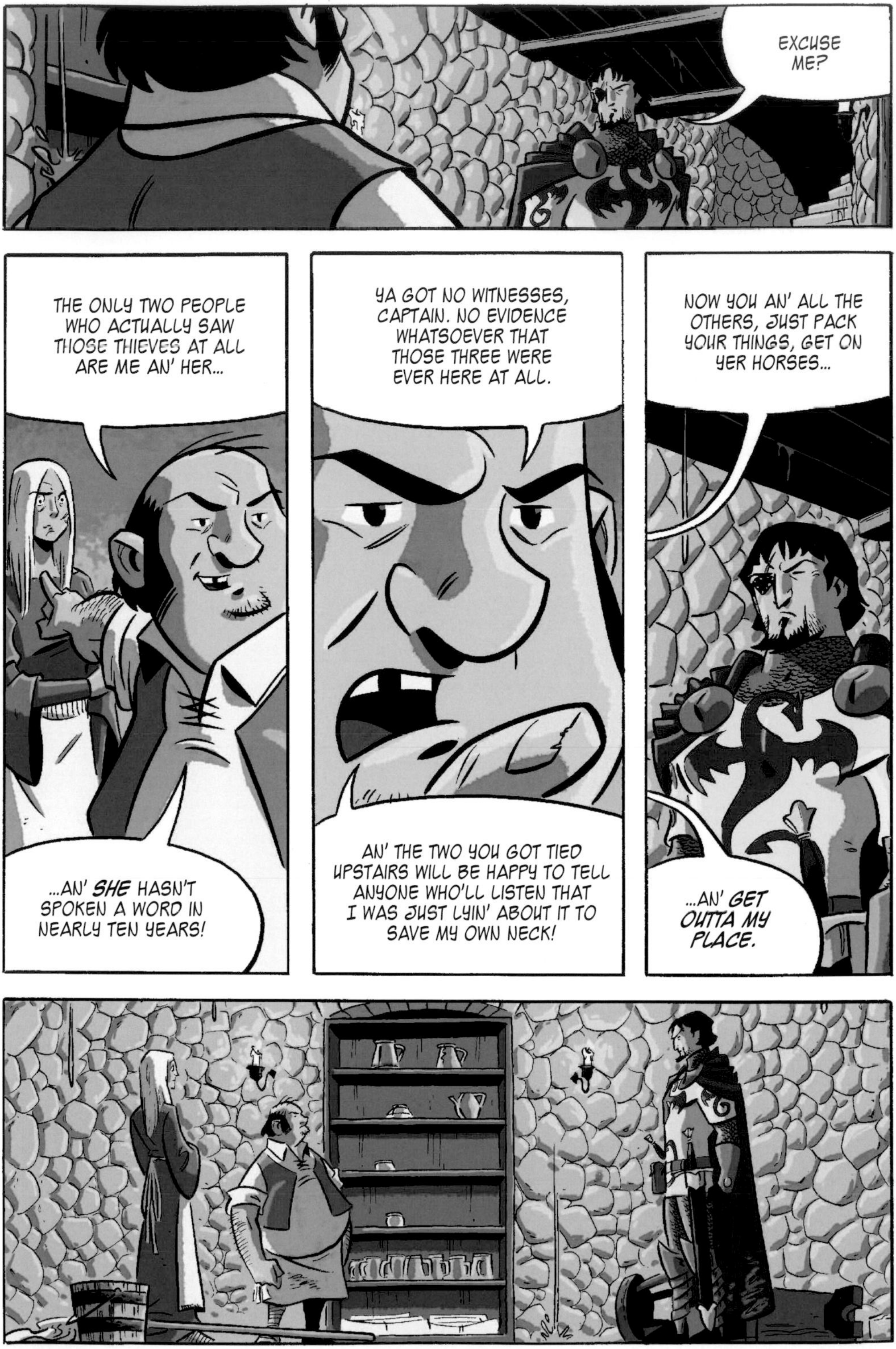
EXCUSE ME?
THE ONLY TWO PEOPLE WHO ACTUALLY SAW THOSE THIEVES AT ALL ARE ME AN' HER...
...AN' SHE HASN'T SPOKEN A WORD IN NEARLY TEN YEARS!
YA GOT NO WITNESSES, CAPTAIN. NO EVIDENCE WHATSOEVER THAT THOSE THREE WERE EVER HERE AT ALL.
AN' THE TWO YOU GOT TIED UPSTAIRS WILL BE HAPPY TO TELL ANYONE WHO'LL LISTEN THAT I WAS JUST LYIN' ABOUT IT TO SAVE MY OWN NECK!
NOW YOU AN' ALL THE OTHERS, JUST PACK YOUR THINGS, GET ON YER HORSES...
...AN' GET OUTTA MY PLACE.

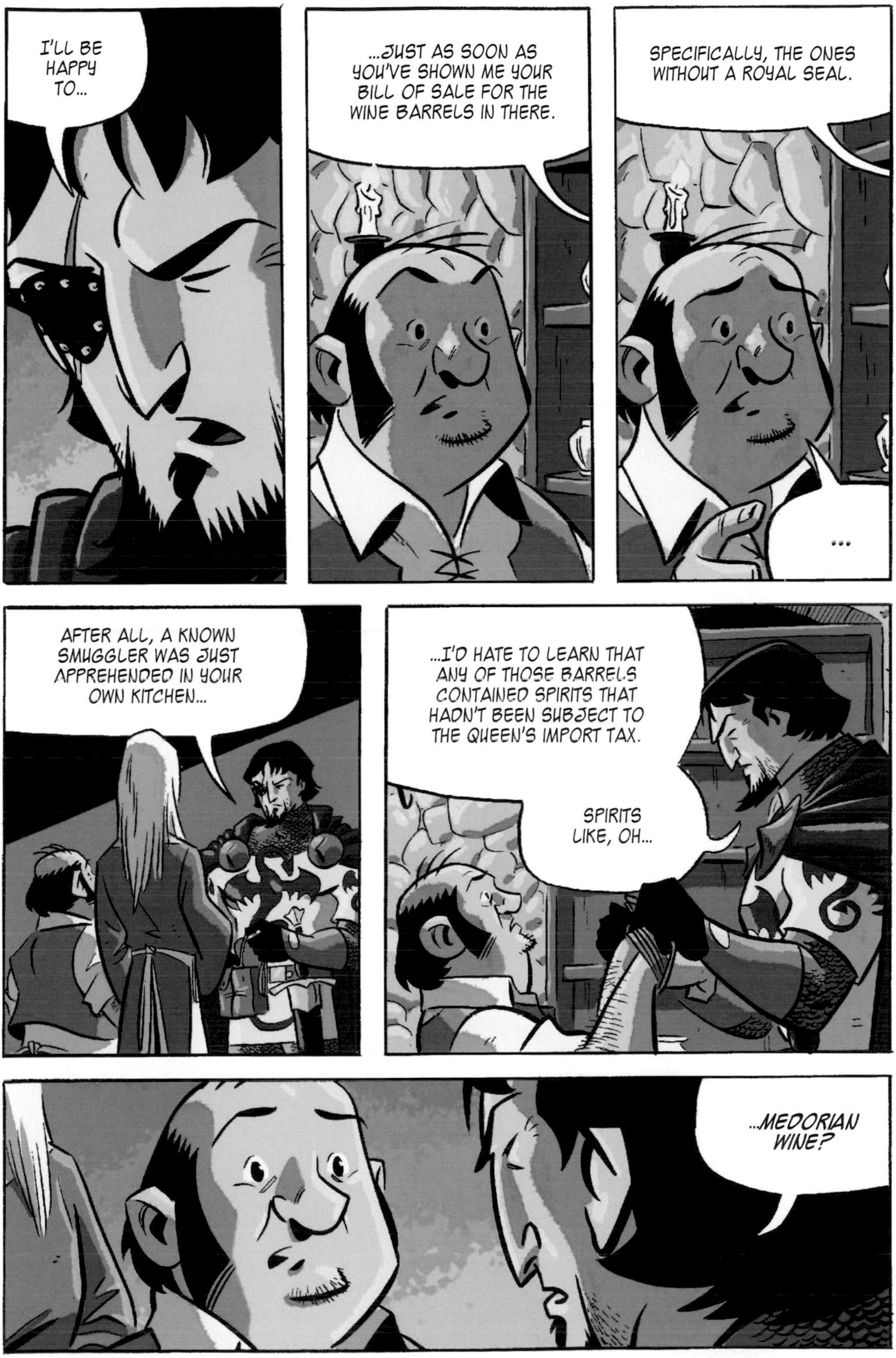
I'LL BE HAPPY TO...
...JUST AS SOON AS YOU'VE SHOWN ME YOUR BILL OF SALE FOR THE WINE BARRELS IN THERE.
SPECIFICALLY, THE ONES WITHOUT A ROYAL SEAL.
...
AFTER ALL, A KNOWN SMUGGLER WAS JUST APPREHENDED IN YOUR OWN KITCHEN...
...I'D HATE TO LEARN THAT ANY OF THOSE BARRELS CONTAINED SPIRITS THAT HADN'T BEEN SUBJECT TO THE QUEEN'S IMPORT TAX.
SPIRITS LIKE, OH...
...MEDORIAN WINE?

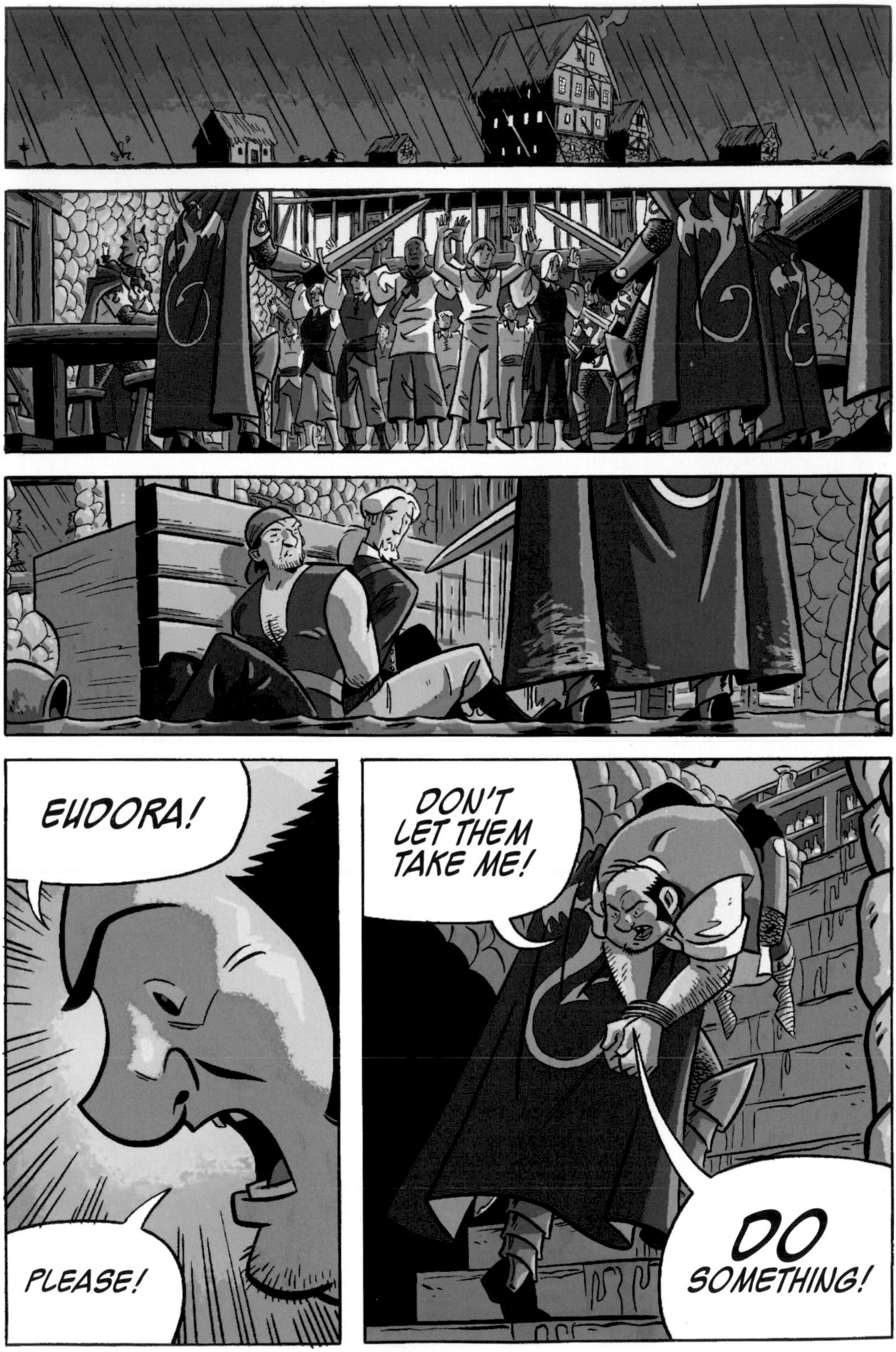
EUDORA!
PLEASE!
DON'T LET THEM TAKE ME!
DO SOMETHING!

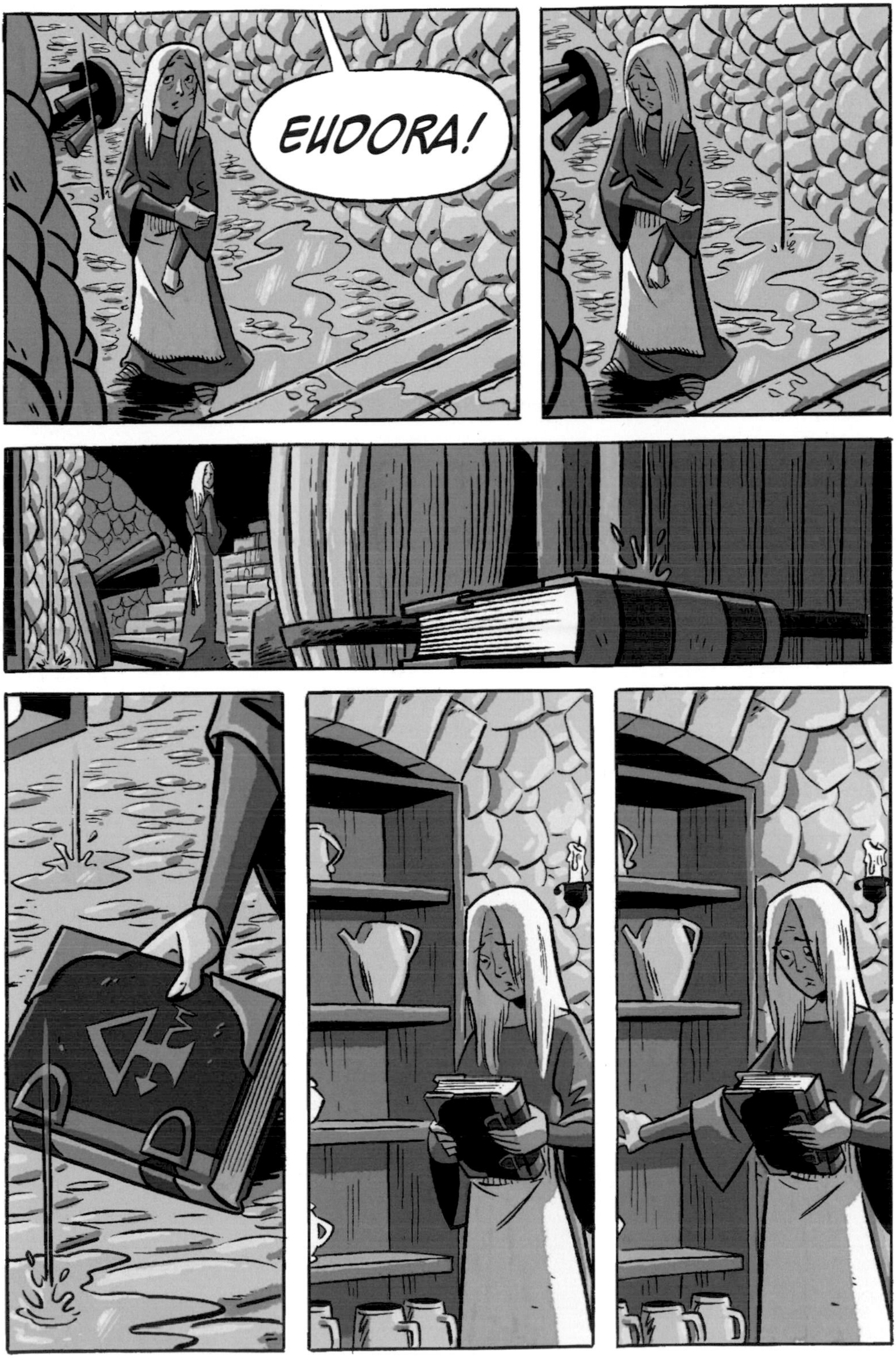
EUDORA!

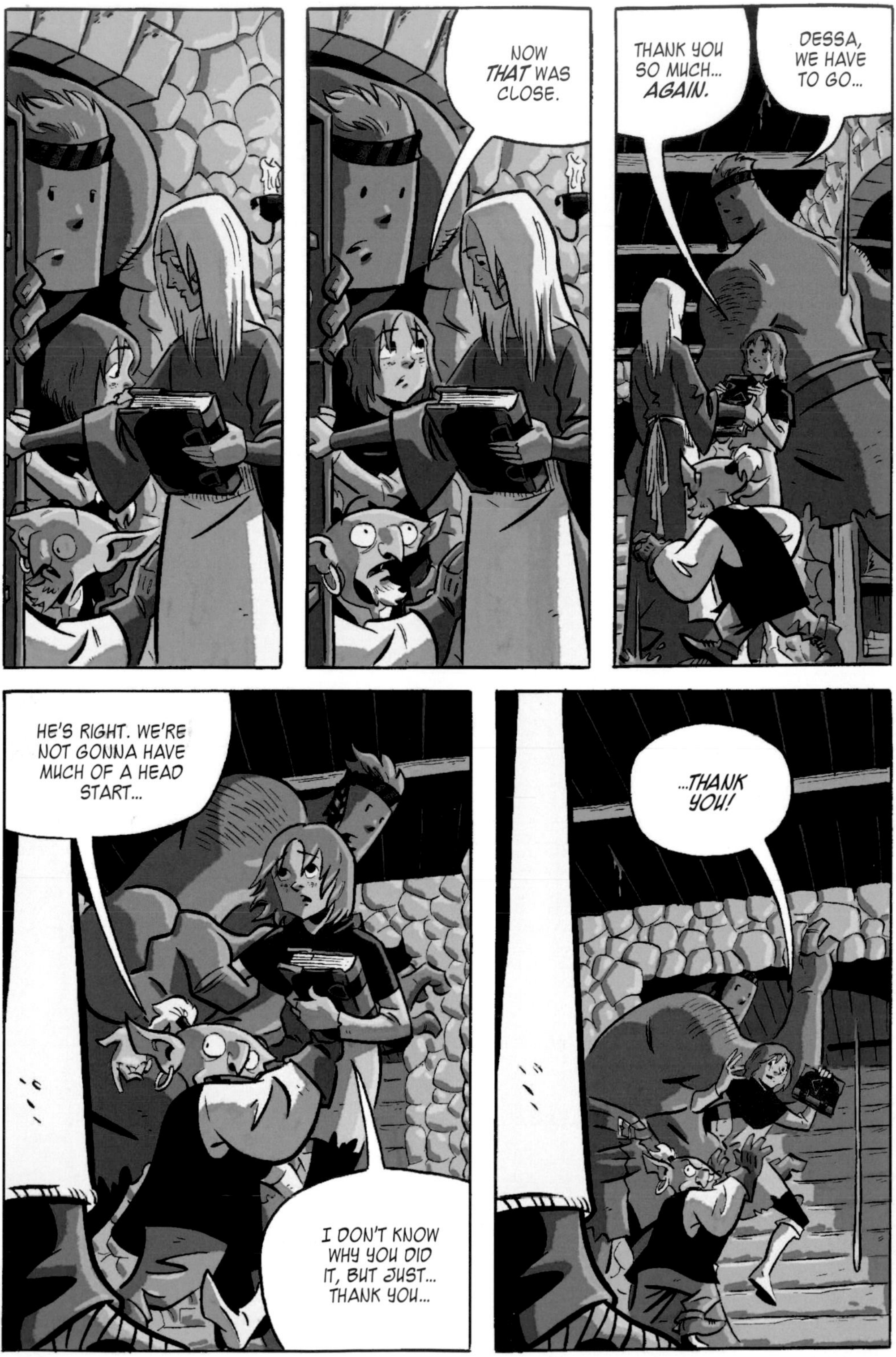
NOW THAT WAS CLOSE.
THANK YOU SO MUCH... AGAIN.
DESSA, WE HAVE TO GO...
HE'S RIGHT. WE'RE NOT GONNA HAVE MUCH OF A HEAD START...
I DON'T KNOW WHY YOU DID IT, BUT JUST... THANK YOU...
...THANK YOU!

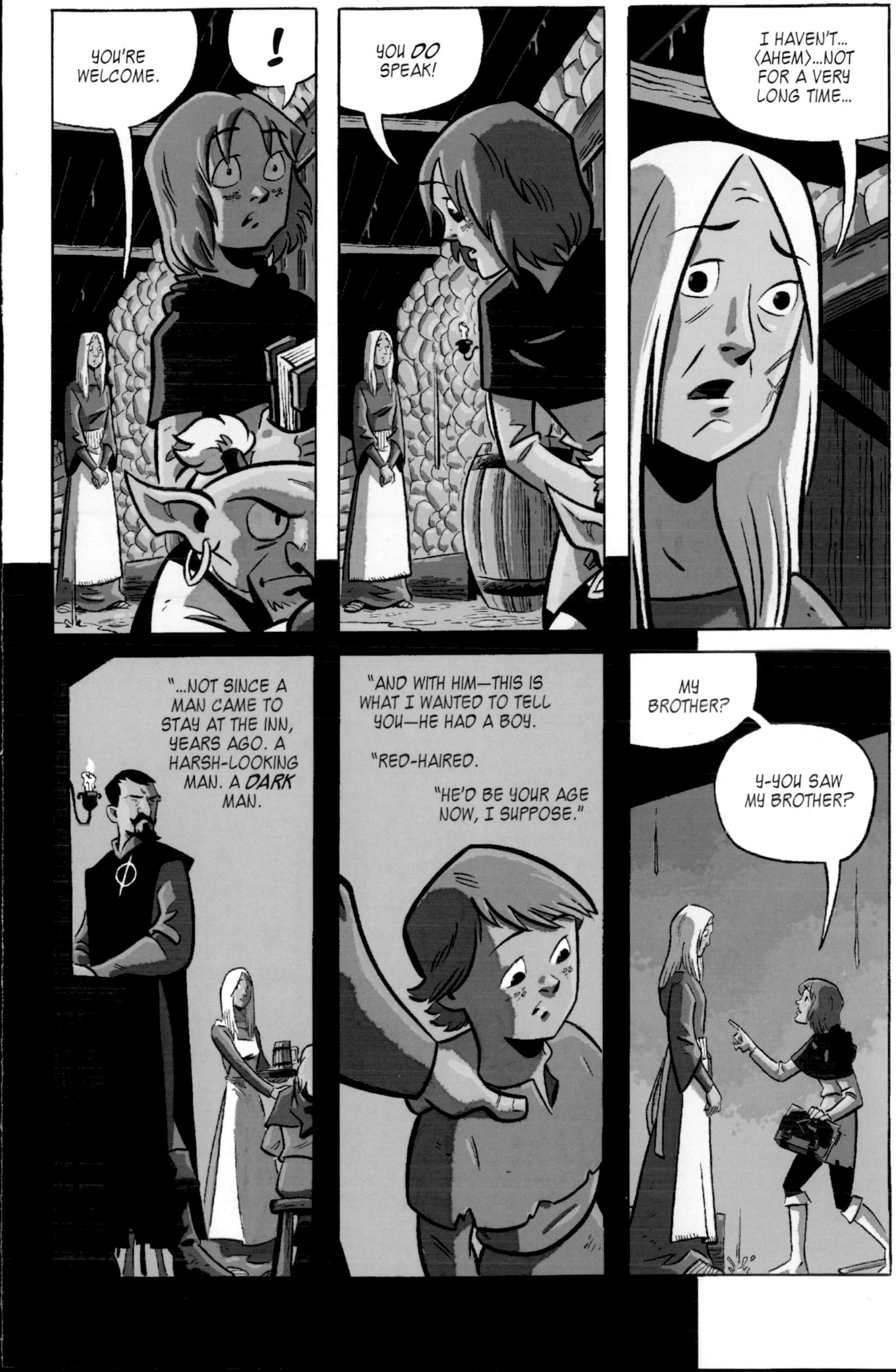
YOU'RE WELCOME.
!
YOU DO SPEAK!
I HAVEN'T... (AHEM)...NOT FOR A VERY LONG TIME...
"...NOT SINCE A MAN CAME TO STAY AT THE INN, YEARS AGO. A HARSH-LOOKING MAN. A DARK MAN.
"AND WITH HIM—THIS IS WHAT I WANTED TO TELL YOU—HE HAD A BOY.
"RED-HAIRED.
"HE'D BE YOUR AGE NOW, I SUPPOSE."
MY BROTHER?
Y-YOU SAW MY BROTHER?

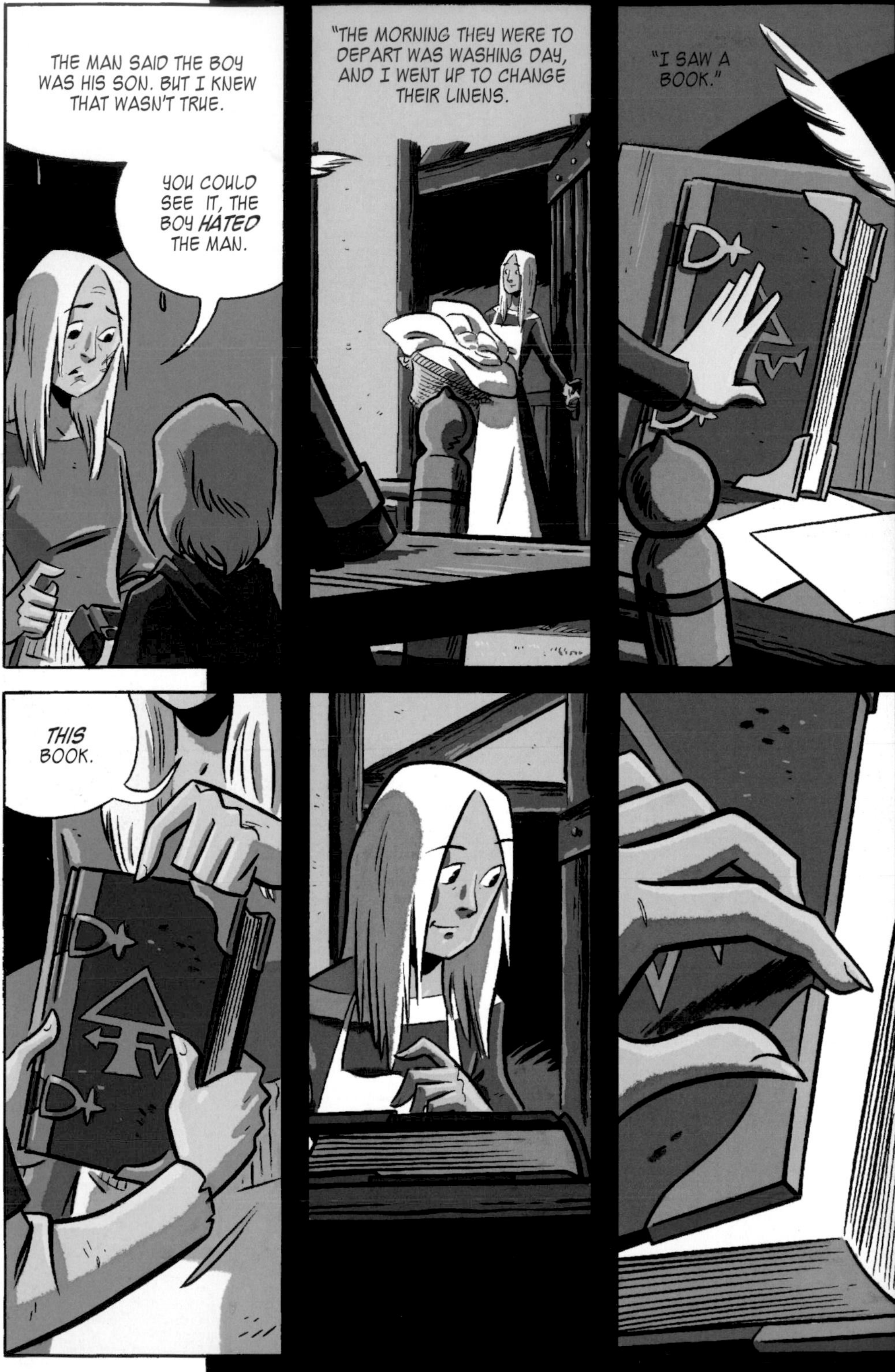
THE MAN SAID THE BOY WAS HIS SON. BUT I KNEW THAT WASN'T TRUE.
YOU COULD SEE IT, THE BOY *HATED* THE MAN.
"THE MORNING THEY WERE TO DEPART WAS WASHING DAY, AND I WENT UP TO CHANGE THEIR LINENS.
"I SAW A BOOK."
THIS BOOK.

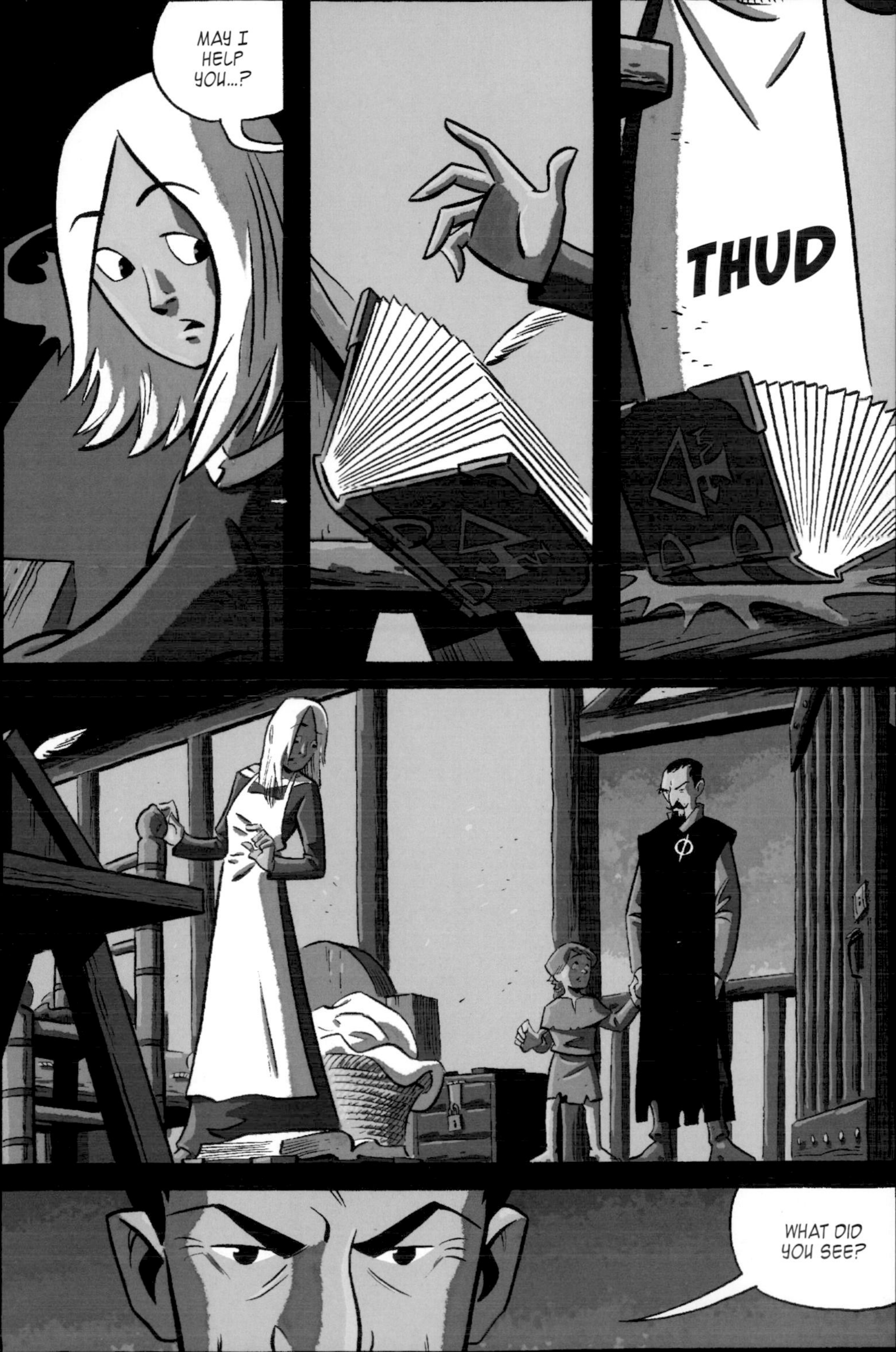

MAY I HELP YOU...?
THUD
WHAT DID YOU SEE?

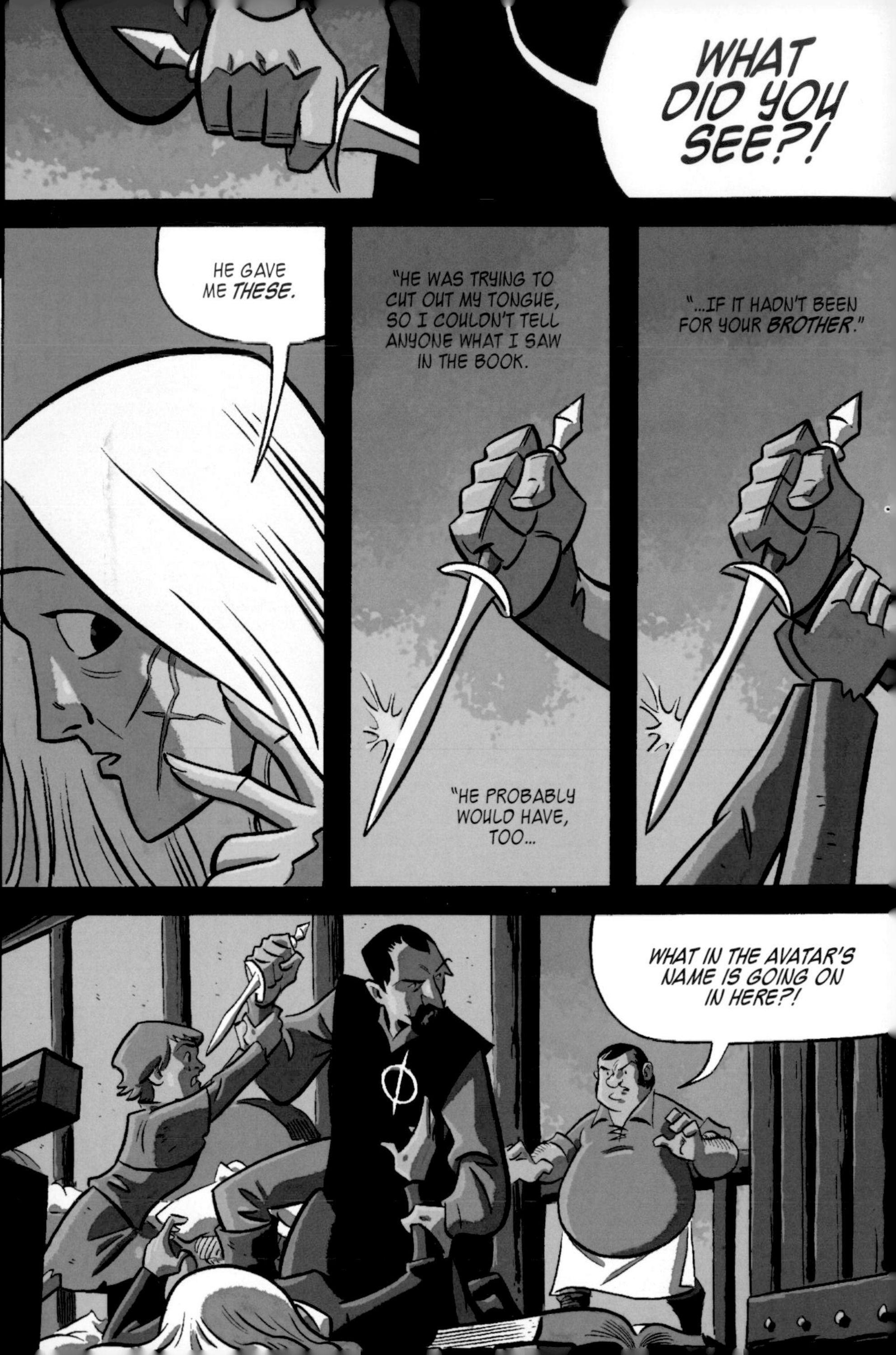
WHAT DID YOU SEE?!
HE GAVE ME THESE.
"HE WAS TRYING TO CUT OUT MY TONGUE, SO I COULDN'T TELL ANYONE WHAT I SAW IN THE BOOK.
"HE PROBABLY WOULD HAVE, TOO...
"...IF IT HADN'T BEEN FOR YOUR BROTHER."
WHAT IN THE AVATAR'S NAME IS GOING ON IN HERE?!

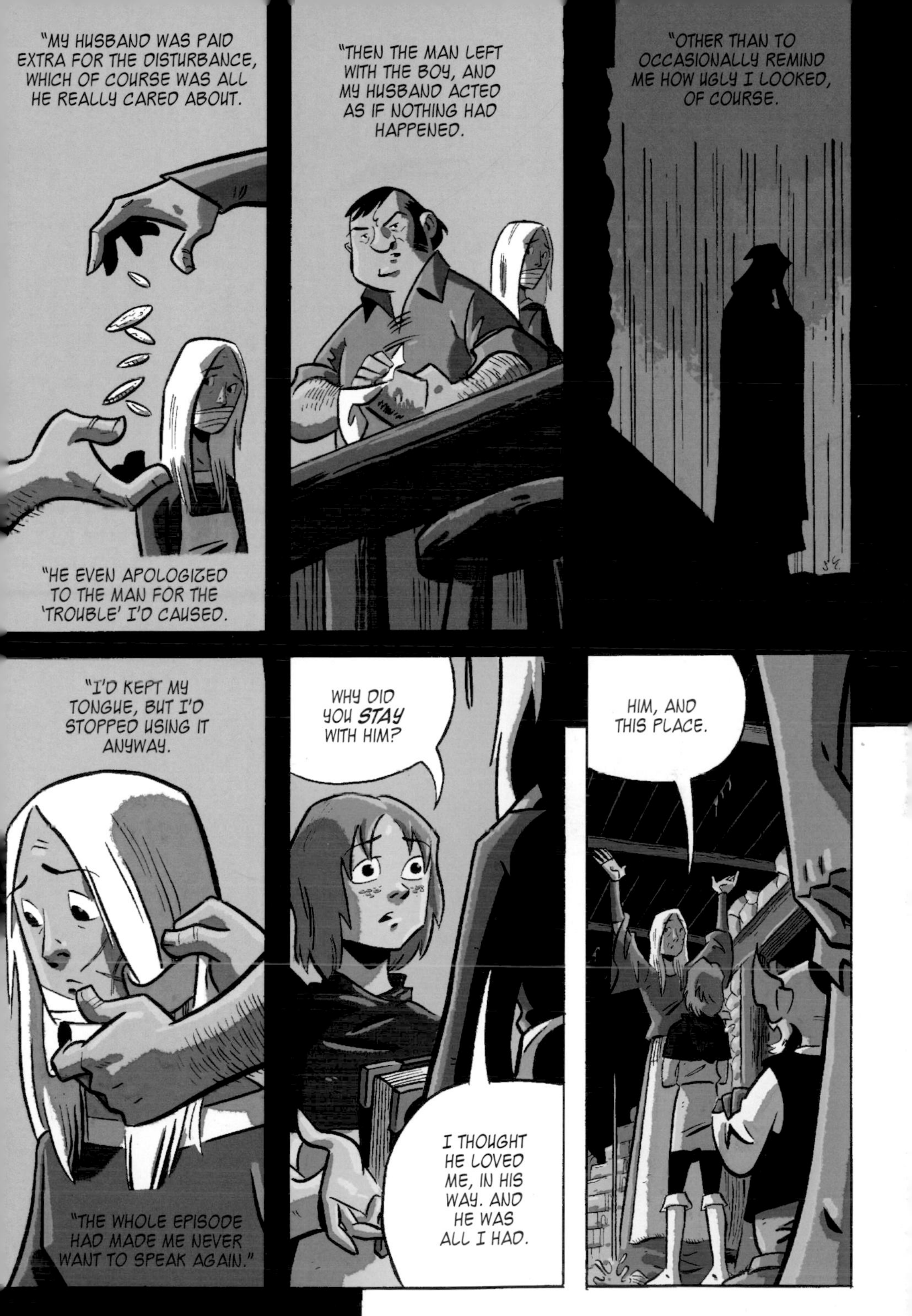
"MY HUSBAND WAS PAID EXTRA FOR THE DISTURBANCE, WHICH OF COURSE WAS ALL HE REALLY CARED ABOUT.
"HE EVEN APOLOGIZED TO THE MAN FOR THE 'TROUBLE' I'D CAUSED.
"THEN THE MAN LEFT WITH THE BOY, AND MY HUSBAND ACTED AS IF NOTHING HAD HAPPENED.
"OTHER THAN TO OCCASIONALLY REMIND ME HOW UGLY I LOOKED, OF COURSE.
"I'D KEPT MY TONGUE, BUT I'D STOPPED USING IT ANYWAY.
"THE WHOLE EPISODE HAD MADE ME NEVER WANT TO SPEAK AGAIN."
WHY DID YOU **STAY** WITH HIM?
I THOUGHT HE LOVED ME, IN HIS WAY. AND HE WAS ALL I HAD.
HIM, AND THIS PLACE.

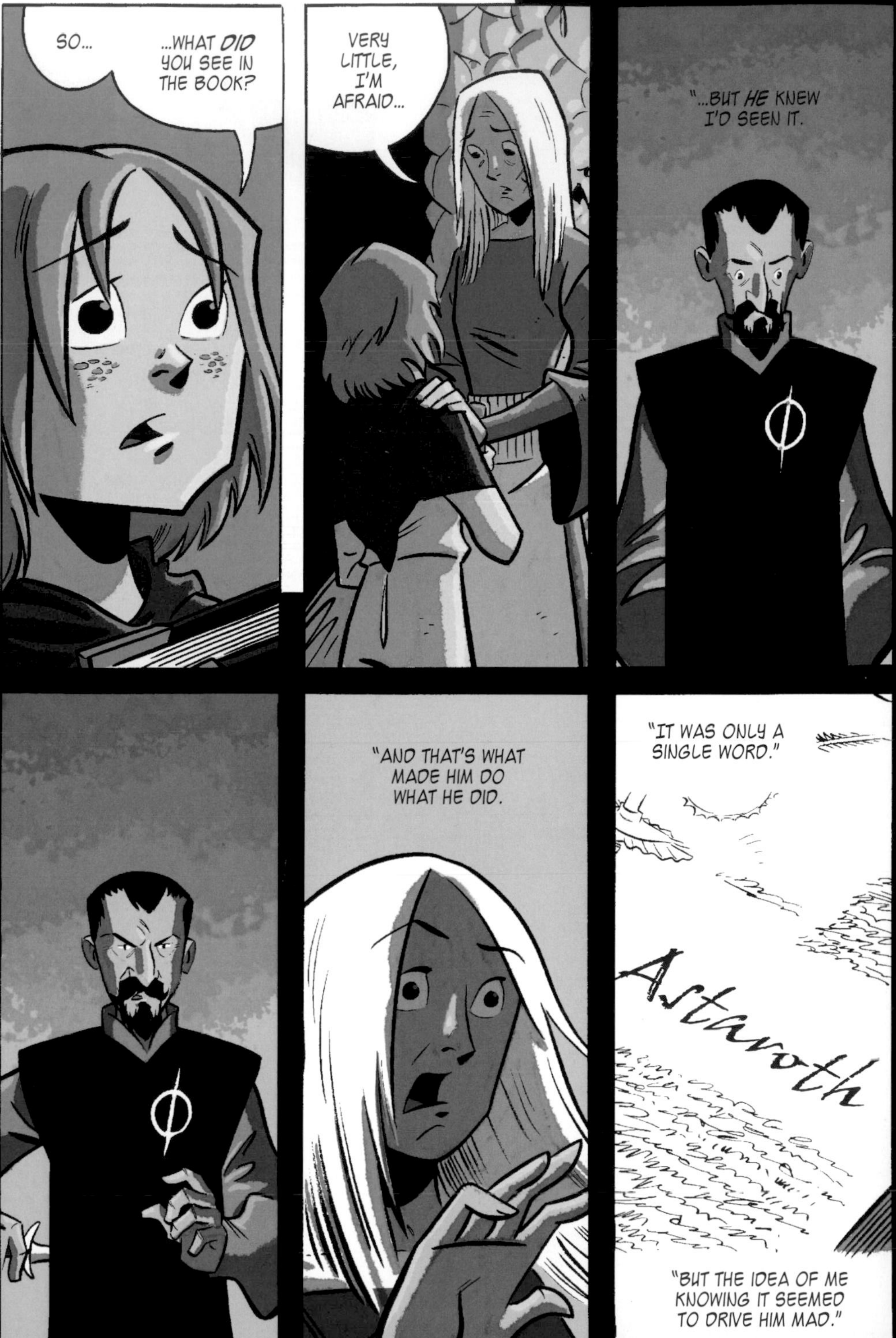
SO...
...WHAT *DID* YOU SEE IN THE BOOK?
VERY LITTLE, I'M AFRAID...
"...BUT *HE* KNEW I'D SEEN IT.
"AND THAT'S WHAT MADE HIM DO WHAT HE DID.
"IT WAS ONLY A SINGLE WORD."
Astaroth
"BUT THE IDEA OF ME KNOWING IT SEEMED TO DRIVE HIM MAD."

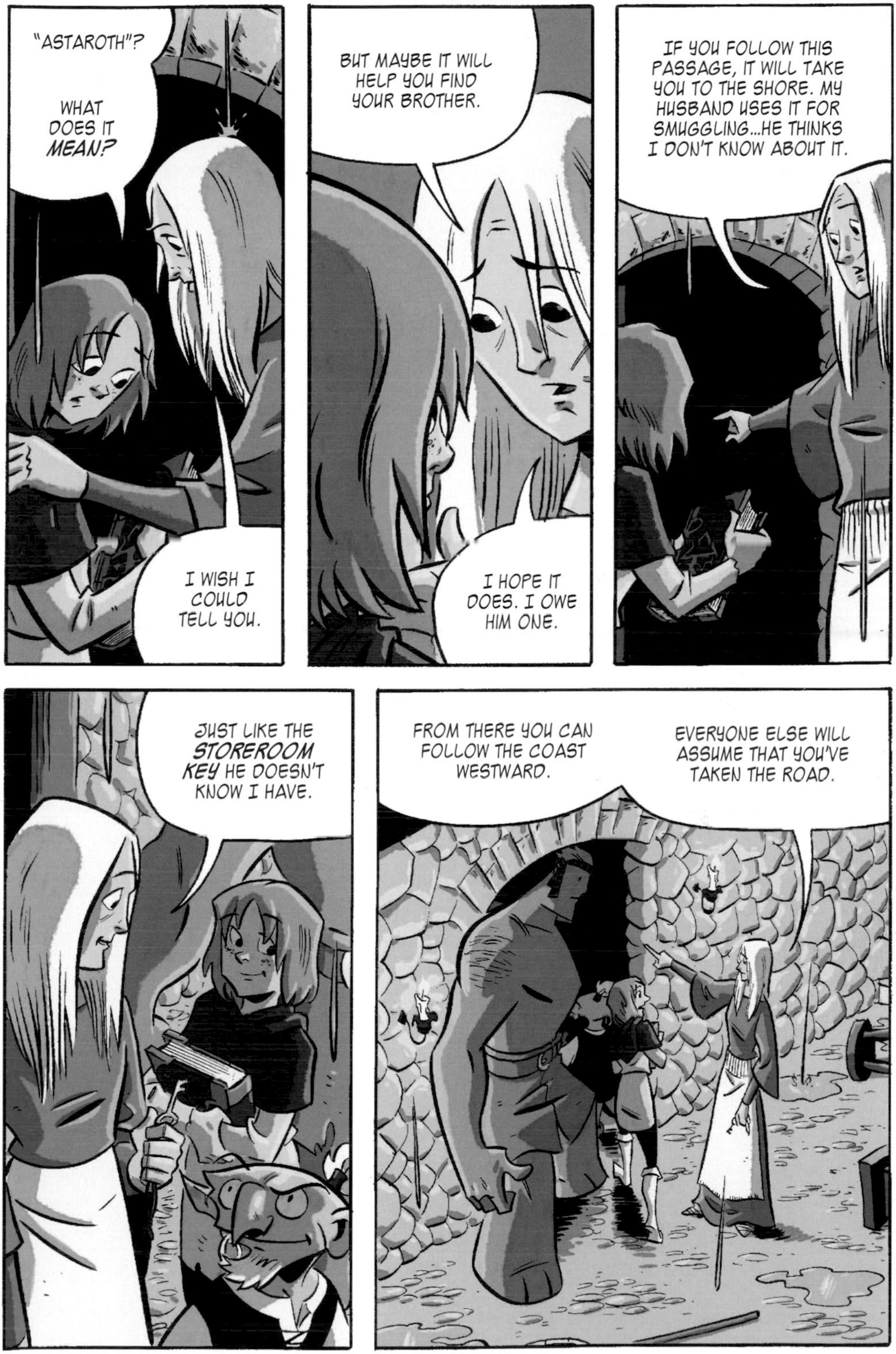
"ASTAROTH"?
WHAT DOES IT *MEAN?*
I WISH I COULD TELL YOU.
BUT MAYBE IT WILL HELP YOU FIND YOUR BROTHER.
I HOPE IT DOES. I OWE HIM ONE.
IF YOU FOLLOW THIS PASSAGE, IT WILL TAKE YOU TO THE SHORE. MY HUSBAND USES IT FOR SMUGGLING...HE THINKS I DON'T KNOW ABOUT IT.
JUST LIKE THE *STOREROOM KEY* HE DOESN'T KNOW I HAVE.
FROM THERE YOU CAN FOLLOW THE COAST WESTWARD.
EVERYONE ELSE WILL ASSUME THAT YOU'VE TAKEN THE ROAD.

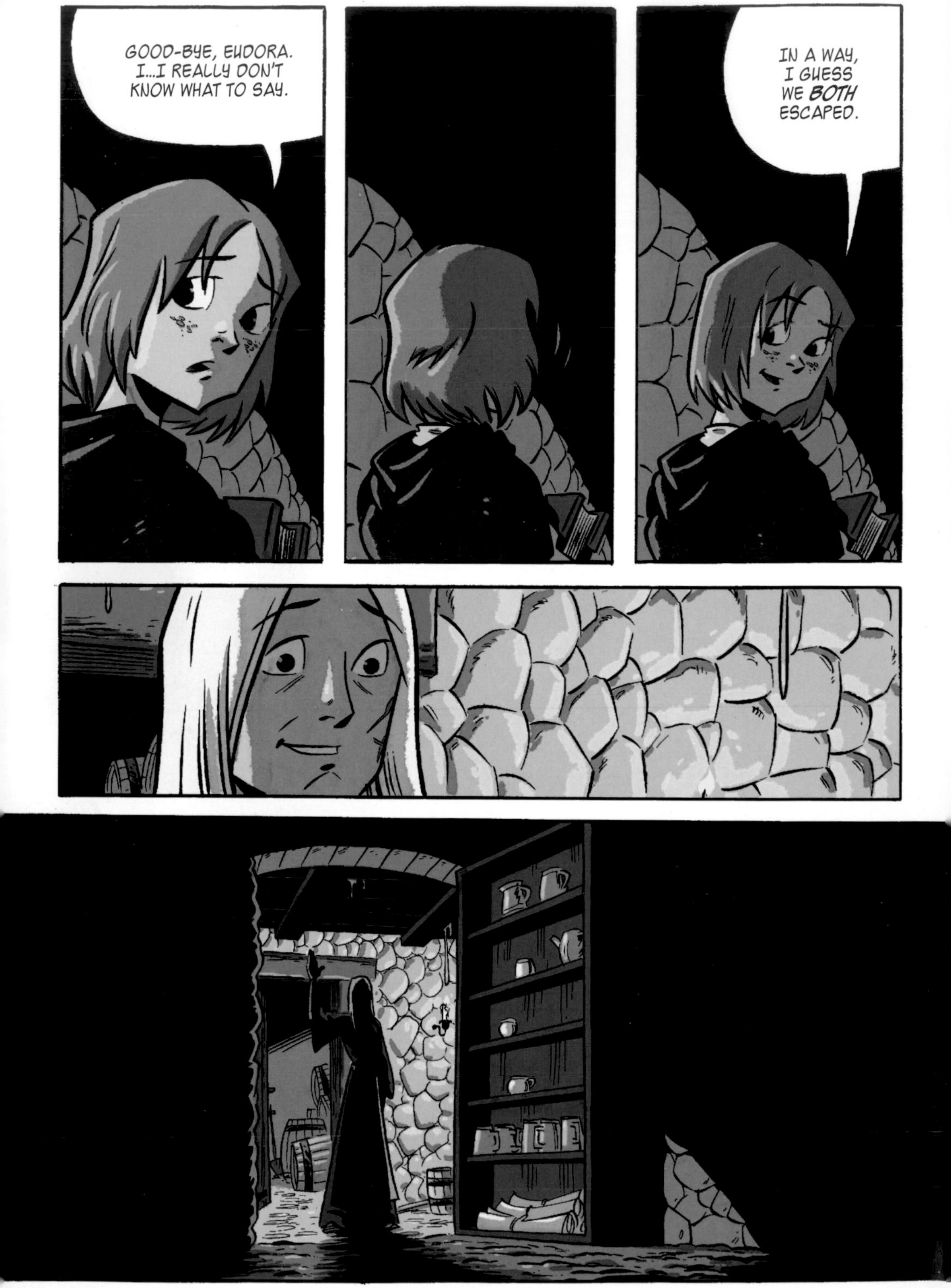
GOOD-BYE, EUDORA. I...I REALLY DON'T KNOW WHAT TO SAY.
IN A WAY, I GUESS WE *BOTH* ESCAPED.

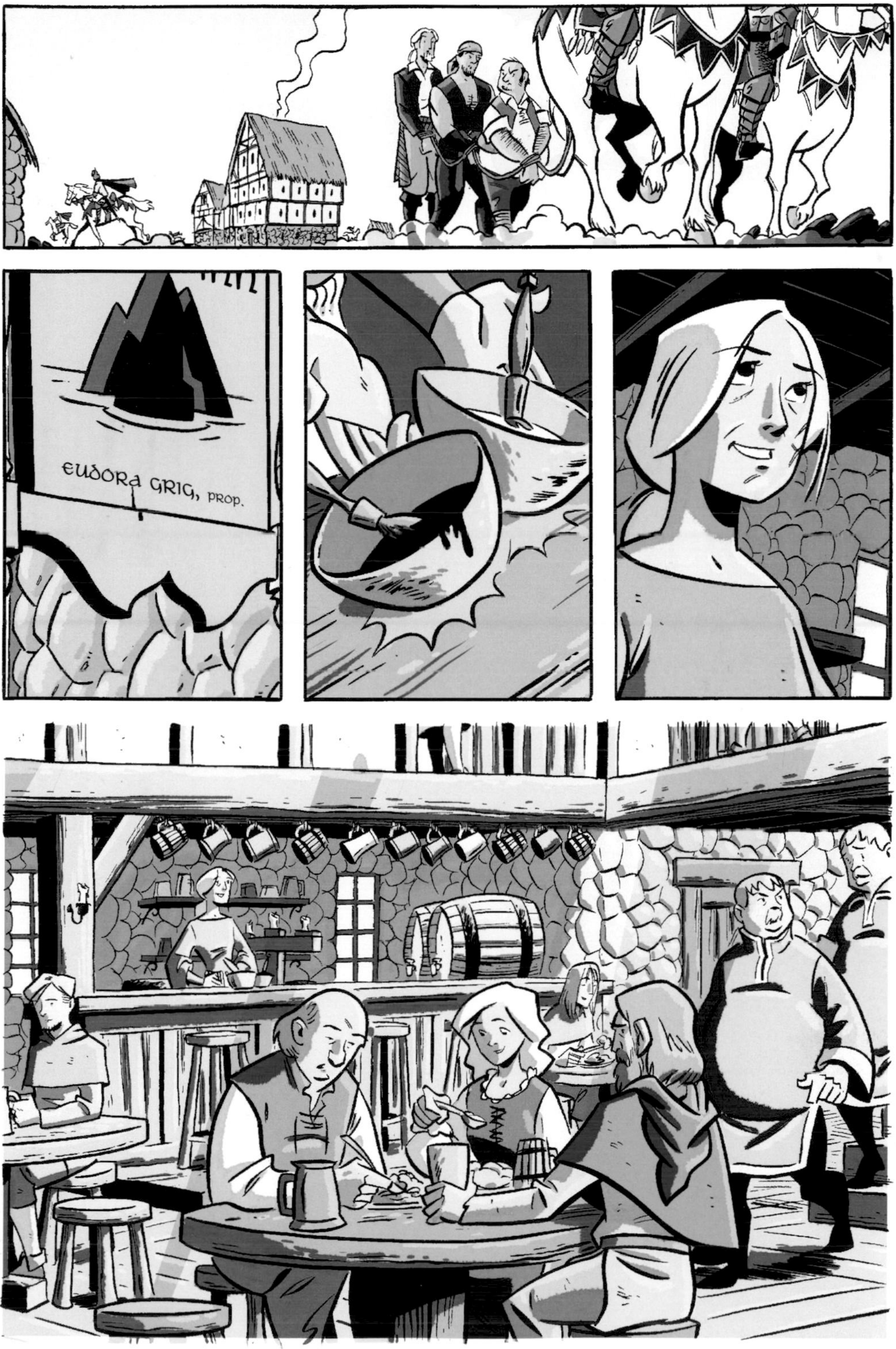
EUDORA GRIG, PROP.

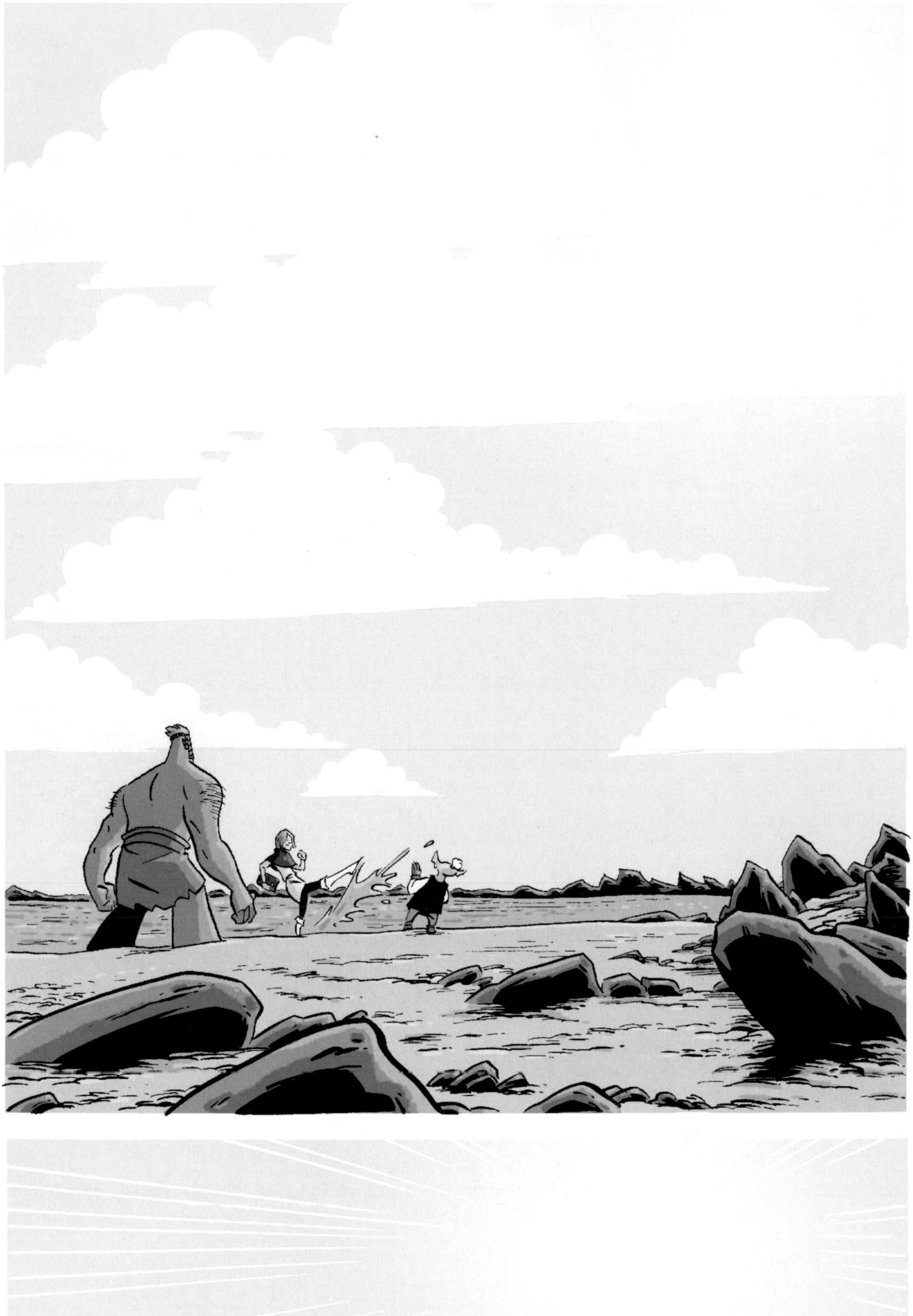